P9-CQE-134

THE AGENCY

THE AGENCY

The Traitor in the Tunnel

Y. S. Lee

CANDLEWICK PRESS

This is a work of fiction. Names, characters, places, and incidents are either products of the author's imagination or, if real, are used fictitiously.

First U.S. edition 2012

Library of Congress Cataloging-in-Publication Data is available.
Library of Congress Catalog Card Number pending

ISBN 978-0-7636-5316-3

11 12 13 14 15 16 BVG 10 9 8 7 6 5 4 3 2 1

Printed in Berryville, VA, U.S.A.

This book was typeset in Palatino.

Candlewick Press
99 Dover Street
Somerville, Massachusetts 02144

visit us at www.candlewick.com

To the LW Quartet

Prologue

Saturday, 11 February 1860

Off Limehouse Reach, London

The old man was all but barefoot, with only a mismatched pair of leather flaps, much eroded by time and wear, bound to his feet with strips of rags. The feet themselves seemed scarcely worth protecting: grotesquely swollen, purple with cold, the toenails entirely torn off—and yet they kept moving over the slick, rain-soaked cobbles. He shuffled crabwise, shaking as with a palsy, a leathery stick of a man rolled in shreds of rotting cloth. Beggars and vagrants were a common enough sight in the seedier parts of the city, yet there was something about this one that made all recoil. Some stared after him. Others, wiser, kept their eyes averted.

None of this signified anything to the man. He couldn't have told the date of his last meal, his last bath, or his last good night's sleep. But he knew what he needed. It was just around this corner—the last endless, filthy corner in this city he detested with all he was and had been. Hate was the only subject that meant anything, the only emotion that lit his eyes, on occasion. But tonight was too cold even for that. With a last gasp of effort, he turned into the alley. The entrance he wanted—a hole rather than a doorway—had a small sign above, for those who cared to read it: AWAN SURGAWI—"heavenly cloud," in Malay. Funny. He'd always known it was here. Scarcely remembered a time when he'd have walked past it with indifference. Tonight, though, he paused and read the sign for the first time. It was a damned lie, like everything else in filthy, freezing, godforsaken London. In England.

The coins were knotted into the hem of his shirt. He'd felt their weight like a promise all evening, every time he moved. Now he stumbled down the narrow, uneven stairs into a murky hell that couldn't have been less like heaven. Of that much he was certain. But it was good enough for him.

Sayed saw him through the gloom and, with a flick of the eyes, directed him to a straw mat. The man stumbled to it, as close to gratitude as he'd ever come, and his bones cracked loudly as he settled himself, as though praying to the battered hookah on the floor. Sayed squatted patiently while the man's gnarled fingers struggled with rotting fabric. Eventually, the coins dropped into the waiting hand.

"Not much here, Uncle," said Sayed dubiously.

The man didn't reply. He'd come with less, in the past.

Sayed sighed and pressed his lips together. "I'll see what I can do." He measured a parsimonious amount of opium—heavily cut with cheapest tobacco—into the hookah's bowl. After a brief pause, during which he refused to meet the old man's gaze, he added a little more. He covered the bowl with a small metal disk, then lit a match. Once the flame caught, he pressed the snake-like smoking tube into the old man's trembling palm. "Wait," he said in a warning tone. "Not yet."

The old man kept an impatient vigil as the water heated and sufficient steam built up. At long last, it was ready. Raising the mouthpiece to his lips, lungs hollow and aching for the thick smoke, he felt a very specific sense of calm amid his frantic need. This was new—an omen. He disliked both those things intensely. Yet as he sucked on the pipe, welcoming the fragrant poison into his body, it was the calm that remained with him. As though his troubles were nearly over. As though tonight, in some way, he would meet his fate.

Pipe dreams, he thought, and drifted away.

One

The same evening

Buckingham Palace

Her Majesty Victoria, by the Grace of God, of the United Kingdom of Great Britain and Ireland Queen, Defender of the Faith, had a lamp shade on her head. Again.

"A lamp!" shouted Prince Leopold. Age six, he was of a literal disposition.

"You've already guessed that, Leo," said Princess Helena. "Give somebody else a go."

"A hot-air balloon?" asked Prince Arthur. He was sprawled across the rug, keeping half an eye on the game of charades while building a model ship.

"A fine guess, but rather disproportioned, don't you think?" said the queen, a twinkle in her eye. "There isn't a lamp shade in the palace big enough to turn me into a *montgolfière*."

"One more guess," said Helena. "Bea, shall I give you a clue?"

Princess Beatrice nodded vigorously and quickly

pulled her finger from her nostril. Helena bent to whisper in her sister's ear. In a moment, the toddler's eyes lit up. "A Christmas tree!" she shrieked, to the family's amusement.

There was a vigorous round of applause for the tiniest princess, and her father smiled indulgently. "Well done, children—especially for guessing before your mother set her hair on fire."

"And before our guests arrived to find me wearing a lamp shade." Her Majesty laughed. "Think of the gossip! The scandal!"

At her station in the corner of the Yellow Drawing Room, where she was arranging a tableful of sherry glasses, Mary bit back a smile. Queen Victoria's public reputation was for demure virtue and domestic bliss. In private, however, her casual high spirits sometimes reduced her family to tears of laughter. In the six weeks Mary had been posted at the palace, she'd heard Her Majesty tease her children, banter with her husband, and even engage in wild games of hide-and-seek, which seemed always to end with shrieking laughter as the queen was discovered beneath a piano, crouched on a windowsill, or, once, memorably, inside a suit of armor.

The queen moved between her roles with ease, and this early-evening gathering was a perfect example. After the young princes and princesses had had an early supper in the nursery, they came down to the drawing room to see their parents before going to bed. It was quite common for Her Majesty to invite a handful of extra-privileged dinner guests to join them at this time, for sherry, before bidding her children good night and proceeding to her state dinner, resplendent in silk train and tiara. Clearly, she was determined to emphasize her domesticity as a central feature of her character as sovereign.

Mary finished arranging the sherry table and glanced about the room. No other alterations seemed necessary, as tonight's dinner was a relatively intimate affair with only two dozen guests. She slipped into the corridor, passing an underbutler bearing a drinks tray. Her progress was arrested, however, when a lady-in-waiting rounded the corner.

Like a well-trained servant, Mary instantly stopped and turned to face the wall—becoming, as it were, part of the furnishings. It was a serious breach of domestic discipline not to do so, and Mary had once been delayed for nearly a quarter of an hour when two of the elder princesses had stopped in the Long Gallery to examine a painting.

This particular lady-in-waiting, though, spoke to her. "Who is that?"

Mary turned and curtsied. "It is Quinn, ma'am."

"Quinn. Tell the butler that the Earl of Wintermarch is prevented by illness from dining with Her Majesty this evening."

"Very good, Mrs. Dalrymple. Is there anything else?"

"What? No, of course not. Why do you ask?"

"No reason, ma'am. I shall tell Mr. Brooks immediately."

"See that you do."

With faint amusement, Mary watched Honoria Dalrymple stalk away. She was a greyhound of a woman in her late thirties—thin and elegant, with cold green eyes and a habit of sniffing whenever she entered a room, as though mistrustful of what might lurk in its corners. Such suspicions were probably well founded: it was generally servants who occupied room corners, and they universally detested Mrs. Dalrymple.

It was no mystery why. Her peremptory ways were normal enough (although the royal family managed to speak with civility to their servants), but she was a known troublemaker. On one of Mary's first days in service, the assistant pastry cook pulled her aside to warn her: the lady-in-waiting changed her mind, and blamed the servants; ordered boiled fowls, then pitched a fit and insisted that she'd said roasted. It was impossible to please Mrs. Dalrymple, and no one tried seriously. The trick, said the pastry cook, was not to let her put you in the wrong before the family.

Mary returned belowstairs and presented herself to the head butler, Mr. Brooks. As she delivered her message, the top of his bald head turned scarlet.

"Did she say what illness he had?"

Mary was startled. "No, sir. Just 'prevented by illness.'"

Mr. Brooks muttered something extremely impolite. The Earl of Wintermarch's absence put a hitch in the seating plan. So did Mrs. Dalrymple's report of his indisposition, as it was only moderately reliable. Would it be worse to have an empty place at table when the company proceeded into the dining hall or to have laid no place at all for such a high-ranking guest? "Get up there," said the head butler finally, "and tell Richardson to keep his eye out for the earl. If he's miraculously recovered, I need to know instantly."

"Yes, sir."

"And tell Potter, too, in case the earl slips into the pen." The pen—the term was short for "cattle pen"—was the staff nickname for the White Room, where less privileged guests were given their pre-dinner sherries.

"Yes, sir."

"Quinn, why are you dillydallying there? I expected you back fully ten minutes ago."

Mary spun about and saw the housekeeper, to whom she officially reported, standing at the end of the corridor, arms akimbo and lips pressed tight. From this angle, she looked not unlike an awkward reproduction of Mrs. Dalrymple. "I'm coming immediately, Mrs. Shaw."

Mr. Brooks may have shared Mary's impression. His tone was frosty as he said, "You mustn't blame Quinn, Mrs. Shaw; she was charged with a message for me, and I have only just finished giving her further instructions."

"I am surprised you should so forget the chain of

command as to give orders to one of my domestics, Mr. Brooks." Mrs. Shaw's military language was habitual and seldom failed to inspire eye rolling when her back was turned.

"It is a matter of urgency," he replied. "Quinn will return the very instant she's relayed my message."

Mary seized her opportunity. "Indeed, sir. Thank you for understanding, ma'am." And she fled.

It was going to be a long evening.

Two

Midnight, the same night

Belowstairs at Buckingham Palace

One of the last rituals each night, after all duties had been completed and staff prayers conducted, was the doling out of hot-water bottles. The servants, weary and eager for their beds, queued in relative silence outside the housekeeper's room. Mrs. Shaw called them in one at a time, inspecting their uniforms and appearances for the last time before permitting them to take a large stoneware bottle filled with boiling water and tightly stoppered. The hot-water bottles were heavy, cumbersome, and pure heaven in an unheated attic room in midwinter.

This evening, when Mary presented herself, Mrs. Shaw had an envelope on her desk. "Quinn, there's a little note here for you. I don't know when it arrived. From your mother again, I presume, though it's a bit early for her weekly letter."

Mary tried not to scowl at the housekeeper's presumption. "It looks like her hand, Mrs. Shaw." All letters and parcels directed to servants were first delivered to their supervisors. Although this was, in theory, for efficiency's sake, Mary had heard from other servants that Mrs. Shaw occasionally opened and read her underlings' letters, citing "morals" as her justification.

Mrs. Shaw paused before placing the letter in Mary's open hand. "Have you laid the breakfast table ready for morning?"

"Yes, ma'am."

"How did you fold the napkins?"

"Into fans, as you said I should, ma'am."

A sniff. "Are there fresh candles in the candelabra?"

"Yes, ma'am." It had been such a cold, dark winter. And Her Majesty breakfasted early—often before sunrise, during these dark months.

"Your apron is dirty." This last was in a tone of satisfaction.

Mary looked down at the tiny smear of orange that marred the edge of her apron's crisp whiteness. From the lily stamens, she supposed, whose dye was indelible. She ruined an apron every other time she changed the flower water. "I shall replace it immediately, ma'am."

"See that you do." Mrs. Shaw dropped the letter into Mary's hand and nodded; Mary was dismissed.

As she climbed the narrow wooden stairs to the servants' quarters, a scalding-hot bottle tucked into the crook of her arm, she wondered again what she'd done to offend Mrs. Shaw. The woman was an exacting housekeeper, an older woman with rigid ways of doing things. But that didn't account for the angry joy she exhibited when Mary was in error. It was quite possible that she resented Mary's sudden appointment; perhaps she'd had a favorite in mind for the plum position of upper housemaid. It was rather a change in the palace for a newcomer to be placed so high. Of course, Mrs. Shaw had no way of knowing just why it was so.

It had been someone high up—Mary wasn't permitted to know who, for her own safety—who'd first approached the Agency about the delicate matter at the palace. Small ornaments and trinkets were going missing. The first, a tiny tortoiseshell snuffbox that had belonged to Queen Victoria's uncle, the Duke of York, might have been gone for some time before it was missed in the densely ornamented Blue Room. But the second, a Dresden shepherdess, had been prized by Her Majesty's mother. Its disappearance inspired a spring cleaning and general inventory of the palace's domestic decorations. Yet despite the heightened safety measures instituted by the Master of the Household—locking of drawing-room doors at night, for example—the thefts continued. No obvious suspect emerged. There was, apparently, no trail to follow.

Calling in the Metropolitan Police was impossible, of course: much too sensational and inclined to stir high-society gossip. And without clear evidence, the Master of the Household declined to sack individual employees. And so, for this pettiest of crimes, Mary found herself posing as a seasoned housemaid in the queen's own household. It was her first assignment as a newly elevated full member of the Agency; she'd completed her training just before Christmas. And while she still dreamed of complex assignments, a hint of danger, and a twisty problem to puzzle out, she had accepted this staid little case philosophically. She was content to pay her dues.

It was a soft landing, as far as domestic service went. Food was plentiful, uniforms were provided, and some upper servants even had their own tiny bedrooms in the attics. It didn't prevent them from grousing, however. The food was too plain: Her Majesty was suspicious of French sauces and pungent herbs. The evenings were dull: Her Majesty had abstemious ways, and so fine wines and spirits were served only to guests. And gossip was forbidden. It was this last stricture that Mary found most frustrating. After nearly six weeks at the palace, she'd heard nothing of use about the thefts. The servants were banned from even mentioning the fact, and so Mary's weekly report to her mother—that is, to the Agency—was very thin indeed.

With a sigh of relief, Mary entered the chilly bedroom and closed the door behind her. It hadn't a lock. Amy, her new roommate, would be up soon, but the current silence was a rare pleasure. The envelope was still sealed. Unless Mrs. Shaw had taken the time to re-gum it, her "mother's" words were still private.

My dear Mary,

I had a letter from my cousin Alfred, who you recall was married last year. He is now father to a little boy called Edwin. The birth was difficult but now all danger is past and the baby is, by the midwife's own report, a healthy babe. Will you travel down to Wimbledon this Sunday to help out?

Your loving mama

They'd agreed to use the simplest of codes, for speed: every eleventh word contained the Agency's real instructions. What she read now—*recall; little danger; report Sunday*—was utterly surprising and perplexing.

The Agency seldom recalled its undercover agents. If it did, it was usually because of grave personal danger: a disguise gone wrong, or a new and volatile element of risk. But this message was the inverse of what she'd been trained to expect. If there was so little danger, why not permit her to stay and achieve what she could?

A new and humiliating thought struck her: perhaps her employers, Anne Treleaven and Felicity Frame, had tired of her lack of results. Five full weeks with nothing to report, and she could only say the same again tomorrow. Mary was too reasonable to think that it was her fault. There had been no subsequent pilferings; nobody gossiped about the original rash of thefts; nobody had behaved suspiciously under Mary's watch. And yet the total absence of results shamed her. She felt, in some obscure way, responsible for producing answers—even if they were provisional.

Or it might be the client. Perhaps Buckingham Palace thought that after more than a month's lull, the thief had moved on. Her Majesty was notoriously frugal. Perhaps Mary's work was simply another unjustifiable expenditure, if the thief was disobliging enough to have gone on holiday. Yet an uncaught thief almost never retired satisfied. After another month, the thefts would begin again, and then where would the palace be? Yet it was impossible to think that Anne and Felicity wouldn't have explained this carefully to their client.

Mary scowled about the spartan room. It wasn't that she'd miss this place, or this rather dreary little assignment. And she hadn't much to pack, or long to wait: she could ask permission to visit her "mother" tomorrow, while the family was at church. Even so, failure stung. Especially as this was her first proper case.

The door handle clicked, and almost immediately the barrage of words began. "Oh, my good lord, what a night! What is that Mrs. Shaw like? Thinks she's the queen of all us girls, don't she? I were that close"—Amy gestured with vigor—"that close, I swear, to telling her where to stick her blooming feather duster."

Mary rolled her eyes. "I wish you would."

Amy's outrage dissolved and she giggled. "Aye, that would be a sight to see. Maybe I'll save it for my last day."

"Got that planned, have you?" Despite Amy's volubility, Mary didn't know her well. They'd begun sharing this room only a few nights ago, after a falling-out between Amy and her previous chamber-mate.

Amy kicked off her shoes and winked. "Well, a girl can't stay in the same place forever. Even if it's quite a nice one."

"I didn't know you were ambitious."

She smiled broadly. "Oh, aye. My ambition's to stop being Miss Tranter and to become Mrs. Jones."

It was a common enough ambition, and Mary nodded, folding up her letter. Amy was well-nigh unstoppable on the subject of her beloved Mr. Jones.

"What's that, then?" asked Amy. Her voice was muffled by the dress she was pulling over her head. "Love letter?"

"It's from my mother."

"Lordamercy. Anything juicy?"

"Not really, but I'll ask permission to go and see her tomorrow."

"Dearie me, you're but a babe unborn. Here, give us a hand with this corset." As Mary obediently began to unpick the fiercely knotted strings, Amy asked, "Why haven't you got a beau? You ain't ugly."

"Thank you."

"You know what I mean, silly. Don't you *want* a beau? No, daft question: every girl wants a beau. But you've got to be sharp about these things, y'know—not just any beau will do. Them footmen—waste of time, all of them. What you want is a gentleman friend. Somebody with a bit of class, a proper gent."

Mary nodded mechanically. She'd heard this before—each night, in fact, as they got ready for bed. It was the Gospel According to Amy.

"No sense in wasting your time with some poor cove in service. What's he got to offer, eh? A life just like this one. No, you want a gent what can set you up in your own home. You want to be the mistress." She prized off the corset and plucked at her crushed, rather damp chemise. "Ooh, that's better! I were like to die in that. Now, you take my Mr. Jones: nice office job—late hours sometimes, but his time's his own when he ain't there. And so soft and clean, his hands are, when he comes round! Never any black under the fingernails. It half makes me ashamed of my own."

Mary hadn't heard exactly this variation before, and her ears pricked up. "He comes round here?"

Amy's mouth opened and shut soundlessly, and her cheeks flushed pink. "Er—not round here, exactly . . ." she finally managed to say. "I mean, only of a Sunday, when he calls to take me for a stroll in the park."

Mary stifled a smile. "Oh, I see. Well, he sounds very nice."

"He's better than nice." Amy smiled. "Tell you what: I'll ask him tomorrow if he's got any friends what might like to meet you."

"Oh, there's no need," said Mary immediately. "Honestly. I don't want a beau. Not right now, that's certain. Maybe one day . . ."

Amy looked at her with genuine pity. "A babe unborn," she muttered, shaking her head. "A babe unborn."

Three

The early hours of Sunday, 12 February

Buckingham Palace

Mary woke with a start, as from a nightmare. She lay in the bed, trembling slightly, trying to think why. She couldn't remember what she'd been dreaming of, but its residue troubled her in an unusual fashion. As she retreated further from sleep, she became aware of Amy's serene snores, quiet and steady, and the relentless clatter of rain on roof shingles. It was still black outside—not that darkness indicated a great deal during a London winter.

She shivered again, now from cold rather than fright. Her hot-water bottle was frigid. She forced herself to sit up and pull on her dressing gown. The palace was completely silent, below and around her. Mary nestled deeper into the bedclothes, willing her tense limbs to soften back into slumber. And yet, what did it matter? She was being recalled from her assignment today; she'd likely be back in her own bed at Miss Scrimshaw's Academy tonight, if she knew Anne and Felicity. She waited another minute for sleep to take her, then grimaced at her own foolishness.

No. If this was her last opportunity to work on this case, she had better exploit it. What was the use in imagining a still, silent palace if she stayed neatly tucked up in bed? Below that logic simmered the irrational hope that a scrap of proof—any sort of lead, however slight—might persuade Anne and Felicity to let her continue. It was a lightweight assignment, true. But perhaps that way of thinking had influenced her approach, had caused her to give it less than her full, thoughtful attention. If so, this was her last chance to put that right.

She dressed swiftly in her morning uniform, a light print dress designed to mask dust and smudges from her cleaning duties. Indoor shoes, which were lighter and quieter than her boots. She hesitated before knotting her hair and added the compulsory maid's cap and apron, both of which made her more visible in a dim light. Still, she could hardly wander around without them and expect to be unchallenged. At least if she wore them, a casual passerby might assume that she was on duty.

The corridor smelled of mildew, sweet and damp. Halfway down the hall, someone snored loudly; the thin doors did little to muffle the sound. But apart from that innocent rattle, all was quiet. The service stairs were narrow, so vertiginous that even in full daylight Mary kept one hand on the banister when descending. Now, in the dark, she moved slowly, establishing a foothold on the next small tread before shifting her weight.

The Blue Room, from which the trinkets had been stolen, was locked each night according to the Master of the Household's instructions. There were three keys, distributed among the queen, the master, and Mrs. Shaw, as the master's deputy. It was locked now. Yet it wasn't as secure as everybody assumed. This was an old mechanism—no bad thing in itself, but one installed before the palace had become the *palace.* Back when it was Buckingham House: a grand home for a duke, to be sure, but without the strict need for safety and privacy required of the primary royal residence. Mary withdrew her special hairpin—a steel needle, fine and strong, and rather longer than one might expect. It was special issue from the Agency, and remarkably useful in a diverse number of applications.

Opening a lock without proper lock picks was a delicate operation requiring patience and a keen ear. She would have to work each tumbler round to the correct position and keep it there. Mary made herself comfortable. But she was only a few minutes into this operation when she was distracted by, of all things, the faint sound of a bell ringing. It was so improbable as to make her shake her head, in an effort to clear it. Surely she was imagining the continual jangle of the service bells belowstairs, her daily life bleeding into her nights?

And yet . . . she froze.

Listened.

After a few moments, it started again, louder and more frantic if that were possible, and continued for perhaps a minute until it broke off midpeal. Mary abandoned her task, slid the hairpin back into place, and stood, wondering what might come next.

She hadn't long to wait.

This time, the rumpus was different—a kind of vigorous hammering. It was much louder now, and she followed the sound to the Ambassadors' Portico, on the palace's east wing. From where she now stood, at the top of the flight of stairs to the second floor, the sound was unmistakable: somebody was pounding furiously on the palace doors, seeking admittance at—the chiming of a nearby grandfather clock conveniently announced—the ungodly hour of half past four in the morning. A Sunday morning, no less.

Mary's course of action was clear. She couldn't possibly have heard the ruckus from her quarters; neither could she explain the fact that she was fully dressed for morning service. So she retreated into the shadows, tucking herself behind the useful grandfather clock, and waited.

The thumping let up for a moment, but only so that the caller could redouble his efforts. In fact—she listened carefully—it was at least two men, hammering slightly out of rhythm with each other. They weren't using their fists—that much was certain; human knuckles would be bloodied and broken as a result of that sort of vigor.

At very long last, a sleepy manservant stumbled into the hall, clutching a single candle. He wore livery trousers, a half-buttoned jacket, and no shirt that Mary could see. "Who goes there?" he said, yawning, clearly not expecting a sensible answer.

"The Metropolitan Police, on a matter of urgency!"

The footman rubbed his eyes. "Now, see here, this ain't the time for a prank. It's a serious business, coming here and disturbing Her Majesty in the middle of the night. If you don't pack up this instant, I'll send for the real Scotland Yard. Go on, then!"

A different voice came this time: a calm male voice, quiet, with real authority. "This is Commissioner Russell of Scotland Yard. I am not trifling with you, my good man. We require an immediate audience with Her Majesty the queen."

The servant blanched and nearly dropped his candlestick. "Just a moment, Your High—er, sir. I'll fetch the key." He scurried off, leaving Mary in the shadows, her heart pounding.

This was a stroke of—not good fortune, precisely, but intrigue. She tried to slow her racing mind. Conjecture was so often harmful. Her role here was simply to observe as attentively as possible and leave the interpretation until later.

It was a surprisingly swift few minutes before a

procession of three returned, led by Mr. Brooks, dignified in a woolen dressing gown and slippers, holding aloft a large candelabra. Behind him stalked a tall woman, also in a dressing gown, whose abundant chestnut hair trailed down her back in a loose braid: Honoria Dalrymple. They were tailed by the hapless footman who'd finished buttoning his jacket, although the buttons were misaligned. He carried a second candleholder with unsteady hands.

Mr. Brooks opened the door with perfect sangfroid, as though the police commissioner had been expected all along. Before the commissioner could step forward, however, Honoria addressed him with considerable hauteur: "Her Majesty is asleep. You cannot possibly disturb her at this hour."

"I'm afraid you don't appreciate the urgency of the situation, ma'am. We require an immediate audience with the queen."

"My instructions, Inspector—"

"Commissioner." The correction was polite but firm. This was a man unaccustomed to refusal.

"Your pardon: *Commissioner*." Honoria sounded arch, as though humoring a child. "My instructions remain unchanged: unless urgently summoned by the prime minister on a matter of national importance, the queen conducts all business at court, during the usual hours. She has the highest regard for the Metropolitan Police Service, and for that reason, she will, I feel confident in saying, agree to see you today."

"Mrs. Dalrymple, can I not impress upon you just how urgent this matter is? It involves the royal family in the most immediate way. It may even have repercussions for the queen herself."

Honoria opened her lips to answer but was interrupted by a new sound: a set of carriage wheels bumping across the cobblestones at a brisk pace. The carriage clattered to a stop and a brisk, middle-aged gentleman carrying a doctor's bag sprang into view.

"Where's my patient, Commissioner?"

"In my carriage. I thought that would be more comfortable for His Highness."

The physician vanished without a word.

At the sight of Mr. William Lawrence, Her Majesty's sergeant surgeon, Honoria's face blanched. And with the commissioner's reference to "His Highness," she tottered visibly. "It's—" She cleared her throat. "It's—not—Prince Albert Edward, is it?"

The police commissioner nodded. "Yes, ma'am. We summoned Mr. Lawrence directly, to save time."

"He is—seriously injured?" Honoria looked in danger of fainting, and the commissioner stepped forward as though in readiness to catch her. Immediately, she recoiled and pulled herself upright, flinching away from the policeman.

"His life is not in danger."

"Oh, thank God."

"But we must speak with Her Majesty immediately."

Honoria pulled herself together with obvious effort. "If—if you would be so good as to wait here . . ." The voice contained only a shadow of its former arrogance.

Mary waited with even less patience than the commissioner. What on earth could have happened to the merry, lazy, pleasure-loving Prince of Wales? Mary had only briefly glimpsed the young man, as she'd begun her work at the palace a few days before he returned to Oxford for his second term. The younger children seemed to adore him, though, begging him to play games with them all day long. When they misbehaved, he pleaded for clemency on their behalf. And while the queen and her husband lectured and admonished him almost hourly, there was no concealing their deep fondness for their eldest son. It was astounding to learn that such an affable scamp was, this minute, in the hands of Scotland Yard.

"Would you be so kind as to clear the entranceway?" It was Mr. Lawrence's voice again. To the policeman standing just behind the commissioner, he added, "Your assistance, sir, would be appreciated."

A moment later two police officers entered the hall, bearing between them the apparently unconscious figure of Albert Edward, the Prince of Wales. He was in evening dress, although much disheveled. Mary wondered whether this disarray was a result of medical attention or if he'd been picked up by the Yard in that condition. She saw Mr. Brooks's nostrils twitch, very faintly, as the heir was borne past him and wondered what sort of malodor could cause the usually impeccable butler to react so.

Within a few minutes, Honoria returned, looking about her for the missing Prince of Wales. When she spoke, her voice was tight. "Her Majesty will receive you in the Yellow Room. If you would be so kind as to follow me."

Four

The invitation wasn't for Mary. Nevertheless, she moved swiftly, keeping ahead of the small, grim delegation as they climbed the grand staircase toward the second floor. The Yellow Room, despite being the most intimate of the drawing rooms at the palace, was a vast, high-ceilinged apartment; she'd never overhear a thing unless she concealed herself inside. It was the riskiest option, of course, but tonight's investigations had nothing to do with caution. In a few hours, she would leave the palace forever. And luck was with her tonight: Mr. Brooks must have unlocked the door, for when she tried the handle, it turned beneath her hand.

The gas lamps were already hissing—Mr. Brooks again—and they defined the area in which the conversation would take place: two deep armchairs, arranged rather like a pair of throne chairs, facing an open space framed by a Persian rug. One of its silk tassels was ever so slightly disarranged—another subtle indication that even the butler, under his neutral facade, churned with anxiety tonight. She had just enough time to whirl behind a heavy curtain and ensure that its pleats remained perfectly regular before the door handle clicked again. Any footsteps were muffled by the silk carpets, but soon enough Mary heard Honoria's voice, scarcely altered by the thick drapes. "Her Majesty will see you shortly."

They hadn't long to wait. The queen was remarkably quick when occasion required, moving with a smooth rapidity that belied her short-legged bulk. Mary wished she could see Her Majesty now, as the door opened and closed once again. It was impossible, though, without disturbing the curtains and giving away her hiding place.

"You bring news of the Prince of Wales," were her first words, spoken in a clipped tone.

"Your Majesty; Your Highness. I am Commissioner Russell, of the Metropolitan Police Service, and this is—"

"We know who you are." The voice was colder than the room. There came a pause. Then the queen continued, in a voice so different that Mary scarcely recognized it. "Where is my"—there was a barely repressed sob—"where is the Prince of Wales? Is he injured?"

"But very slightly, ma'am: one or two bruises and a slight graze. The Prince of Wales is now resting safely in his apartment."

"His apartment here in the palace?"

"Yes, ma'am. A doctor is with him."

"Then we shall go there. You may give us your news afterward."

"Your Majesty—if I may have just a moment, to explain what—"

Queen Victoria interrupted the commissioner. "My eldest son is here, in highly irregular circumstances. You say he is well, yet you have summoned the sergeant surgeon to his bedside. Do not trifle with us further, Commissioner."

There was a tense silence. Mary imagined the policemen frozen with awe and frustration.

And then a new voice spoke. "Her Majesty and I shall not be long," said Prince Albert. As prince consort, the queen's husband but not king in his own right, he had allowed his wife to take the lead. "But we must satisfy ourselves as to the Prince of Wales's well-being." His German accent sounded especially harsh—the only indication of the anxiety he, too, must have been feeling.

There was a sweep of fabric, the click of a doorknob, and then the room fell silent. The commissioner heaved a gusty sigh. After a very long interval—perhaps ten minutes, in reality, although to Mary it felt several times that duration—the second man said, in a hesitant tone, "Shall I try to find the queen, sir?"

"Whatever for?"

"This news—it can't wait much longer."

"And you propose to—what? Romp through the palace, calling out for Her Majesty? Tell her to hurry, as we're on police business?"

"N-no, sir."

"Then be silent. It is Her Majesty's privilege to take all day, should she so desire."

But as Mary had witnessed during her service at Buckingham Palace, Queen Victoria seldom presumed upon her privileges. She was a dutiful, serious-minded monarch whose small frame contained apparently boundless self-discipline as long as she was on state business. This morning proved no exception. Within half an hour, she and the prince consort were back in the drawing room.

"We appreciate your patience, Commissioner," said His Highness. "Our minds are somewhat relieved to have seen the Prince of Wales, resting under Mr. Lawrence's orders."

"Was it on your instruction that he was given a sedative?" asked the queen, a sharp note in her voice.

"Our suggestion, Your Majesty," said the commissioner in his humblest tones. "The prince was gravely upset and very emotional, I'm afraid. We were anxious that he should rest."

There was a charged silence. Then, abruptly, the queen turned the conversation. "This is not a time for riddles. You had better explain exactly what has happened."

"Of course, Your Majesty. We are here to inform you of a grave accident that has happened, this night, to the Honorable Ralph Beaulieu-Buckworth. I believe you are acquainted with this young person?"

Prince Albert's voice was hard. "One could scarcely say 'acquainted.' He is the same age as the Prince of

Wales. They may even have friends in common. But the prince does not associate with the person you named."

Commissioner Russell scarcely paused. "Your Majesty, Your Highness. I am sorry to inform you that your son was in the Honorable Ralph Beaulieu-Buckworth's company at the time of the—tragedy. The time, in fact, of Mr. Beaulieu-Buckworth's unfortunate death." His last word seemed to echo in the silence that followed; a heavy, absolute silence in which the soft *ffffft* of the gas lamps became loud and obtrusive. There was no soft oath, no sudden intake of breath, from the royal couple. When Russell spoke again, his tone was even, measured—the voice of a bureaucrat doing his job. "The Prince of Wales has stated to us that he came down to London this afternoon at the invitation of Mr. Beaulieu-Buckworth."

"You questioned the Prince of Wales in the absence of his parents?" Her Majesty's anger was clear. "He is but eighteen years old."

"We did not formally question him, Your Majesty; I apologize for the false impression my words may have created. The Prince of Wales, in his agitation, gave us to understand a number of facts. We realize, of course, that upon reflection he may be able to correct some of those statements. But we are repeating to you the information he volunteered to us."

A grim, skeptical silence. Then the prince consort again: "Carry on, Commissioner."

"Thank you, sir. The young men's intention was to celebrate Mr. Beaulieu-Buckworth's birthday, and a number of young gentlemen were invited to the festivities. The prince's equerries were in attendance, naturally." A pause.

"It was rather a large gathering. They dined at—"

"Oh, what does it matter where they dined?" cried the queen in a voice so terrible that even the commissioner's dry recitation faltered. "Stop toying with us, man, and tell us what has happened!"

Russell swallowed audibly. "Very well, Your Majesty. You'll understand, ma'am, that the young men had drunk wine with dinner, and continued to indulge in various wines and spirits over the course of the long evening. The Prince of Wales informs us that by two o'clock in the morning, he and Mr. Beaulieu-Buckworth were gravely impaired. They had become separated from their companions, including the prince's equerries, and Mr. Beaulieu-Buckworth proposed a tour of what he called 'the dark side.' Against the prince's better judgment—"

The queen gave a sharp, sudden sob. "Judgment, my God! The boy lacks all common sense and good judgment!"

Commissioner Russell paused, uncertain.

"Pray continue, Commissioner," said Prince Albert.

"The Prince of Wales assented. Mr. Beaulieu-Buckworth led him into east London, through a maze of streets the prince assured us he should never have been able to navigate alone. They eventually came to an establishment catering to the desire for the consumption of opium—" Commissioner Russell paused.

"Even we, with our sheltered lives, have heard of opium dens," said the prince consort with heavy irony.

Russell cleared his throat. "Quite. At any rate, Mr. Beaulieu-Buckworth persuaded the prince to enter, in order to view what he described as 'the scum.' The prince informed us that he was reluctant to enter. However, he feared losing Mr. Beaulieu-Buckworth, who promised to guide him afterward out of the maze of slums. Thus he followed his friend into the opium-smoking establishment.

"The prince tells us that a dark-skinned man—the proprietor of the establishment, we believe—asked them if they wished to smoke. Although they declined, the dark-skinned man proceeded to fill a hookah for them and urge them to sample his wares. Mr. Beaulieu-Buckworth became agitated—remember, he was extremely intoxicated—and either struck or kicked at the smoking device." The commissioner stopped, as though considering how to phrase his next sentence.

The room became perfectly quiet once more, the queen and her consort still awaiting the terrible blow that was surely to come.

Eventually, Commissioner Russell cleared his throat. "At this point, the prince's recollections become regrettably confused, but he describes, in general terms, a contretemps. The proprietor was angered by this destruction of his property, and harsh words were exchanged. There were a number of patrons—Lascars, mainly, on shore leave—smoking opium at the time. Some were, of course, in a drug-induced stupor that left them unaware of the goings-on. But others were more alert, and one seems to have been enraged by Mr. Beaulieu-Buckworth's language; the prince described it as strong. This man—the prince describes him as an elderly sailor and an Asiatic—rose up and staggered toward the young gentlemen. The Prince of Wales was a little closer to the Asiatic and thus caught the first blow. The prince says he attempted to grapple with the man but soon found himself thrown aside with a force that was quite astonishing, given the Asiatic's apparent age and build.

"Mr. Beaulieu-Buckworth said something—the prince does not recall precisely what. The Asiatic then turned to Mr. Beaulieu-Buckworth. It seemed a fistfight, at first, but in a very short time—the prince was unable to say how many minutes, as he was still downed and attempting to make sense of the struggle—Mr. Beaulieu-Buckworth lay sprawled on the floor, facedown."

Mary could well imagine what Beaulieu-Buckworth's "strong" language had been like. England was rarely a comfortable place for Asiatics, or any foreigners for that matter. But since that past summer's aggression and bloodshed between Britain and China, tempers and temperatures had run especially high, particularly for the Chinese community in London. England was not at war with China. Not officially, at least. But English troops were killing Chinese—both soldiers and civilians; the Chinese retaliated, and there had been rumors of torture.

The horrors in China now echoed through Limehouse, where for generations Asians had lived in quiet—if not, perhaps, peaceful—coexistence with their English neighbors. Now there were reports of conflict: service refused to a Chinese woman at market, a Chinese man attacked by a gang of boys, a shop selling Chinese herbs burned down. English outrage was high, and some took that as license to "retaliate"—as though the denizens of east London were responsible for the actions of the Chinese emperor. There could be no doubt as to where Beaulieu-Buckworth stood.

Had stood. That was the key: the pig was dead. And although his name was mud in aristocratic circles—a well-known gambler, whoremonger, drunkard, and coward—he was still one of them. He was, after all, an "Honorable," a scion of a noble house. That his short life had been almost entirely without honor or nobility mattered not. There would be no satisfactory ending to this tale.

"The prince," continued the commissioner, "though alarmed by the general violence, decided this was a good opportunity to persuade Mr. Beaulieu-Buckworth to depart. But when he tried to help his friend up, he found him dying, a knife buried deep in his chest."

A strange, high-pitched sound erupted—a cry that seemed more animal than human. "Murder!"

Mary scrambled to make sense of this scream. It hadn't come from the queen.

"Murder of a young aristocrat, and an attempt on the Prince of Wales's life!"

"Indeed, Mrs. Dalrymple," said Russell. "But we are speaking to Her Majesty in confidence; it is of utmost importance that you keep silence about what you've just heard."

"That goes without saying," said Her Majesty severely. "We do not tolerate tale bearing and idle gossip at our court."

"Forgive me, Your Majesty." But Honoria's voice continued to vibrate with emotion.

"We are glad of your discretion in coming to us first," said Prince Albert, "and we still have much to discuss. But first: you have arrested the vermin, of course?"

"Yes, Your Highness. The miscreant is in Tower jail even as we speak."

"He was an opium fiend?"

"Yes, Your Highness."

"And an Asiatic, you said."

"A Chinese sailor, Your Highness, and a rather elderly one at that. Unless I'm much mistaken, he sailed his last journey some years ago."

A pause. Then the prince consort murmured, "That is useful."

"'Useful,' sir?"

"Surely you understand me, Commissioner," said His Highness in a meaningful tone.

"Mrs. Dalrymple," said the queen suddenly, "you may instruct my maids to draw my bath and prepare my morning dress."

"Very good, Your Majesty," said Honoria in a soft, even voice. A few moments later, the door closed behind her with the softest of clicks, and Mary tried to visualize those who remained: Queen Victoria, Prince Albert, Russell, and Russell's silent subordinate, she thought.

"The Prince of Wales must not be named as a party to this shocking event," said the queen in a rapid and matter-of-fact fashion. "Mr. Beaulieu-Buckworth was alone in his visit to the opium den. The prince and his equerries became separated from the larger group at a much earlier hour, and the prince returned here, to his family, at midnight."

Russell cleared his throat. "There is the small matter, ma'am, of the other witnesses. Patrons of the opium den, for example."

"A ragtag band of drug-addled sots," replied the queen.

"And the owner, with whom the prince exchanged words?"

"He must be convinced of his error. He cannot possibly believe that the Prince of Wales entered his low den and spoke to him."

"We can certainly try, ma'am. But the gravest difficulty lies with the Lascar who attacked Mr. Beaulieu-Buckworth. He will insist that the Prince of Wales was present—perhaps, even, that he joined with Mr. Beaulieu-Buckworth in attacking him. Pure invention, of course," Commissioner Russell added hastily, "but these scoundrels seize upon anything to shore up their defense and muddy the truth."

"He may be certain of a second gentleman," allowed the queen, "but he is clearly mad if he imagines it to have been the Prince of Wales. Did you not say the man was an opium fiend?"

"We believe so."

"And do opium addicts not suffer from fits and delusions?"

"Y-yes . . ."

"Then we have no difficulty." There was a long, meaningful pause. "Have we?"

"And yet we may." Prince Albert's voice was deep, reluctant—and utterly surprising. "The first attack," he said very slowly, "was on the Prince of Wales. And you say the Asiatic sailor recognized him?"

"The Prince of Wales thinks so," said Russell. "He believes he was recognized."

"Then we have not only a clear identification, but a much more serious crime: an attack—most likely a murderous attack—on the person of the future King of England."

There was a prolonged silence, during which the

unspoken word seemed to reverberate about the chilly room. *Treason*—not merely against the state, but against the monarchy. That made it high treason.

"Correct, Your Highness."

"That is true only if Bertie is correct about the identification," objected Queen Victoria. "Could he not be in error? What would an opium-addled foreigner know about the Prince of Wales's appearance to enable him to identify him so confidently, especially in such circumstances?" Her voice grew angry. "It beggars belief that such a villain could instantly recognize—and have the temerity to attack—the future king. This must surely be a grotesque error."

"The Prince of Wales is a public figure," argued Prince Albert. "His portrait appears regularly in society papers. Just as your subjects recognize you, my dear, they recognize your heir."

"Perhaps," said the queen. "And I grant the seriousness of the attack. But if we pursue this route, the Prince of Wales will be subjected to a public scrutiny far too painful for him to bear. There will be scandal, not to mention the horror of a trial—good God, what if he were required to testify? Only think of what people would say—what newspapers might print! I cannot permit this!"

There was another prolonged silence. It was perhaps fanciful of Mary to imagine, sightless as she was behind the drapes, but this pause had a different quality. It was not a standoff but a sort of silent negotiation between husband and wife. Mary had witnessed this before—the rapid, minute flashes of change and exchange in their eyes. The sort of conversation only a close, long-married couple could have.

After a moment, Her Majesty once again addressed the commissioner. "The prince consort and I shall speak with our son tomorrow, when he is awake and calm. We shall ask the Prince of Wales to repeat his impressions of the night's events. Once we have arrived at an understanding, we shall inform you of how we wish to proceed."

A pause. Then, reluctantly, "As you wish, Your Majesty."

The interview was over, bar the formalities. Mary let out a long, silent breath she hadn't known she was holding until that moment. She raised her shoulders and willed her tense muscles to soften. Outside this room, the day was starting. Servants would soon be rising. It was cutting it fine, but she ought to have time to return to the bedroom before Amy woke.

"A moment, Commissioner." Queen Victoria's voice sliced through Mary's thoughts. "What is the name of this opium fiend—the murderer?"

"It's a Chinese name, Your Majesty. Difficult to say—even assuming he gave his real name."

"Do your best."

A pause. Then, haltingly, "It's Lang."

Mary caught her breath. The blood in her veins seemed to freeze for a long moment, then resume its course with a drunken swoop. *Foolish,* she scolded herself. *Utter coincidence.* Lang was a common-enough Chinese surname. What did it matter that it was the same as hers—the real name she'd abandoned, yet another fragment of her lost childhood?

"Why, there are Englishmen named Lang." Prince Albert sounded the *g* in *Lang,* making the name hard and Teutonic, not tonal and Chinese. "The name is of German origin."

"It's the rest of his name that gives trouble, Your Highness," said Russell with an air of apology. "His Christian names—although I doubt he's a Christian. It's something like Jinn High."

Mary swayed and caught desperately at the windowsill for balance, suddenly knocked dizzy by two syllables.

"Jinn what?"

"Spelled J–i–n H–a–i, Your Majesty. Jin Hai Lang."

Her pulse roared in her ears, so loudly she could scarcely hear the queen's terse thanks and dismissal.

Jin Hai Lang, a Lascar in Limehouse.

Lang Jin Hai, his name in Chinese.

An opium addict.

A murderer.

And, unless she'd gone completely mad . . .

Her father.

Mary stumbled back up to her attic room, kicked off her shoes, and climbed back under the bed coverings. Her head ached. Her pulse hammered a single rhythm through her consciousness: Lang Jin Hai. Lang Jin Hai. Her father's name, and one of the few things about him she could remember.

He was gone—lost at sea when she was a small child—risking all on a mission to uncover truth. His death was the reason she and her mother had suffered so. The bone-deep cold and perpetual hunger. Her mother's desperate turn to prostitution and, not long after, her death. Mary's own years on the streets, keeping alive as a pickpocket and housebreaker. The inevitable arrest and trial, and the certainty of death—so very close that she'd all but felt the noose about her neck.

And then, miraculously, her rescue. The women of the Agency had given her life anew. Mary Lang, the only child of a Chinese sailor and an Irish seamstress, was gone forever. She'd been reborn as Mary Quinn, orphan. Educated at Miss Scrimshaw's Academy for Girls. Trained as an undercover agent. An exciting, hopeful, active life had lain before her. Until this morning.

Mary pressed her palms to her temples, as though that might still the roar of her blood. The blood she shared with an opium fiend and a murderer. The father she'd longed so desperately to rediscover. At least while she'd thought him dead.

What if it were a hideous, improbable coincidence? There might be another Lascar who shared her father's name. What else had the police said of him? "Elderly," they'd called him. That was superficially comforting. Yet her father, had he lived, would now be in his late forties or early fifties—old enough, especially for a wind-blown, sun-beaten working man. It was not unthinkable that he might appear elderly. What else did she know of him? Only that in his youth he'd resembled Prince Albert: his nickname around Limehouse had been Prince. Was it possible for such a resemblance to persist, through years of hard living and wayfaring?

Her chances of getting a look at this Lang Jin Hai were slender. He was in prison and soon to be arraigned as the murderer of the dishonorable Ralph Beaulieu-Buckworth. He might be charged with the even graver crime of high treason, depending upon the queen's decision. For the queen, this whole affair was largely a question of propriety, yet nobody was willing to challenge her views—not even the commissioner of the Metropolitan Police. That rankled, too. It wasn't that Mary wanted the Prince of Wales's reputation sullied or the royal family disgraced through its association with Beaulieu-Buckworth. But Queen Victoria's unquestioned authority in this matter raised other, even more dangerous questions about the sort of justice Lang Jin Hai might receive.

A new thought came to Mary: what if the prince was mistaken about what he had seen? What if he'd seen a struggle and a death but leaped to conclusions about the causes? He'd been slightly injured, of course—perhaps breathless and frightened and nursing his bruises when Beaulieu-Buckworth confronted the Lascar. What if

Lang—as she must call him, whether he was her father or not—had attacked Prince Albert Edward first in an opium-induced haze without recognizing him at all? Lang may even have acted in self-defense, protecting himself from what he saw as a pair of aggressive, drunken toffs. Why, Beaulieu-Buckworth might even have picked up the knife and been the first to wield it!

She sat up suddenly, fingertips tingling. She'd been blind—a fool—as bad as the queen herself, in failing to address facts. No, she'd been worse. She, of all people, ought to know that appearances could deceive, that things weren't always as they seemed. How could she have assumed, like all those narrow-minded children of privilege, that Lang was guilty?

Across the room, the lump that was Amy stirred and mumbled something. Mary sprang out of bed. She would have to investigate. Uncover the truth. And, possibly, fight to save an innocent man.

A man who might be her father.

Five

Sunday afternoon

Acacia Road, St. John's Wood

Miss Scrimshaw's Academy for Girls looked much like every other house on Acacia Road: a large, redbrick villa with a high, wrought-iron fence about the perimeter. It was a girls' school in the usual sense, with teachers and pupils and lessons and meals. Slightly less usual was its approach. It selected girls carefully, charging no fees for their education. And its philosophy was, in many senses, revolutionary. It taught that women were more than domestic angels and helpmeets, and prepared its pupils for lives of independence and dignified, skilled work.

But it was the attic at Miss Scrimshaw's that held its most incendiary secret: an all-female intelligence agency that used the stereotype of the harmless, weak-minded woman to its advantage. The Agency placed spies in settings unthinkable for men—kitchen sculleries, ladies' boudoirs, positions as governesses. Its successes were formidable. Twenty-two months after being admitted to its ranks, Mary was still amazed by her good fortune.

Today, however, she let herself in at the gate with a sense of unease. The visit she really needed to pay lay in a different direction. Scotland Yard was holding Lang Jin Hai at the Tower of London—a location that filled Mary with superstitious dread. It was a legendary jail, the sort of place one associated with traitors of the highest order. It even had an access gate into the Thames known as the Traitors' Gate, for all those who had passed through it. She hadn't the faintest idea how one went about visiting prisoners in jail, let alone at the Tower. And even if she had, she was far from ready to face this man who might be her father. Almost anything—even diving into the Thames—seemed easier.

A more appealing, if cowardly, prospect was trying to help him from afar. Yet here was another fine mess. She'd only just been recalled from the assignment (complete with that strange proviso "little danger"), only to find that she desperately needed to stay. How else could she monitor the case against Lang Jin Hai and the royal family's role in it? Remaining on the case was her only chance of overhearing further discussions between the queen and Scotland Yard. Yet Anne and Felicity did nothing lightly. They would require a great deal of persuasion to let her stay on, even in this puzzling absence of danger.

Mary stopped, drew a steadying breath, and resolved to do only what was necessary on this case without letting her emotions overtake her. To solve the mysterious thefts from the palace. To do all she could for Lang, while preserving her distance. And, most important, to keep her mixed-race parentage a secret. It was too complicated. Certain to mark her out as different. Foreign. Tainted. It was a hindrance and a handicap, when all she wanted was to blend in—with the outside world, but especially here.

She walked past the front door and round the side of the building to the Agency's private entrance. She was expected. Only a moment after her coded knock, a thin, bespectacled woman opened the narrow door.

"Good afternoon, Miss Treleaven."

Anne's watchful gray eyes scanned her face. "Good afternoon, my dear." She indicated the stairs. "After you."

Mary felt a sudden impulse to throw herself into Anne's arms, weeping—as though a childish confession would right everything that was wrong in her life!—and she had to restrain herself with real effort before climbing the narrow, four-story staircase to the attic.

The Agency's office looked more like a teachers' common room than a secret headquarters: slightly shabby, with an assortment of mismatched chairs and sofas salvaged over the years. There was the usual tea tray, the brightly polished lamps, and—very happily—a blazing fire.

As Mary entered the room, Felicity Frame turned expectantly. Her eyes widened at Mary's muddy, bedraggled state. "My dear, all this way on foot? Most unnecessary."

"I needed the walk, Mrs. Frame," explained Mary. She

was always slightly shy of Felicity's beauty and rather theatrical manner. "And I don't mind the rain."

Something glinted in Felicity's eye—Mary was almost certain she would ask an uncomfortable question—but she said only, "As you prefer."

"Sit by the fire," said Anne, closing the door quietly behind her. "You'll soon dry." She took one of the two chairs facing Mary, while Felicity remained standing. It was an awkward arrangement, but neither woman seemed aware of it.

There was a strange, hesitant silence. Mary finally broke it, saying, "I was surprised to receive your message."

Anne nodded. "It's a highly irregular situation. I should like first to emphasize that it has nothing to do with your performance on the case."

A weight she hadn't quite realized she carried was plucked from Mary's chest, and she breathed a little more deeply. "That is a relief."

"In fact, it's a damn shame you're so set on recalling her," said Felicity in a velvety but definitely combative tone.

Anne blinked rapidly—a sign of irritation, Mary knew from experience. "Let us explain the situation first, before entering into reproaches and fantasies."

Felicity smiled, her eyes holding a complex blend of triumph and anger. "The explanation is simple enough, my dear." It was unclear whether "my dear" referred to Anne or to Mary. "As you know, London's entire drainage system is to be repaired and rebuilt. This includes the ancient sewers beneath Buckingham Palace, which, according to my contacts at Westminster, are in exceedingly poor condition. I've learned from these same sources the name of the firm engaged to perform these urgent and highly confidential repairs. It is—"

Mary eyed her with disbelief. She wasn't going to say . . . Oh, God, anything but this.

"Easton Engineering."

Mary stared at Felicity for a long moment, willing that name unsaid. Her cheeks, forehead, even the tips of her ears, were scorching hot, which meant that she was blushing furiously. Her heart kicked wildly against her rib cage. Her throat seemed too small. It was preposterous. A prank. Utterly ludicrous, to think that in a city of a million souls, she should keep crossing paths with this one man. She'd never believe it in fiction.

"You see why we were forced to recall you," said Anne, "despite the definite disadvantage it represents to our case. We shall have to place a new operative and start the process again. And we shall have to explain this to our client, of course."

Mary stopped herself from nodding along with Anne's all-too-reasonable logic. Her mind was still spinning, and she said the first thing that came to mind. "Easton Engineering is a small firm. Why were they chosen, above all others?"

Felicity nodded. "You're correct; they are certainly

not the obvious choice, and a number of more established firms would feel their noses out of joint about the appointment—if they knew of it, of course."

Mary fought the urge to bury her face in her hands. "It's a secret appointment?"

"Yes, because the work itself is a security risk. Mr. Easton's work at St. Stephen's Tower this past summer must have impressed the Chief Commissioner of Public Works, for it was at his particular urging that palace officials engaged the firm."

"I don't suppose it's George Easton who's leading this project," said Mary without conviction.

"It's the younger Mr. Easton," said Felicity with some satisfaction. "'James' to you, I believe."

Mary promptly blushed again, even more hotly than before. "No longer," she said—almost snapping, so vehement was her need to establish this fact. "I've nothing to do with him now."

Felicity merely smiled in a maddening fashion.

"So the sewers must connect with the public drainage system," said Mary wildly. Anything to get Felicity off this topic.

"Yes—hence the delicacy of the task," said Anne. She spoke quietly and rapidly, and without glancing in Felicity's direction. "Obviously, it wouldn't do for all and sundry to learn of the existence of these sewers. However, the sewers are in very poor condition—downright dangerous, according to our source. If allowed to collapse, they would not only dam the flow of an underground river, but undermine the foundations of the palace itself."

Mary nodded. "So if the work is being performed under such secret conditions, surely there's no danger of my encountering him?"

Felicity nodded. "True enough; they'd hardly announce it to all the staff." She glanced at Anne. "I rather thought the recall was an overreaction."

"They'd be working underground," continued Mary. "Most of my duties are carried out within a single wing of the palace. The chances of our meeting are almost negligible." She was talking to convince herself as much as her managers.

"I don't like it," said Anne. "A single coincidence—Mary runs an errand, or Mr. Easton steps outside for a breath of fresh air—could destroy the entire ca—"

"Even if they did meet," said Felicity, suddenly leaning forward and fixing Mary with her green-eyed gaze, "would that be so terrible? On that murder case at Big Ben, you managed a chance encounter without destroying your cover."

"All the more reason we mustn't rely on good fortune to preserve our secrecy!" Anne never, ever snapped; she spoke in even, measured tones that were a model of sangfroid. But now, her tone was so unusually vehement that Mary stared at her, speechless.

Felicity, however, only smiled. "Temper, Anne."

Anne swiveled her neck and glared at Felicity. "If you must press your private agenda so openly, Felicity, you might at least take into consideration the safety of our agents. Or is even that too much to expect of you now?"

"Oh, come, now—a chance encounter with James Easton will compromise Mary's safety? Such paranoia and subterfuge are beneath you, Anne."

"Wait!" Mary shot to her feet, so anxious was she to stop the argument. "So the recall isn't absolute? You've not decided precisely what ought to happen?"

"Recalling you was my idea," admitted Anne.

"So much for joint decision making," grumbled Felicity.

"Because there are new developments—not directly related to the case, but with dramatic personal significance for the royal family—that you ought to know, before making a final decision." Mary spoke rapidly, trying to measure the effect of her words on the two women. Although she'd caught their interest, they were still staring at each other, engaged in a separate, private contest that she didn't fully understand.

She pushed on, nevertheless, and informed them of the previous night's events—of everything, of course, except her possible connection to Lang Jin Hai. As she spoke, she felt their interest gradually—inevitably—turning toward her. She kept her voice low, her language matter-of-fact, but it was a sensational tale nonetheless. Scandal! Murder! Treason! Cover-up! It was the sort of story that couldn't be dully told—and a vein of intelligence that, Mary realized with a flash of triumph, the Agency couldn't afford to bypass.

"What if," she concluded, "I were to inform Mr. Easton, in advance, of my presence? That way, in the unlikely event that we were to meet, he would be prepared. That would help to reduce my risk."

"It would reduce the risk," agreed Anne, reluctance and interest clearly warring within her. "But not as much as removing yourself entirely."

"Contacting James Easton," murmured Felicity. "I thought you'd no interest in meeting him again?"

Mary swallowed hard. After her last interview with James—the way he'd refused to look at her when she'd told him of her criminal past—she'd sworn to put him from her mind. That was what she'd told Anne and Felicity, and what she'd instructed herself, too. But here he was again. She'd have to deal with him, in the Agency's best interests. Wouldn't she? She'd learned and changed a great deal over the past seven months. Hardly felt the scars of the wounds he'd caused. Didn't she?

"What are you thinking?" asked Anne suddenly. "There is more at stake for you here than simply the Agency's interests."

Anne was terrifyingly close to the truth. Mary squashed down the rising sense of panic in her chest and forced herself to answer. "Placing a new agent on the case would set the Agency back several weeks at least," she said slowly. "But you're correct. My concern is this: I needn't tell you what public opinion is right now against the Chinese. It's all around us, every time we open a certain type of newspaper. In the current climate, I worry that because the accused is a Lascar, he'll be the victim of a hasty show trial. The queen and prince consort seem less concerned with the general principle of justice here and more anxious to protect their son. That is natural enough, but it is not right. If I stay on at the palace, I may be able to gather information that would offer a clearer view of this man's role in Beaulieu-Buckworth's death."

Anne and Felicity both listened, thoughtful, grave, patient. They'd forgotten their earlier dispute and were now simply listening to her—something they'd both always been good at. Anne was staring into the fire, its flames bright in the glass of her spectacles. Felicity was focused on Mary herself, an inscrutable expression on her beautiful face.

Mary willed herself not to blush, even as she felt the blood rising in her throat, her cheeks. No one ever thought she looked Chinese; not Caucasians, at any rate. Occasionally, a Chinese person might peer at her curiously, somehow alerted to her secret—something in the geometry of her features, the creases of her eyelids. But Mary passed, for the most part, as a slightly exotic-looking Englishwoman. Strangers often asked if she had French, Spanish, or Portuguese blood; Italian was a popular choice right now because Garibaldi's triumphant progress was always in the news. But her answer—"black Irish"—was always persuasive, always enough. She hoped it would continue to be, especially now. "These are the principles you taught me—the importance of justice, and even of second chances for those who never had a decent first chance. It's because of what I learned from you that I need to stay on the case."

The moment passed.

Felicity blinked.

Anne smiled. "You've learned the lessons of the Academy well, my dear. The marginal figure—be it child, woman, or foreigner—is always disadvantaged in our society. It is admirable of you to wish to investigate further, and I find it a sufficiently compelling reason for you to stay on this case."

"Thank you, Miss Treleaven. Might the Agency also provide some information about Ralph Beaulieu-Buckworth? I think a little background research would be useful. For example, knowing to whom he is related. All those aristocratic families are so intermarried. He might be connected to the royal family, through some fifth cousin three times removed."

Felicity nodded. "That's not so easily done, but it's possible."

"Thank you."

"But returning to the original case," said Anne. "Have you anything at all to report?"

"No, Miss Treleaven."

Anne's eyebrows rose very slightly. "Still nothing?"

"The domestic staff was never informed of the original thefts, lest it encourage gossip. I've not observed anyone behaving suspiciously or flush with cash. Until the thief acts again, I can do no more than observe unexpected changes."

Anne nodded. "I see. Well, perhaps a little more time will give the thief the confidence to begin again. But without more evidence, this case may well go unsolved."

"Let us hope not," grumbled Felicity. "It's terribly unsatisfying."

"Not to mention bad for our statistics." The two managers smiled at each other fleetingly, and Mary felt a sudden, lovely wave of relief. Anne and Felicity were all right, then. Perhaps they'd simply been under a great deal of strain lately. Likely she'd read too much into the tension, the disagreements. All colleagues disagreed sometimes, especially when their work was as intense and important as that of the Agency.

Yes. That was surely all.

Her old bedroom had the thick, dusty smell of a place long abandoned. Mary glanced about the space, which was scarcely big enough to hold a single bed, a tiny wardrobe, and a narrow writing table and chair. This room had been hers for years. She knew its every detail—the angled ceiling, the tall, narrow window—better than those of her childhood home. Yet each time she came back from a job, the room seemed unfamiliar. It always took her some time to readjust, to become herself again. She disliked this sense of dislocation and for that reason seldom visited her room while on assignment. Today, Mary almost tiptoed across its length. The desk chair creaked slightly as she sat, and that was new. It was cold in the room, and a thin layer of frost glazed the inside of the window. It certainly didn't feel like home.

No matter. She opened her desk—it was one of the schoolroom sort, with a hinged lid—and looked at the neat nothingness within. Two pens. A bottle of ink. Some blank notepaper, its edges slightly curled from disuse. No mementos, no treasured letters, no girlish diary—nothing personal at all. It was a clean slate that suited her job, and also her status as a lost person. A reformed housebreaker, rescued by Anne and Felicity. An orphan—perhaps.

James's words to her, in their last conversation, still echoed in her mind: *You're still wanted. If you were caught now, they'd hang you. . . .* But much worse than the words had been his expression. Bafflement. Disapproval. Even, perhaps, a little repulsion. James was a purist when it came to telling the truth and the whole truth. And she couldn't afford his high morals, even if she wanted to. It was a damned good thing, then, that there was nothing left between them. She could never explain this new and damning twist to him if they were lovers.

She looked a while longer at the pens, the ink, the paper. Then she closed the desktop with a decisive click.

Writing to ask James for a formal interview would only prolong the agony. It would also give him a chance to refuse. Much better simply to confront him and see what happened. She'd know from the look in his eyes whether or not she could trust him to keep her secret one last time.

Mary walked to the door—it was only five steps—and then paused. Returning to the wardrobe, she selected a reticule from within. She dug into it, fingertips tingling now, and brought out a bundle the size of a walnut. Then she unfolded the square of linen to reveal a small pendant, green like a gooseberry and shaped like a tiny pear. This was all she had left of her father. The rest of his legacy—a letter, a sheaf of documents—was lost, burned in a house fire just days after she'd discovered its existence. But she had the jade pendant.

Mary clasped the chain about her neck and tucked it securely inside her collar so that no trace of it was visible. It was dangerous, wearing personal keepsakes on the job. She'd never done so before. But today, it seemed somehow essential. If her past was going to collide with her present, she would at least be ready in this small, perhaps vital way.

Thus armed, she closed the wardrobe, resisting the impulse to glance in a mirror—it would only confirm what a bedraggled mess she looked. Then she walked out onto Acacia Road and hailed a cab.

"Where to, miss?"

"Gordon Square."

Six

46 Gordon Square, Bloomsbury

The Easton home was one of a recently built row of townhouses, elegant in its proportions without being fashionable. It was nothing, in short, to make a caller quake—except for the knowledge of what lay within. Mary turned away from the cab, which lingered invitingly at the curb, and knocked on the door. She did it quickly so that she'd not have the option of fleeing—although the housekeeper's expression as she opened the door suggested that it would have been her best course of action.

"Miss Quinn."

Mary drew a deep breath and stepped into the hall. There was no retreat now. "Mrs. Vine. Is Mr. James Easton at home?"

With her lips pressed together, the housekeeper showed Mary to the breakfast room, where the fire had gone out and the lamps were unlit, and shut the door with a decisive click. Mary was certain that there were other, more comfortable rooms where a welcome caller might have waited, but this was fine. She'd not been turned away at the door, and that was a start. She stared out of the window into the garden square and tried to compose herself.

Perhaps a minute later, the door clicked open again and an all-too-familiar voice said, "Is that you, Mary? What are you doing, skulking there in the dark and cold?"

She couldn't speak; the sound lodged highest in her throat was a sob, and she certainly couldn't let that out. The best she could manage was a feeble shrug.

He looked . . . wonderful. Partly because he was James Easton, clever, sardonic, intense, and far and away the most interesting man she'd ever met. But even more because he looked healthy once more. The malaria-racked skeleton of their last encounter was transformed. He'd gained some much-needed weight; the edges of his cheeks and chin were thin, but not gaunt. And even in this half-light, he looked astonishingly handsome. No—better than handsome.

She cleared her throat. "Thank you for agreeing to see me," she said in her primmest voice.

"I can't actually see you, though. Come into the study. I can't imagine why Mrs. Vine put you in here in the first place."

Mary could. But she found that she couldn't meet James's gaze, or control the hot flush that sprang to her cheeks when she brushed past him on the way to the study. Here, the fire crackled cheerfully and the gaslight made the cherrywood desktop gleam. She shivered, nevertheless.

"Are you cold?" Before she could reply, he was feeding the fire, angling a pair of logs over the bright flames.

"Thank you."

He brushed off his hands and looked at her, his dark eyes searching her face. "You've already said that."

She tried to smile. "A little politeness never hurt."

His own smile barely touched his lips. "It's new for us, at least."

Us. She'd no idea how to interpret that. "You look very well," she said, then cringed inside: she sounded like somebody's busybody mother.

"As do you."

Liar. She could well picture her winter-chalk complexion, dark shadows beneath her eyes, and the several locks of hair that always escaped her tightly wound bun. "Er—" She didn't dare thank him again, but she could hardly plunge straight into her request.

He stared at her for a moment longer, then let out a whoosh of air. "Mary, aren't we rather beyond small talk?"

Startled, she met his gaze. "You're right."

"Not to mention you're rather bad at it."

"Only with you."

He smiled, then, his features lighting up with pure happiness. "It *is* a pleasure to see you, though."

She caught her breath. "And you." *Pleasure* was the

right word: just looking at him made her dizzy. His dark hair, normally cropped short, was long enough now to hint at unruliness. His locks looked as though they might actually be wavy, and she longed to explore them with her fingers. The lines of his jaw, too: he was still clean shaven, unfashionably so, and looking at him, she couldn't imagine why men might ever want to grow beards.

God only knew how long she'd been staring at him with undisguised hunger when the door opened quite suddenly and Mrs. Vine reappeared. "Do you require refreshment, sir?"

James glanced at Mary, as if to say that the decision was hers to make. She shook her head. Refreshments would mean a long visit. "Thank you, no."

"Very good, sir." Mrs. Vine shut the door with great care, and Mary resisted the urge to pull a face at the closed door. That whole loyal-retainer act was a little excessive. She turned back to James, disciplining her thoughts, drawing breath to explain her errand—only to find herself suddenly, blissfully, enfolded in his arms.

"Let's start again," he murmured, tilting her head back and covering her mouth with his. She gasped, and then felt his smile against her lips. "No small talk, remember?"

Her arms locked round his neck—she couldn't help it. She clung to him, the fixed point in a giddy, tilting universe, and reveled in the taste, the feel, the scent of him. He was the only man she'd ever kissed, the only one she could imagine igniting this trembling hunger, this need, within her. He stroked the length of her back, and she wanted to purr like a cat. Shedding her gloves with clumsy haste, she raked her fingers through his hair and was rewarded by a sharp hiss. He caught one hand and, pressing a fierce kiss into her palm, guided it beneath his jacket so she could feel the heat of him, the mad hammering of his heart against her bare skin. She stroked his chest, the linen warming to fever temperature beneath her hands, and tilted her head back to reach his lips again.

"Mary." His voice was hoarse, the word slurred. "Oh God, I've missed you. I thought I'd never see you again."

His words froze her. Pierced her. Made her exult and then long to weep. After a long moment of stillness, she began to disentangle herself—unwound his arm from her waist, turned her face from his. "James, stop." She became shamefully conscious of her loosened hair, a tangled mass of unmoored pins and stray locks. "James. Please." Where on earth was her hat? And how had she ended up in such an unladylike position, on a desk? "Listen to me."

He blinked, his eyes gradually clearing. "What's wrong?"

She couldn't meet his gaze. "I'm sorry—I should never have let you kiss me like that."

A long, tense pause. Then a dull red flush appeared high on his cheekbones. "You mustn't apologize—I all but attacked you. I *did* attack you."

"It's not that." Honesty compelled her to say as much. "I enjoyed your . . . attentions."

A pause. "If that's so, I don't understand what the problem is."

"I didn't come here for that."

"Not even a little bit of 'that'? I mean, it's more than merely physical between us, but animal passion has its place."

She almost smiled at his hopeful tone. "I came here to speak to you about something important."

He frowned. "You're still angry with me—and I can't blame you! I behaved inexcusably that last time, after the incident at the clock tower. I was a self-righteous prig, and I—" He faltered at her expression. "And I'm attacking you again, with words. I'm sorry; I'll just listen, for a bit."

He looked and sounded more vulnerable than she'd ever seen him. Normally, he seemed much older than twenty-one. Too assured. Too responsible. Too world weary. Now, he was almost boyish. Eager. And for both their sakes, she had to end this madness.

She slid off the desk and smoothed her skirts. Retrieved her hat from the corner of the room to which it had inexplicably rolled. Smoothed her crumpled gloves. When she finally dared meet James's eyes, she could see the resolve, the disciplined patience, shining out at her. They were two of the qualities she most admired in him—and which most terrified her now.

"I didn't come here to revive our—friendship." *Friendship* was such an inadequate word to describe her feelings for James; a cowardly word, even. But then, she'd never been brave where feelings were concerned. "I never meant to suggest otherwise. By my actions, I mean." Her cheeks flamed at the memory. Had James not said those words, where might things have ended? They might still be locked in an embrace on his desk.

He frowned at her, clearly struggling to understand. "I'm listening."

She started. Stopped. Tried again. "I came to ask for a professional courtesy. I believe you're soon to begin repairing some of the ancient sewers at Buckingham Palace."

He let out a puff of laughter. "It's only a top-secret project that concerns the safety of the royal family. Naturally, you know all about it."

She smiled faintly. "Congratulations; you must be very proud."

"We are; thank you." Those dark eyes were still puzzled, but genuinely curious, too.

And now the trickiest bit. "For the past few weeks, I've been working as a housemaid at the palace. I expect to be there for at least another week. Possibly more."

He nodded, comprehension dawning.

"I thought it possible that we might accidentally cross paths at the palace. It's unlikely, given the secrecy of your work, but still possible. And I wanted to ask you . . ." Her voice wobbled here, unexpectedly. This was far from the largest or maddest request she'd ever asked of James.

And yet it was the most difficult to make. "I wanted to ask if you would help preserve my secret. Not actively, of course; I shall be working alone. But I need to be sure that you'd not . . ."

"Not betray you?" His voice was acerbic. Clearly, he'd been expecting a different sort of request.

"I'd not have chosen that word."

"But that's what you meant. You were afraid that either through incompetence or through the spite of the rejected suitor, I'd somehow spoil your game at the palace."

His anger startled her, roused her own latent indignation. "If we're speaking of rejection, it was rather the other way round," she retorted. "I wasn't pure enough to suit your high moral principles . . . although you seem to have lowered your standards a little—but I suppose that was mere animal passion." She regretted the words even as they left her mouth.

James's eyes turned black, a sure sign of anger. "Don't pretend to be stupid. It's more than mere physical passion for me, and you know that."

Mary tamped down her anger. She couldn't afford to let it divert her. "So you say," she said with icy courtesy. "But I don't require protestations of devotion or apologies just now."

"I see."

"Will you be able to pretend that you do not recognize me at the palace?"

A tiny muscle twitched in his jaw. "Of course. I wouldn't dream of obstructing your path."

"Thank you. I'm very grateful." She buttoned her coat—not that she remembered having unbuttoned it—and reseated her hat, careless of how it might look.

In an exquisitely polite tone, he then said, "May I offer you the use of my carriage? It's a most unpleasant day for a walk."

Oh, how she hated the high moral ground when it was occupied by others. "It's very kind of you, but I shall find a hansom without difficulty." And such social niceties made her heartsick. Better never to speak to James at all than talk to him in this way.

"As you wish." He avoided her eyes as he held the study door—a gentleman to the last. "Good day, Miss Quinn."

The wintry sleet came as a rude shock after the warmth of James's study. Mary stalked southward, trying not to shiver as a swift wind picked up, driving the rain against her skin with stinging force. Naturally, there was no hansom cab in sight. And in her anger, she'd left her umbrella in James's front hall. Perhaps it was the cold, but the idiocy of their parting suddenly shocked her. She and James had always been passionate—both in rivalry and in partnership. But they needn't have left things so raw. They would never be casual friends, but she could, at the very least, retract her angry accusation. She stopped, halfway down Torrington Place, and retraced her steps, summoning her courage once more.

Mary knocked again and ignored Mrs. Vine's raised eyebrows. "Is he in the drawing room?"

"Yes, but—"

"No need to show me up." Mary whisked inside and was halfway up the stairs before Mrs. Vine could finish her sentence. She rapped twice on the drawing-room door and barged in. "James, I owe you an apology. I was—"

The words died in her mouth as she registered the scene before her: an extremely lovely young lady of about twenty, with shining red-gold curls, wearing a satin dress that must have cost more than Mary's entire wardrobe. The beauty was sitting in an extremely casual posture on the floor, teasing a kitten with a feather. A second gentleman, with the same reddish-blond hair as the lady, sprawled in an armchair. And James lounged on the floor beside the girl, his back to the door. All three were genuinely startled by the intrusion.

After a long, awkward moment, the two men scrambled to their feet. James's expression was unreadable, the other man's quizzical. The young lady, however, remained where she was, openly staring at Mary.

"I—I beg your pardon," muttered Mary. All her courage, her sensible intentions, dissolved instantly in the beam of the young lady's startled blue gaze. "My mistake." She shut the drawing-room door and plunged down the stairs. She ignored Mrs. Vine's smug expression. Ignored, too, James's voice calling after her down the stairs. She clattered out the door and into the square, forgetting her umbrella once again. Luck was with her, at long last: an unengaged hansom clipped by.

A moment later, she was palace-bound. Ten minutes to cry in peace.

And then she would never cry over James Easton again.

Seven

Monday, 13 February

Buckingham Palace

Amy Tranter took so long over her morning toilette that she was late for prayers—a grave offense under Mrs. Shaw's regime. For punishment, she was sent outside to beat rugs with Mary. In Mary's view, performing this task was a boon—even if the air was far from fresh, it was pleasant to be out of doors and away from the constant domestic clatter. But Amy's round, pretty face was creased and sulky even while she fetched her pattens—wooden blocks strapped to her boots to raise her clear of the mud. It wasn't until they were in the courtyard, however, with a large Persian rug draped over a washing line, that Mary learned why.

"Is any of my hair showing?" demanded Amy, patting at her three inches of exposed face. The rest of her head was shrouded in a huge cap she'd pulled down to cover her ears and eyebrows.

"Only your eyelashes."

"What about my dress?" This, too, was entirely swathed in a dust wrapper that went from her neck to her ankles. The combination of the cap, jacket, and pattens made Amy look like a hot-air balloon about to take flight.

"Can't see any of it," said Mary.

Amy remained unappeased. "The usual work's dirty enough, but this is horrible. I'll be gray with dust in two minutes."

"We'll be done by dinnertime, and then you can have a wash." Something about Amy's expression made Mary pause. "Unless . . . you have other plans?"

Amy flushed and beckoned Mary to her side of the carpet. "I can trust you, can't I?"

"Of course."

"I'm expecting . . . somebody . . . a caller."

"Here?" Domestic discipline was strict, and while letters and parcels were unrationed, staff were certainly not allowed to entertain guests.

"It ain't certain, mind."

Aha. "Mr. Jones?"

Amy flushed and squirmed. "Maybe."

"Oh, come on," teased Mary. "He's all you talk about."

"That ain't true!" squealed Amy, but she looked pleased despite her words. "Did I show you what he give me?"

"You know you didn't."

Amy glanced about in a conspiratorial fashion—totally unnecessary, as they were quite alone in the service courtyard. Opening her dust wrapper, she plunged a hand into her dress and drew out a long silver chain. On it dangled a heart-shaped locket, from which protruded a few wisps of mousy hair. "Ain't it beautiful?" she whispered reverently.

Mary had her own opinions about heart-shaped lockets crammed with hair, but she smiled anyway. "Very sentimental. It looks as though things are serious with your Mr. Jones."

"D'you think so?" asked Amy with eager pride. "I do, but sometimes I can hardly believe it's all real. And listen, tomorrow's Saint Valentine's Day. I want one of them big, beautiful valentines—you know, with real lace and feathers—and that's just the start."

"Are you going to see Mr. Jones tomorrow evening?"

Amy made a face. "I asked Mrs. Shaw for an hour's leave—to see my mam, I said it was—but she wouldn't say until tomorrow. I think she suspects."

Mary smiled very slightly. "I suppose everybody wants to go visit their mother on Saint Valentine's Day."

"But we'll see. All's not lost, even if she don't give me leave." Amy nodded and gave a sly wink.

"How d'you mean? You've worked out a way to slip out at night?"

But Amy only smiled and winked again.

"Well," said Mary, for this was the time to turn the conversation in the direction she needed, "if you want a bit of time in the day, you've only to say. I could dust the drawing rooms for you, and the like." Amy was responsible for cleaning the Blue Room—the one from which the original figurines had gone missing. So far, Mary had managed passing glances in the daytime and a careful nighttime inspection, but it was possible that a leisurely cleaning session by gaslight would yield useful information.

Amy's eyes sparkled. "You're a dear. I don't mind telling you I've high hopes for tomorrow. . . ."

"And so have I, my darling," purred a new voice. Male. Smooth. Educated. And naggingly familiar.

Both Mary and Amy jumped at the interruption, although their reactions were entirely different. Amy squealed and grabbed at her bonnet, whisking off the frumpy dust covers as fast as her shaking hands would allow. Mary, however, went very still. Then, with a grim feeling of certainty, she turned slowly toward the voice. There, smirking at her, was Amy's Mr. Jones: a green-eyed man of middle height, neither fat nor thin, neither handsome nor ugly. He wore a badly pressed suit. Nothing about him seemed likely to inspire squeals of delight or stunned silence, and yet he had done just that.

Mary had first met Octavius Jones, gutter-press journalist and incorrigible busybody, while she was working at St. Stephen's Tower. Admittedly, he'd been a small help to her toward the end of the case. But he'd also been the only person to see through her disguise as twelve-year-old Mark Quinn, and unless she was much mistaken, he'd not let that drop now. Jones was a shameless liar who'd not hesitate to sell his mother for tuppence profit, and boast about it afterward. Needless to say, he was also the last complication she needed on a case such as this.

At the sight of Mary, his face twisted with surprise—but only for an instant.

"Tavvy!" Amy leaped across the narrow space and planted a row of enthusiastic kisses on his face. "I ain't expected you for ages!"

He flinched at the nickname but soon recovered. "I couldn't wait to see you, my dear." "Tavvy" accepted Amy's attentions rather in the manner of a man tolerating the ecstatic licking of a puppy, and his eyes were fixed upon Mary the whole time.

"You say the sweetest things!" cooed Amy.

"Darling, aren't you going to introduce me to your little friend?"

Amy's voice quivered with pride as she made the introductions. "Mary, this is Mr. Octavius Jones; Mr. Jones, this is Mary Quinn, who started as a housemaid in the new year."

Mary dropped a very slight curtsy. "A pleasure, sir."

Jones's eyes were now alight with mischief. "The pleasure's all mine, Miss Quinn. Amy did tell me there had been some changes to the staff in recent months. And if it's not too forward of me, I must say that you look terribly familiar. Where could I have met you previously?"

Beside him—under his arm, rather—Amy stiffened. "I'm sure you can't have met before."

Mary sighed inwardly. It was no more than she expected of him; he was constitutionally incapable of leaving well enough alone. But it was infuriating nonetheless. "I can't imagine. Might you be mistaken, sir?"

"I doubt it; I've an excellent memory for faces—especially features as intriguing as yours. So exotic . . ." He all but smacked his lips. "Have you, by any chance, foreign blood?"

"Quinn is an Irish name, Mr. Jones." She swung her broom in a larger arc than necessary, nearly grazing his knees. His wide grin at this far-from-subtle gesture only annoyed her more.

"Anyway, it's lovely to see you now," said Amy with brisk determination. "I'm sure Miss Quinn won't object to our taking a brief stroll."

"Of course not, Amy. Take as long as you like."

Jones hesitated. "It does feel unkind, though, Miss Quinn, to leave you slaving here all on your own."

"Don't be ridiculous, Tavvy," said Amy, trying to keep her good temper. "Miss Quinn doesn't want to play gooseberry."

"Certainly not," agreed Mary. "I wish you good morning, Mr. Jones."

Amy tugged on his arm, trying to draw him away,

but Jones held his ground. "You do look so very familiar. . . . Are you quite sure we've not met before? Or perhaps you've a sister, or even a brother, who looks like you."

"London's a large town, Mr. Jones. There must be dozens of women who look just like me."

"That I refuse to believe. Never mind—it'll come to me in time," he promised with a cheerful wink. "You just see if it doesn't."

Mary found it very difficult not to bring her broom down on his head. "Good day, Mr. Jones," she said in her frostiest tones.

He finally permitted Amy to drag him away. But as they reached the service gate that led into the park, he glanced back at her just for a moment. He mouthed a sentence: "See you soon."

She didn't doubt it for an instant.

Eight

That afternoon, as Mary approached Her Majesty's private drawing room carrying a tea tray, the first thing she heard beyond the improperly closed door was the Prince of Wales's voice, raised high in a querulous whine. "I tell you again: I cannot remember exactly what happened, Mother!"

The queen's voice was cold and precise and quiet. "You were there. The dead man was your friend. You were surely concerned for his safety. *Why* can't you remember, Edward?"

"Because . . . because . . ." Prince Bertie, as he was known to the servants, heaved a sigh. "Because I was blind drunk, Mother, and—and—hysterical. I was screaming like a woman because I was so afraid. There. Are you happy now?"

"I am far from happy, Albert Edward Wettin."

"It was a figure of speech, Mother."

"I am aware of that. I am appalled to discover that my son and heir is not only a sot but a hysterical coward."

Sullen silence.

"You must try harder to remember. It is all there, in your brain." She paused. "Even such a mind as yours."

The prince made an explosive sound. "For the love of God, Mother!"

"I do love my God, Edward. Your behavior, however, suggests that you do not love yours as much as you ought."

"Oh, what is the use in trying to talk to you?" The prince's words were so anguished that Mary felt a moment's pity. Spoiled and selfish as he was, he was in an impossible position.

"How dare you speak to me like that? I am doing my best to shelter you from the consequences of your own actions! I desire only to protect your good name, spare you the shame of public exposure, eliminate the anxiety of your testifying publicly—and you would speak so to me!"

A long silence. Mary dared not set down the tray, dared not move or even draw a deep breath. "Not before the servants" was an ideal, of course, impossible to uphold in a busy and heavily serviced household such as this. But she very much doubted that this particular conversation would have continued had either mother or son realized she was on the threshold.

Finally, Prince Bertie spoke. His voice was weary and contrite. "I beg your pardon, Mother. I shall try to remember what happened."

"Do your best, my son. It is vitally important."

Another brief pause. Then the prince asked, "Mother, this sailor killed Beaulieu-Buckworth. He'll die regardless of what I remember. What does it matter whether it's a traitor's death or a murderer's?"

The queen's tone sharpened slightly. "Does it matter to you, Edward?"

"Er—well . . . not really!" An awkward pause. "I mean, yes, I suppose it could. Does, I mean. The truth will out, and all that. . . . That's in the Bible, isn't it?"

There was a long, taut silence. Then the queen's voice came again, distant and precise and cold. "'And ye shall know the truth, and the truth shall make you free': the book of John, eighth chapter, thirty-second verse. I believe that is the quotation you sought."

No response.

"You are correct in supposing that whichever is the case, this man will die. He is a bad man, of course: a violent opium smoker. But if he is also a traitor, we must make an example of him. An attack on you is, in effect, an attack on this nation. To permit a foreigner to threaten the crown is unthinkable—especially a Chinese, in the current state of affairs." She paused. "Sift your memories, Albert Edward Wettin. It is no small thing to be the future king, to have a hand in laying the path for justice."

"I . . . I do not know what to say, Mother."

"Do you understand what I've told you?"

Prince Bertie's tone was resentful. "Yes!"

"Then there is nothing more to be said." Her skirts rustled, and Mary heard the prince scramble to his feet. "I have a headache, Edward. I shall not take tea this afternoon."

"Yes, Mother."

"I expect to see you at both supper and at evening prayers."

"Yes, Mother."

At the first swish of Queen Victoria's skirts, Mary retreated round the corner, heart pounding furiously. This was a significant reversal of her earlier position: the queen was interested not only in the truth of what had happened that night, but in the general ideal of truth! What if the prince succeeded in remembering something that might clear Lang Jin Hai of the gravest charge, high treason? Would Her Majesty find a way to make that known to the police? Or what if Lang had acted in self-defense and Beaulieu-Buckworth's death had been a terrible accident? Mary's hopes rose despite her attempts to squash them down. With sufficient evidence, Prince Bertie's memories could even lift Lang's death sentence.

A delicate rattling of china reminded her of the tray in her hands, and it took a long moment to calm herself sufficiently to enter the room and set the tray before Prince Bertie. "Your Highness." She curtsied.

His head swiveled. He looked at her with sightless eyes.

"Do you require anything else, sir?"

"N-no. You may go."

"Very good, sir." She curtsied again and began her retreat.

She was halfway across the vast rug when he cleared his throat. "Er—Her Majesty will not be taking tea this afternoon."

"Very good, sir." She hesitated. "Do you expect Mrs. Dalrymple?"

A morose shrug was his only answer.

In that case . . . "Shall I pour you a cup of tea, sir?"

"Yes, do."

"Would you like a butterfly bun, sir?" It was the nursery choice: the Prince of Wales didn't seem in the mood to appreciate the pungency of a fruitcake.

"Yes."

She chose the fattest, creamiest cake, so thickly dredged with icing sugar that it gave off a puff of white powder as she set it gently on a plate. "Is there anything else you require, sir?"

"N-no. I mean, yes. I mean, I don't know!" The prince let the plate clatter onto a side table and buried his face in his hands. He made a curious, treble sound—a kind of animal shriek—and Mary realized, with wonder, that he was sobbing. His shoulders quaked. He shook and heaved and gasped for breath. But when Mary caught a glimpse of his scarlet face, his eyes were dry.

"There, there," said Mary with caution. She suspected he'd not take kindly to a sympathetic hand on his shoulder or the offer of a handkerchief. Yet she didn't yet want to summon help. He might tell her something meaningful.

She watched the prince a few minutes longer. His was a hysterical sort of sobbing—theatrical, even. Finally, when it began to subside, Mary knelt beside his chair. "It's not an easy life, yours," she said quietly.

"Nooooo," he agreed with a sort of wail.

In other circumstances, it would have been difficult not to laugh. Yet there was so much at stake just now. Every word of Bertie's was precious. "Nobody really understands what it's like."

His eyes welled up with tears in earnest now, and he began to blub again. "I—I'm so miserable . . . and so alone."

"Because there's nobody in your family like you," said Mary. "Nobody with your duties and people's expectations of you." She hated the words even as they left her mouth. The last thing she needed to encourage was the prince's sense of injured entitlement. Yet it was, she felt certain, the swiftest way into his confidence.

He looked at her for a moment, amazed. "How did you know that? How can a servant girl like you understand so much?"

Because self-absorbed man-children are common as weeds, thought Mary. But she said, "I don't know, sir. I only guessed."

"I'm entirely alone, for all I've equerries and friends and my parents; I'm more alone than the poorest orphan ever born." It was fortunate that the Prince of Wales couldn't see the twist of Mary's mouth as he uttered this. "And I'm even more alone now, because of what happened on Saturday night, and I can't even cry for my friend who's dead. I can cry for myself, all right; that's easy. But before, when I was thinking of him, I tried to make myself cry and I couldn't. I just couldn't. What's wrong with me?"

She poured a fresh cup of tea.

He gulped it down. "Eh? You haven't answered me that one."

"I'd not presume to know, sir."

He stared at her through swollen, bloodshot eyes. "What's your name?"

Mary bit her lip, sudden misgivings making her stomach roll over queasily. What was she thinking, addressing the Prince of Wales directly? Servants were sacked for less every day. "Quinn, sir," she said very quietly.

"I meant your other name."

"It's Mary, sir."

"Mary." He considered her, really looking at her now. "You're new, aren't you?"

"I began in January, sir."

"Clever." He looked her up and down. "Nice looking, too."

"Th-thank you, sir." She edged very slightly backward. This was not going as she'd hoped. She'd been mad, trying to gain the prince's confidence.

Just as he leaned forward to speak again, the door flew open to admit Honoria Dalrymple. Prince Bertie snapped back in his chair, as though on a puppeteer's string.

"Your Highness," said Mrs. Dalrymple, making a light, graceful curtsy. "Her Majesty has told me all about your terrifying ordeal, of course. I am so very relieved to see you unharmed."

"Thank you," he said in a slightly strangled voice. He flicked a reluctant glance at Mary, which Mrs. Dalrymple promptly interpreted.

"Enough dillydallying, Quinn," she said, making a shooing gesture with her fingers. "I'll pour for His Highness. You must have a great deal of work awaiting you." Her tone made it clear that she thought Mary the laziest of malingerers.

"Yes, ma'am." Mary retreated with a sense of relief. She'd never expected to be glad to see Mrs. Dalrymple, but the lady-in-waiting's entrance couldn't have been better timed. Mary closed the door behind her with an audible click, then retreated round the corner. She hadn't long to wait: in a few seconds' time, the door opened again and she heard Honoria Dalrymple sniff. This might have expressed either disappointment (that she'd not caught

Mary eavesdropping) or satisfaction (that she was alone with the prince). Whichever the case, the door banged shut again. Mary waited three minutes, then very quietly edged toward it.

"*Such* a nightmare!" trilled Mrs. Dalrymple. "You must be more careful of your safety; you don't know how your nation loves you, my dear sir."

"I—I shall try," said His Highness. He sounded rather bewildered.

"Why, whenever I hear your name mentioned, it's with respect and eager anticipation. Your subjects—your future subjects, I mean—bear you such uncommon goodwill and affection."

Mary listened with bemusement. What did the lady-in-waiting hope to accomplish with such flattery?

"You are too kind." But the prince's tone was guarded rather than gratified.

"Another cup of tea?" persisted Mrs. Dalrymple. "Or perhaps a cream cake?"

"Thank you, no."

"I don't doubt that trauma has quite dampened your appetite. But you must keep up your strength, dear prince. Your country needs you."

"I've had sufficient," said Prince Bertie, sounding a trifle sulky now. Apparently, even spoiled young princelings could tire of gushing concern.

There came a brief pause. When Mrs. Dalrymple spoke again, her pitch was considerably less shrill. "Will not

Her Majesty the Queen be joining us today? I thought she—"

Her sentence was interrupted by the sound of a teacup smashing—and more: "That's it! I've had enough! Why can't everybody just leave me alone?!"

Mary whirled back round the corner. Half a moment later, the door banged open and the tearful prince charged down the hall. Within the drawing room, there was only silence.

Mary retreated belowstairs, there to await her summons. The queen's position was transparent enough. So was the prince's. But what was Honoria Dalrymple playing at?

Nine

Evening prayers were always brief—belowstairs, at least. The domestic staff, weary from the day's labor, generally wanted nothing more than to retire for the night once the late-night supper had been served abovestairs, the royal family settled quietly for the evening, and the kitchens swept and scoured. Amy looped her arm through Mary's as they climbed the narrow service stairs to their attic quarters, her giddy chatter a high note amid the sighing and grumbling of the throng.

Mary listened with patience. It was a genuine puzzle as to what Octavius Jones wanted with silly, gossipy Amy. There was the all-too-obvious, of course, but he needn't have chosen Amy for that; a woman in service was difficult to visit and had little free time. No, he must be after information—and it was surely Amy's place of employment that captured his real interest. But in what?

Of course! She was a bloody fool not to have seen it immediately. Octavius Jones was entirely capable of bending a girl like Amy to his will. And he'd chosen well: not only was Amy malleable and infatuated, but she was the maid who cleaned and dusted the public drawing rooms. Nobody was better poised to steal those ornaments than she. It was simple enough for Amy to carry a snuffbox or a small china figurine in her handbag when she went out to meet Jones. And with Amy running all the risks, Jones would likely be safe even if she was caught. He might even be able to count on her loyal silence under questioning.

This theory led to new possibilities and new motives for the thefts. Mary had always assumed that common avarice was the reason: the items stolen were of good quality, although far from the finest examples of their kind. They would fetch a decent price without calling undue attention to their provenance, and Mary had always assumed they'd long since been sold to unscrupulous antiques dealers. But what if the palace thief was no ordinary thief? What if he was calculating and subtle, and interested in far more than a small profit on a couple of Dresden shepherdesses? If Octavius Jones was the mastermind behind the thefts, there had to be something else to it. The question was, what was he planning?

She could imagine a sort of shrill exposé about the laxity of palace security. Or perhaps on the corruption of antiques dealers—no, too rarefied for readers of the *Eye*. A scandal-mongering piece about the obscene riches amid which the royal family lived? No, too socialist-republican for Jones. Or perhaps he was after the questionable characters of the royal domestics—decrying the corruption belowstairs. That would be a hard blow for Amy, though; was that perhaps too unconscionable a betrayal even for Jones? It would mean significant personal risk if Amy took umbrage. No. It had to be palace security, then, or something similar.

"It's a delicate thing to ask," Amy was saying, already blushing in anticipation.

Mary was recalled with a jolt. "You can ask anything of me," she said.

They had gone into their shared room now, and Amy closed the door firmly behind her. "Well, Mrs. Shaw wouldn't give me leave to go out tomorrow night," she said, rolling her eyes. "The old ninny. Said she reckoned I could go and visit my mother on Sunday afternoon, same as always."

Mary grinned. "*Do* you visit your mother of a Sunday?"

Amy shot her an indignant look. "'Course I do. I just make it quick, like, so's to leave time to meet Mr. Jones. Anyway, there it is: I've an appointment to see my gentleman friend, and I ain't allowed out."

"That's a shame."

"Maybe. But I thought again, and perhaps it's for the best. And that's what I wanted to ask you . . ." To Mary's surprise, Amy blushed again, deeply. "Would you—d'you think I could—well . . ."

"Do you want me to help you slip out?"

Amy shook her head and went from pink to scarlet. "To help Mr. Jones sneak in. And to let us have the room for a bit." Mary's face must have reflected her surprise, for Amy rushed on. "I been thinking, right, and this is the thing to do. He's a lovely man, is my Tavvy, but he's a bit on the shy side." Mary tried not to show her utter disbelief at this description. "And I reckon a little encouragement is just what he needs."

Mary shook out her apron, inspecting it for dirt. "Encouragement to what?"

It was Amy's turn to stare. "Why, to pop the question, you goose! What else?"

Instantly, Mary's thoughts turned to the thefts. "Was this Mr. Jones's idea?"

"Of course not!" Something in Amy seemed to snap. "Ain't you been listening? It's my idea, you dunce, because Tavvy's so blooming slow. If I had permission to go out tomorrow, he'd take me to stupid Astley's to see them stupid horses again, or for another freezing-cold walk in the freezing-cold park, and all I'd get for my troubles'd be a cuddle in a corner and a dress that's all over mud. No, ta—not again."

Mary's lips twitched. She had, indeed, been sluggish on the uptake—nearly as slow as Jones. "So by giving you a bit of privacy . . ."

Amy smirked, all embarrassment evaporated. "Right you are. A little encouragement and a nice warm bed, and I'll be the future Mrs. Octavius Jones by Wednesday morning."

"Sounds as if he hasn't a chance."

"Not even half." Amy wrestled mightily with her corset and pulled it off with a groan of relief. "Oh, that's heaven, that is." She waved the giant pink lobster's-tail bustle at Mary with a disgusted air. "He ain't never even seen this, y'know; that's how behindhand the man is."

Mary grinned. "I'd never have guessed." Amy's plan was far from original, but her brazenness was endearing.

Amy rubbed soap onto a flannel and washed herself with brisk, decisive gestures that spoke of her determination. "I once suggested—you know, coy, like—going to his place, but he says his landlady's a right old sourpuss, and he daren't cross her. We'll move into a proper house, of course, once we're married."

Mary knew better than to challenge Amy's fantasy of escape: a woman intent on freedom through marriage wouldn't listen to a naysaying spinster. Amy was only following the usual script. Yet Mary couldn't resist a gentle question. "D'you think you'll be happy, married to Mr. Jones?"

Amy looked at her, all astonishment. "I'll be the lady of the house and never wipe out a chamber pot again. If you don't call that happy, I don't know what's wrong with you."

"I meant with Mr. Jones."

"Oh, Tavvy. Aye, he's an all-right sort, I reckon. But he's a gentleman, and that's what's important."

Mary gave a philosophical shrug. At least Amy wasn't blinded by visions of romance. "Well, then—about tomorrow night. What d'you want me to do?"

It was only after Amy had rolled herself into a ball and fallen into the sleep of the just schemer that Mary's amusement faded. She'd been dreading her next task all evening. The habits of discipline she'd learned at the Academy were strong, though, and so she pulled a thin folder from beneath the bed, took out a sheet of cheap paper, a pen, and a bottle of ink, and prepared to write a letter.

Her father could read and write adequately. His reply—if he replied—would be an immediate first test of his identity. Unless, of course, he was too weak to write and had to dictate a letter. Or the opium had addled his brain. Or they didn't trust him with a pen. The possibilities were several. Nevertheless, she would begin with a letter.

Dear Mr. Lang—

She stared at the words and then at the expanse of blank notepaper beneath. She could hardly start with *I may be your daughter*. She gazed at the page until her eyes lost focus, until she could see and smell the bittersweet poverty of her childhood home. A loud snore from the other side of the room made her jump, and she returned to the present.

Finally, she dipped her pen again and wrote:

I may have information that could help your case. Please reply as soon as you are well enough to receive callers.

Yours sincerely,
A friend

She blotted the page in one swift gesture, not pausing to reread the letter. A moment later it was sealed, the address written, and a penny stamp applied, and she was pulling on her coat and hat. Slipping out to the nearest pillar box after hours was a risk, but a far lesser one than keeping that letter overnight. And if she got the response she needed, it was the least of the risks she'd have to run in the next few days.

Leaving the palace without Mrs. Shaw's permission was strictly forbidden. But, like many forbidden things, it was also rather easy. At night, as was the custom in grand houses, the footmen slept outside the storerooms, the better to guard Her Majesty's valuables by night. Any thief who evaded the Yeomen of the Guard outside the palace would then have to bypass at least one large, cricket-bat-wielding manservant before getting near the royal candlestick holders. However, Mary had discovered early on that the footmen nearest the service door were the youngest, the newest, the hardest worked—and thus also the deepest sleepers. One could tiptoe past them with perfect confidence. In fact, she'd wager that if she lit a string of firecrackers beneath their trundle beds, the commotion would only cause them to push their faces deeper into their pillows.

So Mary let herself out through the servants' entrance without much concern for the inner guardians of the palace. Outside, however, were the real sentries—the Queen's Guard, whose duty it was to protect their sovereign, not her silverware. They were trained, armed, disciplined. Mary shivered. At this moment, she still had a choice. The first possibility was to play the dizzy, naughty maidservant, tripping out after dark to post an illicit letter. Her success in that case, however, would depend on the character of the soldier in the guard box. If he was lenient, he might let her get away with it. But that route left far too much power in the hands of one unknown man. What if he was dutiful? Worse, what if he required payment for his silence?

It was too uncertain. She set out—westward into the gardens, away from the grand entrance gates. In the open courtyard, fat raindrops thudded heavily against her hat and fell, startlingly cold, onto her cheeks. Between the dark and fog and steady sleet, it was difficult to see anything. The mass of shadows in the middle distance, however, was certainly a stand of densely grown hawthorns, perhaps twice the height of a man. She had seen the young princes and princesses playing in front of them, using a natural hollow as a sort of playhouse. And she knew that they grew against the tall iron fence that encircled the palace grounds.

The night was unnervingly still. In the elegant streets beyond, there was only silence—not even the clatter of a dustman's cart—and the outlying parks filled with carriages only during the fashionable hours. After her early years around Limehouse and Soho, Mary had thought St. John's Wood—home of the Agency—quiet and peaceful at night. But the northern suburbs positively bustled compared with her current streetscape. It was all about density, she supposed. In east London, it was common for several families and their animals to share a pair of rooms in a ramshackle tenement. Here, one family with its domestic staff occupied a few acres of palace and park, making for a peaceable hush at night. Yet the hollow emptiness of Westminster made her feel edgier than did the seedy violence of Soho or the Haymarket. Nobody about. No one to hear her scream.

A slight rustling in the hedge made her start. She stared furiously into the shadows, willing whatever it was to move again. It did not. A change in the wind, perhaps, or a bird. She would not permit herself to speculate further. She moved steadily, holding herself in readiness—for what, she didn't know. Perhaps that was the point. As she reached the play hollow, she stopped and listened again. Nothing. Was it possible she'd imagined the first rustle? She was certainly jumpy enough. After waiting a full three minutes, she pressed on. The branches were long and tangled, and although she could shield her face with one hand, their thorns caught at her hat and sleeve, pulled at her skirts. She'd be a fine mess when she got in. With time and patience, however, she pushed through. In a way, the tearing thorns affirmed that no human, at least, could be lurking within the hedge, for all her vivid suspicions.

The fence was surprisingly low, a wrought-iron affair perhaps one and a half times a man's height. It was details like this that reminded Mary of the palace's history as a grand home and pleasure palace rather than a state residence. It was no wonder that the occasional lunatic managed to wander into the grounds. One could hardly expect a fence like this, abutted with shrubbery, to keep out the determined. Or to keep them in.

Mary found a toehold at waist level, pulled herself up, and balanced with care over the rather spiky top. It was a simple matter of using her arms and hoping her petticoats didn't catch as she went over. When she dropped down on the other side, she wasn't even breathless. The hawthorns had been the greater challenge. From here, it was only a hundred yards or so to the nearest pillar box. Then back over the fence. In ten minutes, she'd be in bed.

She fought her way through the brambles for a second time, cursing the tiny hooks that gripped her clothing with such tenacity, and emerged annoyed but warmed by her little adventure. Then she looked across the garden toward the palace, at the yellow lights winking from the odd exposed window, and felt suddenly cold. All the feelings she had long suppressed overcame her at last, making her stagger. It was like a physical blow: she was not just alone, but lonely.

The solitary state was nothing new, of course. But she was lonely now for different reasons. She was lonely despite the possibility of family—perhaps because of that very likelihood. Because she might not be absolutely, truly alone, after all, and she might have preferred it so. Her fingers went to her throat, touching the reassuring lump of her pendant. She found it uncomfortable to wear now. Not literally, for the pendant was small and weighed very little. But each time she touched it or felt the slither of its chain about her neck, she writhed and tried not to think of the man who might be her father.

She'd considered taking the necklace off, of course. Or throwing it into the river. She had the power to erase the last tangible link to her past, just like that. But she couldn't quite bring herself to do it. Too frightened to face the truth. Too afraid to bury it. When had she become such a coward?

Mary stopped short. She'd always despised cowardice. Found it difficult to understand in others, much less sympathize with. But here she was now, sidling away from the real problem. A man called Lang Jin Hai was locked in a prison cell, old and ill, likely abused by guards, awaiting trial for murder—and all she'd done was write him a letter. What a stupid, useless thing she'd chosen—hoping he'd not reply, hoping she could salve her conscience by saying that she'd tried. When she considered the problem in theory—the injustice of a man being falsely accused—she burned with anger. Yet the shame of being related to such a man—a killer, an opium addict—made her shrivel. She was wasting her time tiptoeing about the palace and hoping that Prince Bertie might remember something, that his mother might extend leniency to this foreign criminal. But even if they did—a vast and unlikely assumption—such so-called success would bring her no closer to the real problem. Whatever happened to Lang Jin Hai, she wouldn't have come anywhere near dealing with him as she ought to. As she needed to.

She had to confront Lang Jin Hai. She would have to gain access to his jail somehow and speak with him. Only by seeing him could she know whether he was in fact her father, or whether it was all a grotesque coincidence. She'd no idea which scenario she might prefer.

Ten

As she reentered the palace, Mary was cold, distracted, brooding — three reasons why she nearly walked into the furtive figure creeping along the servants' corridor. It was only her training that saved her — had her stopping behind a door frame even before she knew why. For this was no ordinary prowler. Not a footman investigating a strange noise. Not another maid on an illicit errand. The tall figure was instantly recognizable, her elegant posture thrown into relief by the candle flickering in her hand. It was, of all people, Honoria Dalrymple.

Mary gave her a short lead, then followed with soundless steps. The lady-in-waiting had no reason to be in the servants' quarters. Even in the unlikely event that she had wanted a cup of hot milk before bed, she had only to ring for her maid. Yet here she was, picking her careful way past the butler's pantry until she reached a flight of stairs. She paused, as though summoning courage. Then she opened the heavy door and began her journey into the subterranean kitchens.

Mary rubbed her eyes. It was almost too perfect to be true, as though her tortured brain had produced a hallucination spectacular enough to distract her from thoughts of Lang Jin Hai. Yet even as she paused, she heard the soft *clop* of Honoria's shoes against the rough stone steps. Honoria had left the door slightly ajar, rather as though she didn't expect to be long. Mary thought about her choices—but only for a moment. Nothing in the world could have kept her from following the Honorable Honoria Dalrymple into the bowels of the palace.

Mary waited a few seconds longer, then peeked down the stairs. Smiled widely. And descended. The stone floors were worn smooth, here in the heart of the original Buckingham House. It had undergone generations of renovations, including very recent ones to create nurseries for Her Majesty's young family, but the kitchens had remained unchanged. It was perhaps a shame—they were dank and smoky, desperately small for the large staff, and, Mary imagined, a positive inferno in the warmer months. In present circumstances, though, they were cozy and warm, the coals from the banked-down fires offering just enough light for Mary to track Honoria's movements across the sloping flagged floor.

As the heel of Honoria's shoe scraped loudly against an uneven section of flagstone, she glanced down and sniffed. Tense as she was, Mary couldn't repress a smile.

So the snobbery wasn't an act put on for the queen's benefit: even a humble square of stone could be found remiss. Honoria halted before what Mary thought of as the herbarium—not that any of the staff called it by such a grandiose title. It was a small space, like an open room, near the two vast bread ovens where all the palace baking took place. At summer's end, the cook maids hung large, bushy bundles of thyme, rosemary, sage, and tarragon from the ceilings. These dried in the heat of the nearby fires, then were packed into dark cupboards for the winter. Now the small space was empty, although perfumed by the ghosts of those aromatics.

Holding her candle aloft, Honoria began to look about—not suspiciously, but with earnest inquiry. The upper halves of each wall were fitted with open shelves where less frequently used equipment—jelly molds, especially large basins—were stored. Below were cupboards that held, presumably, the dried herbs and other goods. Her large, elegant hands skimmed the shelves and she peered into cupboards as though searching for just the right cake tin. It was a most unlikely sight.

Honoria searched methodically from left to right, from top to bottom. When she reached a small cupboard in the darkest corner, she paused, her sudden stillness as clear as any announcement. She selected a small jug—it was glazed white earthenware, with a scene painted on it in blue—and, holding her candle closer, peered at the shelf on which it had stood. The candle's wick was long, and it produced a high, bright flame that illuminated her features beautifully. Mary was surprised to realize that Honoria Dalrymple was a handsome woman—at least while her features were lit with excitement and anticipation, as they now were. Whatever she'd sought was very near. She smiled—a feline look of satisfaction.

Mary took three careful steps back around the nearest corner, preparing to retrace her steps with some speed. Once Honoria had her prize, she would leave as swiftly as possible, and the last place Mary wanted to be was in her path. Such caution had its difficulties: she could no longer see what Honoria was doing. She heard a distinct click, and then a low scraping sound, rather as though something heavy was being dragged over flagstones.

Honoria took two audible steps, then gave a sudden, high gasp. Mary tensed, ready either to fly or to confront her. There came that scraping sound once more, punctuated by a second metallic click. Time slowed in inverse relation to Mary's wild impatience, and she strained her ears for more information. Yet as the seconds crawled past, she heard nothing more. Incredible as it seemed, the room fell still and quiet. The perfect silence was marred only by the faint sounds of mice scurrying in the kitchens' deepest recesses. Mary waited ten seconds, and then another ten. This might well be a trap. If Honoria suspected she was being watched, this was a classic strategy for flushing out an inept follower. Only after a full five minutes did Mary feel secure enough to inch forward again, moving slowly and poised to freeze at any moment. When she gained the corner, she took a moment to focus, to listen with renewed attention to the peculiar stillness of the room. Then, taking a smooth, quiet breath, she peered round the corner—to discover the impossible.

Honoria Dalrymple was gone.

Mary blinked, reluctant to believe the evidence of her senses. Honoria was a tall woman—not the sort who could tuck herself neatly into a cupboard. Yet the herbarium was undeniably empty. There was only one logical explanation, and Mary approached it with caution. She knew about secret doors, of course—there was one in the attic of the Agency, for heaven's sake, that had impressed her no end when she'd first been recruited. Yet it seemed far-fetched in this context.

In grand houses of the sixteenth and seventeenth centuries, it was not uncommon to have a "priest hole"—a specially built hiding place for persecuted Roman Catholic priests. But Buckingham Palace was a new palace, and Queen Victoria the first monarch to use it as her official residence. Even these kitchens, original and unmodified, were only a hundred and fifty years old—nearly new, in comparison with most other palaces and châteaux. So an old-fashioned escape route—built in times of religious conflict and dire need—was impossible. Yet there Mary stood, in the herbarium, very much alone.

With a careful, light touch, Mary found the shelf that had so fascinated Honoria, and the blue-and-white jug she'd inspected. It was a coarse piece of pottery—the type used for food preparation, but never service, in a house as grand as this. Without more light, she couldn't decipher the scene, but surely it wasn't the jug that had caused that clicking sound. The jug was merely a signal, a place marker. She lifted it carefully from the shelf, noting its precise angle and placement. One had to assume that everything was a snare. The shelf was unpainted wood, somewhat dusty—another potential trap, Mary realized, since it would render visible even the slightest touch. Yet Honoria had already disturbed the shelf. It was worth the risk.

She felt about delicately, unsure of what she was seeking. But the instant her fingertips met something sharp and metallic—colder than bare wood—she smiled. It was a latch, invisibly mounted at the very edge of the shelf. In her experience, that meant a simple sort of door—nothing that would fool a team of professionals out for blood, but a concealed entrance all the same.

She pressed gently against the shelf. Nothing.

But when she pulled it toward her instead, she immediately felt it give. It was only a small shift—a fraction of an inch—but it moved, all the same. Mary's pulse, already rapid, leaped so strongly that she felt it throb in each fingertip, in her throat. A secret door in Buckingham Palace! And Honoria Dalrymple had just walked through it. She controlled a ferocious impulse to dash after her in pursuit. Not now, when she hadn't a clue, or even a candle. Mary replaced the blue-and-white jug with care, turned, and left the kitchens.

Eleven

Five minutes later, she was properly equipped: coatless and wearing soft-soled shoes, carrying a candle, a box of lucifers and her hairpin lock pick. As she went back down the service stairs, with more than usual care, a distant clock struck midnight. It was early yet, she told herself, trying to contain her sudden simmering anticipation at the prospect of adventure. It was quite likely that Honoria would remain behind the secret door for some time. She couldn't just blunder in. She would have to improvise. Yet that was one of the things that made her happiest, and so it was with a very real lightening of spirit, if not physical discomfort, that Mary settled in to wait at the other end of the kitchens near the larder.

It was a deeply familiar situation—sitting on her haunches, in the dark. She'd spent countless hours on "watch training" at the Agency, learning to maintain her sense of time's passing without even the skies for reference, remaining alert but not overfocused, keeping her limbs from falling asleep without the privilege of movement. It was, on the surface, a simple matter but one she had struggled with. Her propensity was either to remain so furiously alert and still that she found her joints stiff and seized just when she most needed them or to ponder the possibilities of each case so intently that she lost track of time. As Anne and Felicity noted, she was a creature of extremes.

Neither of these occurred tonight. Instead, she committed a new and astonishing error: falling into a daydream. It was something she'd never done before, and something she'd never quite understood. It had always seemed impossible to become so distracted in uncomfortable, high-tension situations where nearly all questions remained unresolved. But this evening, Mary was a few miles and many years away, sifting through fragmented memories of Limehouse and her father, when she became aware of the scraping sound of the hidden door. She started and, compounding her error, gasped slightly.

There was a second gasp, like a magnified echo of her own. Then, Honoria's voice: "Who's there?"

Mary was instantly awake and furious with herself. However, there was nothing to do but remain perfectly still and silent.

"I know you're there," said Honoria after another pause. Bold words, but her voice was higher and thinner than usual.

Mary's tension eased a fraction. Fear was good—for

her, at least. The next few seconds must have stretched endlessly for Honoria, but Mary's internal clock was working once again. She heard an uncertain shuffle, and then another. Impossible to know in which direction.

"Show yourself, if you're there," said Honoria, and this time her voice held a distinct quaver.

Perhaps half a minute ticked silently past. She could see little of Honoria—primarily the dazzle of her candle, and her general shape behind that. But she was safe enough: as long as Honoria continued to hold that candle at arm's length, all beyond it would appear black. And even if she extinguished her flame, Mary would have time to move away silently before Honoria's eyes adjusted. So Mary remained poised but relaxed now and waited for Honoria to act.

The lady-in-waiting hesitated a minute longer. Took a half step, as though to investigate. Mary tensed, readying herself for action. But after another pause, Honoria turned on her heel and hurried away. She *had* sounded thoroughly rattled. And she was snooping about a part of the palace she'd no business being in, going through concealed doorways. Mary wondered, again, about Honoria Dalrymple's position within the ranks of the ladies-in-waiting and made a note to check with the Agency about her history. Come to think of it, they'd not yet supplied information about Honoria's possible connection to Beaulieu-Buckworth, either. . . .

When Honoria's footsteps had receded and she was

definitely alone once more, Mary moved decisively toward the secret door. She loved these moments, when endless possibilities of action and adventure stretched before her. It was tempting to savor them, to play at heightening her suspense. But this wasn't a game, and she, like Honoria, was trespassing. They both risked severe punishment if caught, although it was a fine debate as to which was the graver penalty: social disgrace for a lady-in-waiting or loss of livelihood for a housemaid.

Mary shook her head, both figuratively and literally. She was wasting time. And, she reminded herself sternly, it was possible that nothing of real interest lay behind that secret door. Neat rows of jams and pickles, perhaps. Or a child's play closet. Yet even as her fingers found the catch, she didn't really believe that.

The door swung open with a faint creak. A new smell, thin and cold and sharp, filled her nostrils. This was a surprise—she'd expected claggy damp, perhaps mildew or mold. But not this aroma, which was more reminiscent of riverbanks than anything else. She frowned into the darkness, unable to discern any sort of depth or detail. Even so, she was reluctant to strike a light. As Honoria had just demonstrated, a candle in the darkness illuminated only the things nearest. And it alerted possible observers for hundreds of yards all around.

Instead, she stepped through the doorway and felt about the frame with her fingertips. One of the Agency's first rules was *Secure your exit*. Her fingers moved swiftly, carefully over the unpainted wood. There: set into the top of the frame was a sturdy metal latch that, when depressed, would release the door. Mary tested the catch. Then she swung the door closed behind her and pressed it again. So far, so good.

Now, inside the secret door, she listened for clues as to what sort of hiding place this was. The floor gave slightly beneath her shoes—not packed earth but wooden floorboards, springy and rotting with age. How old did that make them? Perhaps thirty or forty years, depending on what lay beneath and how damp it was. Safely during the reign of George III, at least, who'd used the palace as an occasional home. Mary's mind whirled. The old King George and Queen Charlotte were reputed to have had an ideal marriage—congenial and affectionate and dignified—and had had fifteen children, if she remembered her history lessons correctly. It made a concealed entrance of this sort less likely than ever—unless it had been built for someone other than the king.

A small sound—a rattle or a trickle of some sort—recalled her to the present. It wasn't an echo, but it sounded distant—as though where she stood was merely the starting point of a long corridor. And so it was. Certain now that she was alone, Mary lit her candle and, blinking against its sudden dazzle, was astonished to find herself in a narrow, low-ceilinged tunnel. The cobwebbed brick walls curved up to become the ceiling, which was scarcely taller than Mary herself. She touched the ceiling thoughtfully: a film of greasy dust coated her fingertip. The floorboards were indeed rotting but bore no particular signs of heavy use: the edges were nearly as worn as the centers, so she could at least discount the possibility of tens of thousands of urgent footsteps wearing them down.

She moved carefully through the tunnel, the yellow glare of her candle skittering wildly off the walls, making her dizzy. It was her hand, she realized: it was shaking with excitement and nerves. She relaxed her fingers about the small grips she used to carry the candle—the only sensible way to avoid being continually burned by hot wax—and its light steadied perceptibly. Better.

Her progress through the tunnel felt timeless. She couldn't have been more than fifty yards from the secret door, yet the still, stale atmosphere made it seem endlessly distant. It was the tunnel's shape, too—a series of short, straight lengths with sudden forty-five-degree turns that seemed designed to disorient its occupant. Then, quite suddenly, she came to an end—or, as she quickly realized, a beginning. It was a large hole in the tunnel floor, neatly circled with brick. It was much too large and distinctive to fall into, unless one were tumbling pell-mell through the darkness. On peering inside, Mary saw an ancient, rusting iron ladder set into the bricks that lined its walls. It was a vertical continuation of the tunnel, nothing more. What troubled her was that with a sole candle, she couldn't see its end—only the ladder disappearing into blackness. She paused for a moment. Then, transferring her candle to her left hand and accepting philosophically the inevitable damage to her dress, she began her descent.

The rungs weren't painfully cold: a surprise, until Mary remembered the insulating properties of being underground. They did, however, leave a thin coating of slime against her palms, her sleeves, and her cheek when she accidentally brushed too close. She descended twelve rungs before her searching foot encountered only emptiness. Damn. She crouched—no mean feat on a ladder, in a crinoline—and shone her inadequate little light downward. It flickered wildly, and this time it wasn't due to her shaking hand. Yet it revealed nothing—no visible floor, no detail that gave a clue as to what lay below.

Mary snuffed out the flame and put away the candle, heedless of the dripping wax that promptly made a small pool in her pocket. Gripping the lowest rung tightly with both hands, she lowered herself down with a smooth, athletic motion. Felicity and Anne had sometimes remarked on her uncommon strength—her ability to pull herself up by the arms, even when encumbered by ten or fifteen pounds of clothing. But tonight, her arms felt bruised and shaky. She was grateful when her toes brushed something solid. She tested the surface and found it wide and even.

Releasing the rung and resisting the temptation to wipe her hands on her skirts, she listened to the new atmosphere about her. It had a slightly hollow sound.

She relit her candle and raised it, the better to inspect her new discovery. It was a small room, apparently an antechamber of sorts, with a doorway at the other side. Unlike the tunnel she'd just come through, it had a brick floor. In fact, it was a tube of a room, with curved walls that led up to a low, curved ceiling—another tunnel fashioned in bricks.

Mary shook her head slowly, a small smile curving her lips. How utterly unlikely, how preposterous, to think that Honoria Dalrymple was mixed up in all this grime and skulking about. The room was empty, and it was unclear what purpose it served. A clandestine meeting place? A storeroom for illicit goods? A secret escape route? She would write to the Agency for more background detail. Perhaps she'd not allowed enough time.

She crossed the room slowly. The second opening was barricaded with closely spaced wooden planks, fixed in place from the other side. There were, technically, gaps large enough to peer through, but her candle showed nothing but blackness. She'd no idea whether she was looking at a wall, six inches away, or another endless tunnel. Mary frowned at the barrier. She could remove a plank easily enough, she imagined, by kicking it loose. Yet after that, she'd have no way of replacing it in an unobtrusive fashion. It would obviously have been tampered with.

Even so, it was instructive. The wooden planks were recent and solid, not ancient and rotting. They weren't even that grimy. Someone else had been here in the past few months and seen fit to barricade the tunnel. Someone else had accessed the tunnel from its other end. And—as she could see now as she peered through the planks from a new angle—someone had affixed a sign that said:

DANGER

ABSOLUTELY

NO ACCESS

she blinked and glanced back into the chamber. There were no obvious hazards, of course, unless one counted spilled poisons. Or the tunnels suddenly caving in.

At that, a small, distinct chill rippled down her back—and it had nothing to do with the threat of being trapped underground. She turned back to the sign and frowned at the lettering. It was difficult to say, of course, reading backward by candlelight—and she'd seen so few examples of his handwriting, and never this sort of block printing. Yet there was something about the way the letters were formed that raised her suspicions. She felt a rush of warmth. A sense of dread. A thundering in her ears, her throat, her pounding pulse. All this, at the mere thought of the man.

She leaned against the wall, feeling suddenly weary. It was a sickness of hers, dreaming up James Easton in the unlikeliest places. But flowing beneath that fear was the knowledge that he was, indeed, at work beneath the palace. She pushed the thought away with difficulty and looked at her candle: burning low. She sighed—and then paused. Closed her eyes as the truth struck her. She was a fool for not realizing it earlier. *That* was the source of the wet, almost metallic smell: she'd just entered the underground sewer system.

It was warmer than she'd expected. Less smelly, too: the air was dank, but not suffocating or nauseating. The Thames smelled worse on a daily basis than this sewer drain did. Standing at one point within this vast underground maze of tunnels, Mary felt her choices dwindling. The case was closing in on her.

She looked again at the notice. Now that she knew where she was—knew that it had to be his—it seemed surprising she'd ever doubted the handwriting. Denial was a waste of energy, but at this hour, she simply couldn't contemplate more. She had to go—to bed, to sleep if possible, and, at some point, to consider two inevitable tasks that lay before her.

James Easton.

Lang Jin Hai.

Both men she'd have to talk to in the near future. She couldn't imagine anything she'd like more. Or less.

Twelve

St. Valentine's Day

Buckingham Palace

Morning came far too soon, but sleep not at all. Mary lay awake through the cold night, listening to Amy's breathing and the muffled chiming of a distant grandfather clock, measuring out the quarter hours. At six, she pulled herself out of bed, feeling utterly bruised in spirit. Appropriately, she was also somewhat damaged in body: the hawthorns had made their mark, leaving a number of deep scratches on the backs of her hands and one on her neck. She pulled a face at her reflection to gruesome good effect, the dark circles beneath her eyes made more macabre by the way Amy's cheap looking glass swelled her chin and shrank her forehead. She'd always dreamed of being reunited with her father. Now that it was a possibility, she looked like a ghoul and he was in jail. Perfect.

While the queen had breakfast, Mary was responsible for cleaning and airing Her Majesty's private parlor. She was crouched down, laying a new fire, when the door clicked open. Mrs. Shaw, of course, checking up on her again. But when she stood and turned, it wasn't Mrs. Shaw at all.

"Oh, I say—is that you, Mary? It *is* Mary, isn't it?"

Her eyes widened as she stared into the sheepish face of the Prince of Wales. Dropped a reflexive curtsy. Stifled a curse. "Your Highness. I didn't know you wanted the parlor."

"I—er—was just on my way to breakfast."

"In your dressing gown, sir?" She cringed. Too impertinent, by far.

And yet he smiled. "Actually, I was hoping for a breakfast tray." That was logical enough: if he kept to his room, he needn't face his mother.

She kept her tone demure. "Very good, sir. I'll ask Mrs. Shaw straightaway."

"Actually . . ." His hand fluttered in the air for a moment, arresting her movement, before dropping to his side. "I'd like *you* to bring it. Yes."

Her stomach lurched. Trouble snapped at her heels from all directions. After a few moments, she found her voice. "Very good, sir."

Prince Bertie muttered something and fled.

When Mary relayed the message to Mrs. Shaw, the housekeeper's eyes widened. "He asked for you particularly?"

"Yes."

The sharp eyes raked her appearance, lingered suspiciously on her scratched neck. "You're quite certain."

"Yes, ma'am."

A pause. "That's not the way to promotion in this household, my girl; that's the swiftest path to a home for fallen women."

Despite Mrs. Shaw's fears, one didn't say no to the Prince of Wales—not directly, at least. A quarter of an hour later, Mary was treading noiselessly to the prince's apartments—a rather glorious term for a bedroom with a small sitting room attached—carrying a tray heavy with breakfast delicacies: cold roasted meats, coddled eggs, deviled kidneys, both bread and butter and toast.

As she'd suspected, the prince was alone in his apartments—a suspicious circumstance, as he was, at least in theory, constantly attended by one or two equerries. He was seated in a wing chair, studying a French newspaper with an expression of great wisdom. As she approached, he glanced up with elaborate surprise. "Oh. That was prompt."

She dipped her head. "Mrs. Shaw sent a little of everything, sir."

"Leave that tray for a moment, Mary, and come here."

She hesitated briefly, then advanced two small paces, keeping herself well out of arm's reach. "What is it, sir?" She couldn't decide whether or not to look him straight in the eye. Doing so would be a defiant stance on her part, and one the prince might misconstrue as bold invitation.

"Come and sit by me." His hand waved vaguely to

the place beside his armchair—although there was not, of course, a second chair or stool.

"I'll fetch a chair, sir." Mary turned aside, wondering for one crazy moment what her chances were of simply fleeing the room. Would Prince Bertie chase her down the corridor? Invent a story to have her dismissed?

But just as she began to move away, the prince said, "Just—never mind the chair—it's only—I'd like a word." His voice sounded small and shuttered. She glanced down: yes, his eyes were suspiciously bright.

She felt a sudden easing in her chest. "Of course, sir." She returned to stand beside the chair again, wondering if she ought to offer him a handkerchief.

Prince Bertie took several deep breaths, which seemed to keep the tears from rolling. "It's ridiculous, isn't it?"

"What is, sir?"

"Expecting you to be kind to me. But the other day—was it yesterday? I forget—you seemed so sympathetic. As though you understood what it must be like, being me."

Mary pressed her lips together to keep from making a face. "I don't know, exactly, but I can imagine, sir."

He looked up at her through bloodshot eyes. "Then you've a devil of an imagination. Most of the time, I can't even imagine what's required of me—even as I'm doing it."

It was that sudden, as though he'd pulled off a mask.

Mary stared at the Prince of Wales, her irritation suddenly submerged by a wave of pity. Prince Bertie was still a ridiculous figure, to be sure. His plump cheeks and heavy eyelids gave him the air of a sleepy schoolboy—the class dunce, even. But what else was he, really? Other people's expectations were rather beside the point just now. With bloodshot eyes and slumped posture, he was really just a very young man in disgrace, suffering under the weight of family disapproval and his own guilty conscience.

She knelt beside the wing chair. "There, there," she murmured, and as if on cue, the prince's face crumpled. His eyes welled over, the tears forming fast-running rivers down his cheeks. Mary felt his breath, hot and childlike on her fingers, as he clasped her hand and wept, his whole frame shuddering with the effort.

They remained locked in their awkward clasp—he was hugging her arm like a favorite doll—for only a few minutes, at most. Then, as though recalled to himself, Prince Bertie released her and sat back in his chair, trying to stanch the tears.

Mary fumbled for a handkerchief. She never had a clean handkerchief. But His Highness was already shaking his head and gasping, trying to master himself. His forced smile was grotesque—more of a fright mask than a facial expression. But it was an attempt. He found his own square of beautifully monogrammed silk—so infinitely superior to her own meager scrap of hemmed cotton—and mopped himself. When he blew his nose, he honked so loudly that she blinked.

He winced. "Apologies." He glanced at her damp arm. "I mean, for everything."

"Not at all." It was partly reflex—what else could she say?—but Mary meant it.

He was silent for a moment. "It's quite pathetic, what I did, isn't it? Asking you up here for a friendly bit of chat. As though you've a choice: my family pays your wages."

"No," said Mary quickly. "It needn't be like that."

Prince Bertie looked at her through bulging, red-rimmed eyes. "Really?"

She shook her head. "I'm just somebody you happened to run into. I mean, it was quite by chance that I was in the parlor just now. It could have been any other servant."

He studied the floor, almost shy now.

"Forget that I'm the parlor maid. If you'd like someone to talk to, I'll listen." The words felt awkward in her mouth. This was a new role for her, the sympathetic confidante. And she had her own, highly suspect motives for playing it: she was talking to an eyewitness—the most important eyewitness—to Beaulieu-Buckworth's death. What might he remember, or reveal by accident? She couldn't allow herself to hope. But here she was, nonetheless.

The prince's gaze floated back up to her face. "It's not

very regal of me . . . not manly, either. His Royal Highness the Prince Consort would be scandalized." Deep sigh. "But then, what's new about that? Father's appalled by everything I do."

Mary stayed silent. This was a strange, one-sided intimacy. He was so unsteady, so childlike — if she pressed him in any way, he'd turn on her a moment later. He still might, if she couldn't help him.

He slouched deeper in his wing chair. "What is all the staff saying?" He saw her hesitation and forced a playful smile. "I'll not tell anybody what you say. Promise."

Mary knew better than to believe that; one well-chosen word from Queen Victoria and the prince would spill the lot. Nevertheless . . . "They're all a bit confused. They know something serious has occurred, but nobody knows what, exactly."

"Come on . . . there must be more gossip, even in a household as strict as this." His smile was more authentic, now that he was on familiar ground: pleading, pestering, teasing. "Don't you girls talk about us?"

"I couldn't possibly say, sir, gossip being strictly forbidden." Her small smile undercut the severity of her words. "But one or two people have mentioned how you're not generally here during term time."

"Have they said why?"

She made her eyes wide and round. "They'd never have made so bold about the Prince of Wales, sir."

He winced. "Ah. Yes. Me and people's expectations."

"You don't sound happy, sir."

"Would you be, if you were me?" he demanded, voice rising. At her shrinking back, he softened his tone. "Though, of course, you don't know the truth." He sighed heavily. "I can't possibly burden you with that. . . ."

It was such a transparent invitation. "And is it such a heavy burden, sir?"

He snorted. "Oh, aye. Heavier than you could imagine, my dear."

She remained perfectly still, eyes modestly lowered. If she didn't break the spell . . . If nobody interrupted them . . .

"What would you say, Mary, if I told you I witnessed something truly terrible on Saturday night? Something so nightmarish I can't think of anything else, can't sleep, can't eat. . . ."

She met his gaze with wide, compassionate eyes. "I'd feel right sorry for you, sir, for I can't think of a person who deserves such a thing."

"Really?" His eagerness was difficult to take—she'd never met anyone quite this powerful yet fragile. Or maybe that was the difficulty—he wasn't actually very powerful at all but was assumed to be so because of his mother. "Because—I probably oughtn't say—it's not your concern, and you're a nice girl . . ."

Time to clinch the confession. But she couldn't repress a stab of guilt as she said, "You mustn't say or do anything that troubles your conscience, sir. But I'd count it a privilege to help you, as far as I can."

It was that easy. Through Mary's simple, almost entirely selfish illusion of kindness, the Prince of Wales began pouring out his troubles: his sneaking down to London, the ill-advised abandonment of his equerries, the excursion to Limehouse. He was, however, much hazier on the facts and timing of events inside the opium den.

Through the course of his rambling monologue, two things became clear to Mary. The first was that, despite her delicate attempts to sift for facts, the prince's recollection of events was too muddled to be of use. He'd not been simply evading Queen Victoria's questions yesterday. The second was his assumption that Lang Jin Hai had to be a murderer simply because he was a foreigner and an Asiatic. Such prejudiced illogic was familiar to Mary, of course. English racial superiority was a common assumption, and she generally encountered it with superficial calm. It was also the reason she never acknowledged her parentage, lest her status as a "dirty half-caste" become the sum of her identity in others' eyes. This time, however, Prince Bertie's heedless slurs stung. And even worse, Mary knew why: she already felt protective of Lang Jin Hai, without even being sure of who he was.

Eventually, the prince's ramblings wound down like a clockwork toy. He stared into the middle distance, limp. His features were puffy and his pallid skin marked by painful-looking red pimples—signs of strain that stirred in Mary equal amounts of distaste and compassion. "You must be half mad with grief, sir," she said at last.

He seemed not to hear her.

She poured him a cup of coffee, now only lukewarm, and proffered it gently. "Sir?"

He blinked, as though remembering her presence. He drained the cup, expressionless, then held it out for more.

"Would you care for some breakfast, sir? Mrs. Shaw sent deviled kidneys."

He shook his head, as though sickened. "Take it away." He was unable to look at her, and Mary thought she understood that, too. In breaking down before her, he'd humiliated himself and betrayed his station. It was no wonder he couldn't eat before her.

"As you wish, sir." She packed up the tray and retreated to the kitchens, wondering how Mrs. Shaw would interpret her return. She'd been gone nearly an hour, and here she was with a tray full of uneaten delicacies. Not to mention a Prince of Wales who'd dodged breakfast with his mother. For the first time, Mary thought of the queen with a distinct twinge of pity. Monarch, head of state, empress of the globe—and mother to a weak, tearaway heir with a scandalous murder and a question of justice to address.

Really, a few missing ornaments were the least of Her Majesty's concerns.

Thirteen

Mrs. Shaw's estimation of Mary's moral condition sank even lower before the midafternoon meal. Each day, after the royal family had finished their luncheon, the servants gathered belowstairs for their dinner—a hot, cooked meal that was ample even by palace standards and undreamed of by the urban poor outside its walls. Today, Mary lowered herself into her place at table to find half a dozen others staring at her. She nodded awkwardly at these near strangers. "Hello."

"Go on, open it!" said another parlor maid, a rosy-cheeked woman called Sadie, with masses of russet hair barely contained by her cap.

At Mary's place lay a square envelope, larger than her plate and addressed in a flashy, unfamiliar hand.

"Didn't know you had a sweetheart," said Amy, from across the table and a few places along. There was a sullen edge to her tone, and Mary noticed that Amy had a much smaller envelope on her own plate. It had already been opened.

"I don't," replied Mary. She eyed the packet with suspicion.

"Go on—I'm dying!" squeaked Sadie. "I never seen one that big!"

"Sadie, my sweet," drawled one of the footmen. "That's what you said to me last night."

Sadie sniffed. "Only in your dreams, you nasty little toad." At this, the other footmen roared with laughter, which was quickly quelled by the head butler.

Mary picked up the valentine, holding it as though it might burst into flames at any moment. She could feel Mrs. Shaw's dour gaze trained on her face. Was there anything she could do to make herself less conspicuous?

"Go on!" squealed another maid. "It ain't like to bite you."

Mary tore open the vast white envelope and, to the squeals of several maids, pulled out the gaudiest valentine she'd ever seen: a garish confection of lace, feathers, ribbon, and paint that unfolded into an elaborate heart shape. At its center was scrawled *From your secret admirer.*

"Oh, lordy, it's a stunner," gasped Sadie, half covering her mouth in reverence.

Amy sniffed. "It must have cost a pretty penny."

"Penny, my eye!" snorted another. "That's four bob worth of paper and lace, if ever I seen it."

Glancing down, Mary noticed a second letter on

her dinner plate: a small, very ordinary one that she instantly pocketed. Finally, word from the Agency. Fortunately, the maids' attention seemed fixed on the valentine.

"But who's your beau?" sighed another. "And how'd you trap a rich one?"

Mary shook her head. "I don't have one." Her denial sounded stiff and implausible, even in her own ears. It certainly wasn't good news, this ostentatious valentine. Angry as he was, James wouldn't taunt her in this way—drawing unwanted attention to her, encouraging others to ask questions of her. Besides, his interests were already engaged. He'd not wasted much time, going straight from kissing her blind in the study to flirting with that young lady in his drawing room. Mary swallowed hard and met Sadie's eyes. "I don't know who it's from."

From across the table, Sadie snatched at the valentine and read the message for herself, her eyes growing rounder as she puzzled through the handwriting. "My stars! That's a flash valentine from someone who's too shy to sign his name!"

"He must be madly in love with you," said a thin little maid Mary saw only at mealtimes. "Oh, fancy. It must be lovely."

"Or maybe four bob's naught to him."

This was a juicy subject for the whole table, and while speculation bloomed, Mary caught Mrs. Shaw's eye on her. This much was certain: the housekeeper had definitely, unofficially, put her on probation. Amy, too, had a dangerous look in her eye—an intimation that her Saint Valentine's Day was not going according to plan.

"Here, you coy thing." The woman beside Mary passed her a large earthenware dish of boiled potatoes. "You really got no idea who sent that card?"

"Not the faintest." Mary took a potato and looked hopefully up the table. There was a meaty hash of some sort and cold poached fowl left over from last night's dinner abovestairs. A couple of tureens of vegetables. Something that looked like salmon patties. A boiled ham. Slices of bread and butter. Even a quivering aspic which Sadie seemed to favor, judging from the portion she served herself. There was more food than they'd ever consume at this meal. It seemed wrong, at a time of such privation. With last year's poor harvest and this long, cruel winter, the Cockneys on the streets looked thinner and more haggard than ever.

Sadie turned and subjected her to a cool, full-length appraisal. "You're bonny enough. Got spindle shanks, though. Men like a bit of meat on a girl's bones." She shimmied her own ample curves suggestively. "Something to hold on to. Though it don't seem to have hurt you any."

Mary spooned some boiled turnips onto her plate and thought about the envelope in her pocket. "I don't think it means much. The valentine, I mean."

It was a long lunch, dominated by conversation about

who got what and what it might mean—not unlike a schoolroom full of twelve-year-old girls, thought Mary. It was rather more difficult to interpret the significance of her own unwanted valentine. When it had traveled the length of the table and back, Mary stuffed it back into its envelope and laid it on the chair behind her. She tried to catch Amy's gaze, but the girl's eyes were fixed on the tablecloth, her mouth a grim line: clearly, Octavius Jones's valentine hadn't met her expectations. And then, suddenly, it was so patently obvious that she jumped slightly.

Sadie glanced at her, only half interested. "What's the matter with you?"

"Nothing." Mary took a deep drink of Mrs. Shaw's excellent cider—another palace luxury. Then she joined in with the cheerful, idle conversation all around her. One of her difficulties, at least, was within her power to address.

After dinner, there was an hour's respite before her afternoon duties began, and Mary slipped up to her bedroom. She wanted a little privacy to read this second letter—the one the others hadn't noticed in their excitement over the splendid valentine. But when she arrived, Amy was already sprawled belly down on her bed, face turned toward the wall. Mary stifled a sigh as she saw Amy's crumpled valentine on the blanket. As she stood there, wondering how on earth to begin a conversation, Amy turned a wet, tear-stained face toward her.

"You didn't even look pleased to get that blooming great valentine."

"I'm not. I don't even know who it's from, and that makes me nervous."

Amy lifted her head at that. "Nervous? You should be bloody over the moon!"

Mary shrugged. "What if it's a prank of some sort?"

"A pretty expensive prank! No, I reckon whoever sent that really meant it."

Privately, Mary agreed—but not the way Amy thought. "Are you all right, though? You seem disappointed."

Amy sniffed, scrambled to a sitting position, and flicked her crumpled valentine onto the floor. "You'd be, too, if that's all you got from your stupid gentleman admirer."

Mary looked at it. "May I . . . ?"

"'Course. It ain't special."

Mary picked up the card and smoothed it. "It's pretty." It was, too—fine paper with a picture of red roses, and real lace glued round the edges. But it lacked the show-stopping garishness of Mary's.

"It ain't the card what bothers me—just read it!"

Mary obeyed. "'To my darling Amy—Happy Saint Valentine's Day, my sweet girl. Very affectionately yours, Tavvy.'"

"'Very affectionately!'" howled Amy, suddenly furious. "It ain't much, is it?"

"Well, it's *nice*. . . ."

"I don't want nice! I don't want pretty! I want a bloody wedding ring on my finger!" Amy yelled this last sentence so loudly that the window rattled.

Mary considered her irate roommate. Pity was certainly out of the question. "Well . . . what will you do, then? D'you still want my help?"

Amy stared at her for several long moments in outright astonishment. Then, to Mary's relief, she snorted. And flashed her a determined grin. "Yeah. He ain't getting away that easy."

"Did you send him a note this morning?"

"Of course!"

"Right. Then where's that spare uniform you mentioned last night?"

Fourteen

Less than a quarter of an hour later, Mary was in the servants' courtyard, keeping an eye out for one of the people she most detested. She spotted him idling along, hands in pockets, hat tipped back at a disreputable angle. She took a deep breath. She'd not be bested this time.

"My dear Miss Quinn," he trilled, sweeping her an extravagant bow. "*Such* a pleasure to meet you like this, at this hour. And by *appointment*!" She opened her mouth to speak, but he swept on. "I've so many questions for you, my dear girl. Still digging away in the trenches of truth?"

"You know very well I'm researching the lives of the working poor."

"So you claimed the last time we met. Yet you're not entirely devoid of sense: surely you've given up such a weary, stale, flat, and unprofitable little notion."

"I fear not, Mr. Jones." Especially as she hoped to continue the ruse with James, too. "My investigations are coming along splendidly. But I'm not here to discuss that."

"Tell me something delightful, then."

She inclined her head very slightly. "I received your card."

He feigned innocence. "I beg your pardon?"

"The very large and expensive valentine you sent, signing yourself a 'secret admirer.'"

"Did you? And if so, what makes you think it was I who sent it? I'm Miss Tranter's beau, not yours."

"You're the only gentleman I know with the taste and budget for such a valentine."

His smile seemed to escape against his will. "The truth will out, it seems."

"Sometimes it does," she said, unsmiling. "I've something for you." She pushed the bundle into his hands.

"My! A personal token of your affection? I'd no idea my little valentine would be so effective. . . ."

"From Amy. It's a maid's uniform in your size. At ten o'clock tonight, you're to enter the servants' courtyard in costume. I'll see you safely indoors."

Jones's reaction was wonderful to behold. Surprise, comprehension, deep embarrassment, confusion—all paraded across his face in what Mary thought might be the only sincere response she'd ever seen from him. Completely at a loss, he finally looked at Mary. "Was this Amy's idea?"

"Certainly," snapped Mary. "Nothing else would induce me to play the bawd for the likes of you."

"In which case, I'm honored," he said, trying for insouciance.

"See that you're on time." She made as if to leave, then paused. "And Jones." He blinked at her, still off balance. "If you do or say anything to jeopardize my research—anything that draws attention to me, like that piece of childish nonsense with the valentine—I'll tell all. Possibly while you're still wearing petticoats." And with that, she stepped smartly round him and continued on her way.

The nearest post office was on Old Cavendish Street, roughly a mile away by the most direct route. She'd thought hard about the risks of using it as her *poste restante* address. The General Post Office in central London was so much larger and offered a real chance at anonymity. But today, she was glad of her choice: it was unreasonable to expect Amy to shield her absence for too long.

In this sleepy lull before teatime, there were few ladies or gentlemen in the streets. It was too late for a morning ride, a shade too early for afternoon calls. And yet the streets hummed with butchers' and bakers' boys delivering their wares, fully laden drays making deliveries. The town felt astoundingly open and anonymous after the constant confinement of palace life. Mary walked on, a little giddy with her temporary freedom. Such illusions promptly vanished as she crossed Oxford Street, its glass-and-brass-fronted shops gleaming valiantly through the fog. Just beyond this glamour lay yet another test of her identity, the very idea of which made her stomach churn.

Old Cavendish Street was quiet, a back lane for the

hectic shopping thoroughfare of Oxford Street. She passed a gentleman in a fur-collared overcoat who goggled at her unabashedly, despite her repressive frown. She was too well dressed to be an ordinary working woman, who could stroll about unaccompanied, yet she hadn't a companion or a maid in tow. In the post office, though, her presence excited no comments or stares from either staff or customers, many of whom also looked like respectable domestic servants.

"Poste restante?" said the yawning clerk when she reached the front of the queue. "What did you say the name was again?"

"Lawrence," she said clearly. "Miss Mary Lawrence." She'd chosen a false name that used the initials of her birth name, Mary Lang. Impossible, however, to hope that they held any significance for Lang Jin Hai. Not after all these years.

He swung down from his stool and ambled to a filing cabinet, taking his time rifling through the envelopes within, yawning all the while. Mary saw a future dependent upon this anonymous clerk's alertness and intelligence, and despaired. At least his lips didn't move as he read. At length, he returned to the window, empty-handed. "Nothing under that name, miss."

"It's very important," she said, trying to control the tremor in her voice. "Please, could you look again?"

He scowled and looked at her—really looked at her, for the first time. Something in her expression made him pause. After a moment, he sighed. "All right. Not that it'll do any good."

Privately, Mary agreed. Nevertheless, she watched him retreat to the filing cabinet with gratitude. This might be the one thing of which she could be certain. He performed the second search with exaggerated care, pulling out the occasional envelope and squinting at it in a pantomime of reading. One. Two. After a tantalizing pause, a third. Just as he was about to stuff it back into the drawer, however, the clerk paused. Frowned. Brought the envelope closer to his nose.

Mary shook her head, angered by this ridiculous bit of playacting. Even as she scowled, however, the clerk returned to his stool with an expression of slight embarrassment mingled with avid curiosity. He stared at her. "Bit irregular, this one, but it might be yours, miss."

Mary tried not to snatch the envelope from his grasp—the same envelope, she realized, that she'd posted the previous night. Her careful address—*Mr. J. H. Lang, care of HM Tower of London, Tower Hill, The City*—had been scratched out. On top, in crude letters, was written, *Miss M. Lawrence, Charing X post office.* "Yes, that's it," she said in the calmest voice she could manage. "Thank you."

"Irregular, that, miss," said the clerk again. "The address isn't as clear as it should be. It ought to say, 'To be called for.' "

She nodded, scarcely hearing his words. "I see."

"I'll need to see some proof of your identity, miss."

She fumbled in her handbag and pushed a forged letter across the counter—a testimonial of character from Mrs. J. G. F. Spencer of Muswell Hill, for her paid companion, Mary Lawrence. "It's all I've got," she explained humbly. "I've no passport, you see."

The clerk skimmed the letter, and Mary hoped he noticed the elements she'd incorporated: the good but not lavish notepaper; the slightly cramped penmanship of an older, respectable lady; the well-worn creases of a much-produced "character." Eventually, he nodded and gave it back to her. "That's all right, miss. That's twopence, then, for the postage."

She paid and fled.

The city streets were far too public for her to stop and examine her letter. That didn't prevent her from turning it over and over in her mind, however, until she reached the parks. The fact that she'd received any sort of reply meant that Lang—or someone else—had opened the letter and found her false name and *poste restante* address. Yet the omens were otherwise bad: the sloppy address and the reuse of her old envelope suggested not only that Lang was uninterested in outside help but also that he wanted actively to repudiate it. If he were apathetic, he'd simply have made no reply—that was the result she'd expected. But this pointed rejection complicated matters.

In the peace and relative quiet of St. James's Park, Mary stared at the fateful envelope. As a child, she'd often dreamed of being found by her father—a kind, affectionate man she'd elevated, over the years, into a model of wisdom and noble sacrifice. She'd imagined his daring escape from a band of pirates or his heroic return from a secret mission for the Crown, after all hope was gone. Lang Jin Hai would leave no stone unturned searching for his beloved and only child. Their reunion would be the stuff of children's fairy tales, of serial novels, of dreams.

Her lips twisted. And so it was. If indeed this man was her father, he'd succeeded in undoing every fantasy she'd ever cherished: she'd first heard his name implicated in violence and scandal. She'd made the effort to seek him out. And now he wanted nothing to do with her. A tear rolled down her cheek, and she dashed it away, suddenly furious. Why was she being so passive, waiting for a paternal white knight to ride in and save her? Whether her father was a murderer or not, an opium addict or no, the one thing he'd bequeathed her was the habit of fending for herself. It was her only legacy.

She tore open the envelope. It was precisely as she'd thought, no worse: her original letter had been torn in half. It was the clearest possible message that her attention was unwanted. And that was fine. She was interested not only in helping Lang Jin Hai but also in laying to rest questions from her own past. And for that, she did not require this man's blessing. She would present herself to him, uninvited, and ascertain whether or not he was her father.

If he wasn't, she could once more assume that her

father was dead. If he was her father, she could ask what had become of him. And if he was hanged for murder, her father would again be dead. There was a lunatic logic at work there. Her eyes were dry as she tore the letter to shreds, and then into dozens of tiny pieces, and pushed them into her pocket.

As she did so, her fingers rediscovered her other mysterious letter—the one lurking beneath the valentine at the dinner hour. She'd quite forgotten but now drew it out hastily. It was about time she heard from the Agency. However, the handwriting on the envelope was neither Anne's nor Felicity's. Not even close. And yet it was familiar. Even as her eyes traced the first *M*, the flashing *Q*, she felt that painful double thump of her heart once more, a tangle of elation and caution. She traced her fingertip along the letter's corners. Perhaps she'd mistaken the handwriting. Yet she knew that thought, too, was merely a rationalization. And such fear was foolish: after the way they'd last parted, what was another confirmation of James's disdain? Nothing could be worse than how she now felt. She tore it open swiftly, without ceremony.

My dearest Mary,

Both my words and my conduct at our last meeting were ungentlemanly—born of haste and high emotion rather than friendship and good judgment—and yet I cannot find it within me to apologize. I am glad I kissed you; glad to have reveled in your scent, your taste, the touch of your hands; glad, even, to have quarreled with you, because during those moments of anger, I was in your presence.

Mary, you are the most singular woman I know: intelligent, brave, and honest, and I crave your friendship. I confess to only the haziest notion of what I ask, having never been friends with a woman before. My friendships are male and conventional, pleasant and without distinction. But a friendship with you would be a bright, new, rare thing—if you would do me the honor.

I expect that what I ask is impossible. But it is sweet to dream, Mary, and thus I tender one last, insolent, unapologetic request: write to me only if you can say yes.

Yours,
James

Mary read the letter three times, fingers shaking as she held the page. He reveled, craved, dreamed—words she'd never dare imagine in connection with James. Yet even as she floated in the sheer delight of being thus addressed, frustration seeped in. Came to dominate.

It was a beautiful, maddening, flattering, insulting little epistle. No apology—utterly James-like. A vast request, airily phrased—ditto. And most important, no mention whatsoever of that damned girl in the blue dress. Even so, she couldn't help melting, and that was perhaps the worst part. Was she so susceptible, so utterly without pride, that she'd go charging back to him whenever he crooked his finger? She could sit still no longer. As she walked back toward the palace, she forced herself to think about, rather than feel, her response.

She ought to tear up the letter and forget all about it.

Impossible.

She ought to send it back to him, as Lang Jin Hai had done with hers.

She'd broken the seal.

She could pretend she'd never received it.

But how would she let him know? If he heard nothing, James would assume that she was too hurt, too fragile, to contact him again. Damn and blast his apparently boundless egotism.

And yet—she'd thought just the previous night of contacting him. She needed his expertise, or at least his collection of sewer maps. And for the first time since she'd left the palace, something like a smile tugged at the corner of her mouth. So she could. Just as she'd seen off Octavius Jones—just as she would resolve the question of her relation to Lang Jin Hai—she'd settle another overconfident male.

She walked back toward the palace, sprinkling the paper fragments of her father's rejection into the shallow lake. They floated at first, then slowly became sodden and sank beneath its murky surface.

And that, too, was entirely apt.

Fifteen

The same day, 11:15 p.m.

The service entrance to Buckingham Palace

Although the usual needs of the royal family consumed the rest of her working day, Mary found time to scribble and post a short note she'd composed while serving afternoon tea. She wanted it to be brief but also to encompass cool indifference, taunting ambiguity, and a degree of callousness, all encompassed by a businesslike tone. After much thought, she wrote:

Dear James,

I hope this note is not entirely offensive to you after our last conversation, parts of which I sincerely regret. Recently, I came upon some information about the palace sewers that may interest you in your professional capacity. Are you free to meet this evening? I shall be unengaged at any time after eleven o'clock.

Yrs sincerely,
Mary

His response, in a note delivered early that evening by the penny post beneath Mrs. Shaw's raised eyebrows, was almost too perfect:

11:30 by the works entrance.

J

She was now loitering in the chilly courtyard, watching for Octavius Jones. Although she knew what to expect, she still broke into a broad grin at the sight of a tall, awkward figure in a maid's uniform, clomping through the courtyard with a furtive expression on his face.

At the sight of her, his face grew even longer. "How do you walk around all day wearing so many skirts?" he whined. "The weight is impossible!"

"Good evening, Miss Jones," she said in her sweetest tones. "You look perfectly ridiculous."

"Tell me something I don't know," snapped Jones. "And don't call me Miss Jones."

"How about 'Tavvy'?"

He scowled more deeply. "Just Jones will do."

Mary was enjoying herself even more than she'd imagined. "You certainly don't look like a gentleman about to consummate his love."

Jones turned on her. "Keep your voice down!" He looked genuinely scandalized.

"You're on my territory, Tavvy; you'll do as I say, if you don't want to be caught."

He scowled. "This is absurd. I'm going."

Mary allowed him three steps' retreat before asking, "What message shall I give Amy?"

Jones froze. Waited. Turned round so slowly she could almost hear his joints crack with reluctance. The hatred and shame in his expression ought to have given her pause but instead filled her with satisfaction. "Never mind," he said, his voice hoarse with contained fury. "Lead the way."

Mary conducted him through the servants' entrance, past the snoring footman and to the service stairs. She was careful not to point out potential hiding spots or teach him which steps squeaked at the center, but she knew him to be a keen observer. It had not escaped her attention that she might be leading Her Majesty's chief burglar into the heart of the palace. And yet the thief had been careful and choosy thus far—much too discreet to be caught. Without some sort of encouragement, her assignment might end without her having uncovered a thing.

As they reached the second-floor landing, she heard a quick, mincing step on the stairs above. She touched Jones's elbow and gestured. He moved fast—no protests here. A moment later, they were standing very close together round a corner, watching Mrs. Shaw make her dignified way down to the kitchens. They waited for a full minute after she'd passed. Then, stepping away from Jones, Mary said, "Let's go."

"Wait." His hand closed round her upper arm in a

hard grip, reminding her that, costume aside, there was nothing feminine about Jones. "Why are you doing this?"

"As a favor to Amy."

"I don't believe you."

"That's fine," she said, quelling her impatience. "You needn't."

He stared at her for a long moment, eyes narrowed.

It was an unpleasant shock to realize that Jones was, in his own way, attractive. Neither handsome nor pleasant, but with a sort of diabolical charm that went well beyond the surface—even when that surface included a bonnet.

"I could have had you sacked just then. When the housekeeper passed by."

So he'd not missed the enormous bunch of keys tied to Mrs. Shaw's waist. "But you didn't."

"Not in your interests."

"Nor in yours."

"What I still can't work out is, what *is* your interest here?"

She smiled and set off up the stairs again, so he was forced to follow. "I've already told you."

"You don't expect me to believe you're still researching that book!"

She turned. "You expect *me* to believe you're courting Amy Tranter."

He couldn't quite meet her gaze. "Yes. Well. She enjoys the attention." They ascended another flight of stairs in silence before he said, "You're much too clever not to understand that I could be of very material assistance to you."

"I do understand that, Jones. You were rather helpful during that excitement at the clock tower—right up to the point when you broke your word."

"You're rather touchy about that little slip."

"Because it wasn't merely a little slip." She was relieved when they reached the attic landing. "Here we are. Third door on your left. Amy's expecting you."

He made no move to continue. Instead, he touched her again, cupping his palms behind her elbows in a startlingly intimate gesture. "Mary. We could do great things together."

She forced herself to meet his gaze. Tried not to blush. "I very much doubt our ideas of greatness would coincide." She plucked his hands from her person and made a show of dusting off her sleeves. "And now, I believe you've an appointment to keep."

What James called the "works entrance" was simply a manhole in a little-used side street a quarter mile from the palace—hardly what one would expect for a royal building project. Yet it was exactly right for a job shrouded in such secrecy. Mary would have thought herself in the wrong place but for the sight of James's carriage, embarrassingly familiar to her from partnerships past. It stood perhaps ten yards from the manhole cover.

As Mary approached, the man hunched atop it swung his face toward her. Her cheeks flamed. The last time she'd seen James's coachman, Barker, she'd been at a distinct disadvantage: sprawled on the belfry floor of St. Stephen's clock tower, dressed in boys' rags, kissing James. Not that she regretted the last. But if she had any sense remaining, it'd not happen again.

"Evening," she said, acknowledging Barker.

He nodded very slightly. His features remained perfectly still but seemed to frost over a degree with recognition.

The carriage door swung open, and James hopped out, folding down the steps as an afterthought. He looked at her for a moment, opened his mouth, then closed it again. Finally, he said, "You're late."

"I can't just come and go as I choose," she explained with demure patience. "I have to wait until everybody else is settled for the night before I can slip out. And good evening, by the way."

"Oh—good evening."

She placed one hand on the carriage steps. "I don't want to waste your time. Shall we begin?"

He blinked. "The carriage?"

"It'll be warmer and more comfortable than talking in the drizzle," she said, hiding a smile. "What did you think I meant?"

His blush was visible even in the foggy night. "Er—let me help you up."

Once inside, they sat facing each other on the benches, awkward as innocents on their honeymoon night. James was, at least.

"Thank you for agreeing to see me," said Mary. "I wasn't sure you would read my letter, after our last meeting."

A small frown appeared between his eyebrows. "We've had tiffs in the past and always managed to sort things out."

She smiled. "True. But I don't want to talk about us, whatever that might mean; I want to talk about sewers."

It was clear he'd not been expecting that, even after her note. But a moment later, he raised one eyebrow. "You want information."

"And to share it."

"You're assuming I want to know," he said in a bored tone.

"True." She paused. "I thought it a safe assumption, since somebody's been using a tunnel beneath the palace that connects with your sewers."

He came alive at that, all pretense at relaxation gone. "How do you even know where I'm working?"

"Last night, I was in that strange little room off the sewers and I saw your 'keep out' sign."

"The sign says 'keep out' for a reason, you know: that entire section's structurally unsound. What the devil were you thinking, mucking about down there?"

"I followed someone. And I wasn't there long." Mary

waited for him to scold her. Snap at her carelessness. Grab her shoulders. All the things that would signal that she and James were back once more in their strange, compulsive to-and-fro.

Instead, he frowned. Leaned back. Folded his arms across his chest. "You know, Mary, I've been thinking about something." He considered her through narrowed eyes, studying her features as though they were new to him. "Everywhere you go, trouble follows. That business with the Thorolds in Chelsea. Those thefts at the building site of St. Stephen's Tower. And now this."

Mary unclenched her fists. Tried to breathe evenly. "What are you saying?" She was a complacent fool who should have seen this coming long ago: James was too intelligent to believe her journalist ruse for long.

"Mary." His voice was careful, neutral. "I think there's something you need to tell me."

She cleared her throat. Tried to speak. Found her voice on the third try. "You're right." She struggled for a full minute to find the words to begin. "When . . . ?"

James's gaze was merciless in its intensity. "I completely believed you last year, when we met on the building site. I think I even believed you on Sunday, when you first told me about your new project at the palace. But this new coincidence . . ."

Mary nodded. Her stomach churned. So this was all her own stupid, arrogant fault.

Another minute, and yet another, elapsed. James tilted

his head, the faintest of smiles on his lips. "Don't look so stricken, Mary. I doubt guilty conscience is permitted in private detectives."

She thought she'd been embarrassed before. But now a new surge of blood heated her face; she could feel even her forehead going hot. "Truly," she said, cringing at the inadequacy of language, "I never wanted to lie to you."

"Never?"

"Not when we met again, after you came back from India."

"But you didn't think you could trust me yet." His voice was careful, probing—he might have been a physician investigating the pain in her side.

"I did," she said desperately. "I knew I could. But it wasn't—I had—I simply wasn't in a position to tell you everything. And I thought it better to say nothing rather than tell you a small portion of the improbable truth." Such limping, inadequate honesty. Yet it was the closest she could come to disclosure without openly implicating the Agency.

James's expression did not change. "When might you have told me? The next time our paths collided?"

She tried not to squirm. "It's preposterous, isn't it? Three coincidental meetings—it beggars belief."

"I'd never believe it in a novel."

"Nor I."

"But here we are."

"I don't know when I'd have told you. I'd been

hoping not to run into you again." She saw the flash of hurt in his eyes, controlled though his features were. "Not like this, I mean," she added. But the qualification was too feeble, too late.

"Is there anything else I'm permitted to know?" he asked in a crisp tone.

She gestured uselessly. "I watch people. Ask questions. Try to learn things others would prefer to keep hidden. Yes. It's a filthy sort of living. Entirely apt, I suppose, for a convicted thief." James opened his mouth to reply, but she'd not give him the chance to hurt her like that again. "And now I'm here offering to exchange information. I can't imagine you'd want to, but you may find it necessary to dirty your hands once again. You're already implicated."

"Then I suppose you'd better tell me what you know. And what you want."

She closed her eyes for a moment, trying to control the pain. This was what she'd wanted, wasn't it? For James to know the truth about her. Then she opened her eyes, met his gaze as best she could, and told him about last night's adventure with Honoria Dalrymple—the secret door in the herbarium and Honoria's empty-handed trip. "She may have been acting on instructions. She certainly expected to find the door."

"So there's an outside mastermind plotting . . . what, though?"

Mary decided against mentioning the thefts. This

was still the Agency's assignment, and she'd no business telling James anything beyond the essential. "That's what we need to discover."

"'We'?"

Her stomach churned, and she felt herself blushing yet again. "I beg your pardon—force of habit. I've no intention of luring you into something that doesn't interest you."

"Assuming I could be lured."

"Naturally." She tried not to sound too defensive. She was, after all, the author of this disaster.

He was silent for a long moment. Then, abruptly, he asked, "What do you want from me?"

Again, she forced herself to look him in the eyes. "A map of the sewers. I can't reasonably anticipate Mrs. Dalrymple's next move without knowing what the possibilities are."

"I haven't a map I can part with."

She'd not be dismissed quite that easily. "Could you spare yours for half an hour? I'll make a copy."

"Perhaps . . ."

Oh, at times like this she hated the man. Almost. Folding her arms, she propped her feet with a thump on the facing seat. "Do let me know once you've given sufficient thought to such a complex question."

James blinked at her boots, then seemed to repress a smile. "Ladies' boots for a change."

"I could hardly wear boys' boots with female attire."

"Do you miss wearing breeches?"

"Sometimes. They're awfully convenient."

"It's very strange seeing you in a maid's uniform."

"You're stalling."

"It's a big decision."

She let out a puff of disgust. "What utter balderdash! You're the most appallingly decisive person I know."

He sighed dramatically. "Still rubbish at compliments. You know, Mary, the way round a man is to praise his unequalled discernment, not insult his skills."

She blinked. He was supposed to be cold and brusque, not relaxed and teasing. But if he was coming around . . . "So if I compliment you—"

"Lavishly."

"Right. If I flatter you to the skies, I can have a copy of the map?"

"Why don't you try and see?"

"Now you're just trying to irk me." She rose and dusted off her skirts. "I hope the information I gave you is useful, James. Good night."

She got as far as opening the carriage door before his hand closed over hers, pulling it shut again. "Wait a moment," he said, very quietly.

She froze, that treacherous blush heating her cheeks once more. Even through her gloves, she knew what his touch would feel like, skin to skin. "I've been waiting," she said. Her words were meant to sound haughty but instead came out with a tremor.

"I'm in your debt now."

"You're not." She couldn't look at him.

"You proposed an exchange, but I've only taken."

"I'll make a present of that information," she said. Again, she sounded breathless rather than careless. "Let me go, James."

He uncovered her hand.

She didn't move.

"I don't have the map with me."

"That's fine," she said, rather desperate now.

"But I'll take you on a tour of the sewers."

She looked at him then, stunned. But there was no mockery in his dark eyes, no censure. "W-when?"

"Right now, if you can spare the time."

She couldn't look away. Tried for levity, but couldn't quite manage it. "You always did know how to charm a girl. . . ."

"I even have special oilskin waders. Nobody ever says no to those."

Her mind spun uselessly, trying to find a reason she couldn't spend more time in his company. She wanted a map, not a personal tour with all the freight it threatened.

"I thought you needed information."

"I do. A map would suffice."

"I'll give you more knowledge than any map. Come, Mary—cowardice doesn't become you."

"It's not cowardice; it's good sense."

He shrugged. "Well, that's my final offer: a sewer tour, tonight. Take it or leave it."

She glared at him and gripped the door handle with renewed determination. "Why are you doing this? You can't find my presence any more pleasant than I find yours."

His gaze locked with hers. A lazy smile curled one corner of his mouth. "I don't think *pleasant* was ever the word." He touched the back of her hand, and she trembled, despite her best efforts. His smile turned wolfish. "I'll get the oilskins."

"I'll wait outside."

"Suit yourself."

Sixteen

It must have been cold outside. It was always cold outside. But for once, she couldn't feel it. As Mary paced up and down a small patch of cobbled road, she ran through the reasons she ought to go. Flee. And never look back.

"Here. They're a bit large."

She stared at the vast swathes of stiff oilcloth. "A bit?"

"Did you think they came in women's sizes?"

"What about for boys?"

He shrugged. "I did my best, at short notice. Had you given me more warning . . ."

"You expected me to need a tour of the sewers?"

"Not specifically. But when I received your note today, I did wonder."

Perfect. She was a totally predictable secret agent. The best thing she could do now was keep her mouth shut. She took the bundle, climbed back into the carriage, and closed the door behind her. Thick canvas trousers with braces to keep them up. A coat that would fall below her knees. Tall, waterproof boots. All much too large. Nevertheless, they were her only choice. She began with the trousers, knotting the braces until they would stay up. The coat was ridiculous, but with the sleeves rolled up three times, she at least had the use of her hands. And the boots seemed impossible until she pushed her already booted feet inside and found that they would stay on that way. While they were much too tall and loose, she folded them down and cinched them tight until she had a serviceable—if cumbersome—pair of thigh-high oiled boots.

When she swung open the carriage door again, James was pulling on his own hip waders. For a moment, Mary watched, startled. It was a remarkable moment of false intimacy that felt parodic yet meaningful—at least until he glanced up and caught her peeping. A smug grin crossed his face. "Here's the finishing touch." He handed her a deep hat with wide strips of cloth hanging from its back—the sort of fan-tailed hat worn by dustmen—and a pair of oversize thick leather gloves. "Regulation wear for sewer flushers," he explained. "Your choice, of course—but it protects the back of your neck from, er, anything that might drip down from overhead."

She promptly donned the hat. "Let's go."

He refused her help in levering open the manhole cover. "It's all right—it wants more skill than brute force."

Watching him carefully maneuvering the huge cast-iron disk, Mary was struck once more by how healthy James looked. Seven months ago, he'd been a gaunt, shivering, feverish mess. Today, while still thin, he looked strong and capable and very convincingly recovered. Yet what she knew of malarial fever suggested that he ought to continue to be careful: one major relapse meant that he might be susceptible to more. Perhaps that latent fragility was part of what made it so difficult to tear her eyes from him. He glanced up and caught her gaze, and she felt her color rise again. Or perhaps she was just hopeless. She cleared her throat. "I'm surprised the cover isn't guarded."

"It's just an ordinary manhole cover; putting a guard on it would signal that something was up."

She nodded. "But . . . even from a distance? I'd post a concealed one, if I were in charge of the royal family's security."

He shrugged. "Entirely possible. I suppose we'll find out."

It was a practical—if uncomfortable—stance to take. If confronted, James could easily prove his presence was legitimate. Mary had no such hope.

With a shivering, grinding sound, the manhole cover slid to one side, and James flexed his hands with relief. Clearly, moving it had required strength as well as skill. He lit a pair of dark lanterns—lamps with metal shutters, to contain the light when it was unnecessary—and handed one to Mary. "Shall we?"

There was a ladder fixed to the wall of the manhole, slick with a thin, accumulated layer of moisture that Mary preferred not to analyze too closely. With her lamp closed for safety, she began her careful descent. Reaching the bottom rung, she was suddenly enveloped—not by the smell but by the intense warmth of the sewer. It was a different atmosphere entirely: thick and cloying, compared with the biting cold damp above, much like in the tunnel Honoria Dalrymple had discovered. Even the dank, almost salty smell was a more intense version of that which pervaded the palace tunnel.

The instant her feet touched solid ground, Mary opened the lantern just enough to create a small, concentrated beam of light and shone it about. The sewer was a brick tube, its floor only slightly damp. At its tallest point, it was perhaps seven feet high—more than ample for even a very tall man to stand upright in, as long as he remained in the center of the tube. This was surprising: Mary had expected a low, slimy series of caverns, noxious to smell and dangerous to navigate. And while it was true that they had a distinctly sulfurous odor, they were far from repugnant. The roads above ground were far muddier and more litter strewn.

James jumped the last couple of rungs, landing beside her with a quiet thud.

"You're feeling lively."

"Just trying to make you envious of my well-fitting waders." He opened his dark lantern all the way, bathing them in a sphere of warm, yellow light.

She blinked, dazzled—by his playfulness as much as by the lantern. When had they become friends again? It was a dangerous idea, given their previous relations. Not to mention the risk of that meticulously banked ardor's reigniting itself.

They set off at a moderate pace through the sewer, James in the lead. He walked carefully, surprisingly light-footed in his protective boots, and clearly familiar with this subterranean road. As they went, he noted points and objects of interest, composing for her a sort of condensed history of the sewers.

What she'd first thought to be a small private tunnel beneath Buckingham Palace was, in fact, one of London's primary sewers, which started in Hampstead and ran eastward along the course of the ancient underground river Tyburn. It was a startling realization: that anyone working in the sewer—the "flushers"—had unguarded access to the queen's private residence.

When she said so, James nodded. "That's why this job's been so secretive."

"Well, that's perfectly obvious. But I can't believe that no one thought precautions necessary before now!" Did the Agency know of this? She ought to have been told.

"It's not an open sewer," he reminded her. "There's a

locked gate at the bottom, where it empties into the river. You'd have to know your tide tables, pick the lock, navigate part of the sewer by boat . . ."

"All right, so it's not something you'd try on the spur of the moment. But it's still awfully vulnerable for a palace."

He glanced back at her, just for a moment. "We know. That will change, once this job's done."

She thought of Honoria Dalrymple. "Who's 'we'?"

"'We' is Easton Engineering, advising the Chief Commissioner of Public Works."

"The same one you worked with on St. Stephen's Tower?"

He didn't hesitate. "Yes. That's why I was offered this contract."

They walked on in silence for a few seconds. Then she asked, "And how's business in general?"

James glanced back. "Are you actually curious, or just making small talk?"

"Genuine interest. Does it matter?"

"Business is fine. I'd never say no to more work, but after the Indian disaster, I'm happy just to be busy."

"And your brother?"

He snorted. "Now I know you're only being polite."

"Just because your brother disapproves of me doesn't mean I dislike him," she said primly.

"*Hmph.* Very high minded of you." James paused, as though wondering how to answer such an apparently simple question. "George is quite well. He's engaged to be married, so visiting his fiancée takes up much of his time these days."

Mary's thoughts flew instantly to the lovely girl with red-gold hair. And there was something ambivalent about James's tone. . . . "Do you approve of his fiancée?" God help the would-be bride if he didn't. James was very protective of his genial, blustering elder brother—and the family reputation. She'd learned the lengths to which he'd go on her first case, when he'd broken into a merchant's study seeking proof of corruption on the part of George's intended father-in-law.

James shrugged—a slight hitch of one shoulder that lacked his usual conviction. "She's acceptable."

She couldn't help but laugh. "Not a very generous statement."

"No," he agreed, with a smile in his voice. "But an accurate one. She's not very bright, and inclined to triviality. But she doesn't seem unkind or deceitful. Of course," he added, "I've met her only a handful of times."

"Is her family important?"

"What, socially? Oh, no. Nothing to speak of."

"But useful to you?"

He spun about suddenly, so that she almost walked into him. "You've a very low opinion of me, haven't you?"

She ground to a most inelegant halt, just managing to avoid bouncing off his chest. "Of course not. I've just followed you into a sewer."

His smile was sardonic. "You know what I mean: you think I'd only value George's fiancée if she had a substantial dowry and came from a well-connected family that could help Easton Engineering."

"Well, that is what you claimed when we first met."

His brow creased. "It is?"

Oh, how she enjoyed having the upper hand in conversations with James. "Of course it is. You told me, with perfect conviction, that marriage was a business matter to be negotiated with the head, not the heart. You were very scornful of your brother's affection for Angelica Thorold."

"Oh. Well, I've revised my opinions a little since then." Even in the dim yellowy light, she thought she could detect a slight blush climbing his cheeks. "The lady's family is very respectable. I suppose people who care about that sort of thing would say that George has done well."

"Well, then, what's the difficulty?"

He turned and resumed walking. "Who said there was one?"

"You did—not in words, of course, but by your tone. Not to mention your general lack of enthusiasm."

"Damn. I thought I'd gotten better at social hypocrisy."

She smiled at his back. "Perhaps very slightly."

"Thank you. I think." They trudged on for a minute. The water level in the sewer was rising slowly, and liquid now swirled about their ankles, gleaming with grease. "There's nothing properly wrong with Miss Ringley. It's just that she giggles incessantly—her conversation is beyond inane—she listens to everything George says as though he's, I don't know, Moses delivering the Ten Commandments, and then says either, 'Really?' or 'How true!' I swear, I've never heard her say anything else in response." James's voice rose in agitation. "I don't know how George hasn't gone mad by now, but instead he's enchanted by her."

"She's very beautiful."

James spun about, fully interested now. "How might you know? Have you been trailing George about town?"

Mary felt an absurd, unfounded flash of guilt. "Of course not. I saw her. She was at your house—on Sunday." Even as she said the words, a deep blush welled up within her. Impossible to forget what else had happened on Sunday.

"She wasn't."

"The girl in the blue dress? Strawberry-blond curls?"

James snorted. "Oh, that wasn't Ringley. That was—never mind. On Sunday afternoon, George was at the Ringleys' home."

Mary felt a wave of humiliation settle over her like a pall. Of course George would call on his fiancée. Of course James wouldn't dally on the rug with a girl he disliked. And of course he was free to flirt with, to court, whomever he chose. She was mad to have let their conversation stray into such personal matters: this was the inevitable price. "Where are we now?" she asked, feigning deep interest in the smeared and greasy brick walls. She'd not been paying attention and had no idea how long they'd been walking or the distance they'd traveled.

James looked at her for a long moment, but she didn't dare meet his gaze. When he spoke, his voice was neutral, impersonal. "We've been moving south beneath the palace. We're nearly at the disused tunnel you found the other night. Did you say you accessed it through the scullery?"

"From one of the lesser-used walls in the kitchens."

"Right. So it's quite recently built—within the last few generations, I mean. Any idea why?"

She shook her head. "If Buckingham Palace were genuinely old, it'd be quite obvious—a priest's hole, or something like that. But it's a new palace. George III used it as a family home, and I can't see him getting away with building a secret tunnel, even after he went mad. Wasn't he under the very strict control of his doctors and advisers?"

"We could speculate endlessly. But are there any physical clues as to why the tunnel was built?"

"By which you mean iron rings bolted into the wall for a secret torture chamber? Or racks for secret wine storage? Nothing of the sort. It's a very blank, anonymous-feeling sort of tunnel." She shook her head. "I can't believe I'm discussing the characters of various underground tunnels with you."

"Well, we're here now."

She squinted into the gloom, and, sure enough, there was a black gap looming ahead that signified the mouth of a side tunnel. "What's your theory?"

"Haven't a clue. The tunnel doesn't appear on any official diagrams or sewer maps, and it wasn't mentioned to me by palace officials. I thought I'd gone mad when I first noticed it."

"What did you do?"

"I hadn't much choice. The laborers have begun work at the tunnel's mouth, for security reasons. I notified the Master of the Household, who's equally mystified. We're stuck until he decides what's to be done."

She blinked. "It's been a couple of days, though. Surely he's gotten back to you by now?"

"You'd think. But apparently he needs a decision from Her Majesty, and she's somewhat preoccupied." He fixed her with a sharp look. "By what, I'm not privileged to know. But I imagine you are."

She'd known it would come to this. And this, at least, was not trespassing on the Agency's territory. "This is in absolute confidence."

"Of course."

"The Prince of Wales was involved in a violent incident on Saturday night. He's physically unharmed, but there's a very real possibility of scandal attaching to him."

"What sort of scandal?" He frowned. "And how could that possibly consume all Her Majesty's attention?"

"He was drunk and in an opium den. A Lascar attacked him and killed his friend. It's unclear whether the murder was accidental."

James whistled. "The Prince of Wales was friends with Ralph Beaulieu-Buckworth's set? I'm surprised he's permitted that sort of fast company."

Her eyes widened. "So you know about the murder?"

"Of course. All of London's abuzz with it—although there are plenty of rumors and variations about who may or mayn't have been at Beaulieu-Buckworth's side at the time." He looked at her curiously. "Haven't you read about it? Don't the servants talk?"

Mary's stomach twisted. She'd been so thoroughly distracted by the problem of Lang Jin Hai that she'd forgotten to consider public speculation or read the scandal sheets. The sorts of high-society gossip and newspaper coverage she needed were firmly suppressed both abovestairs and belowstairs. It was like living in a specimen cage. But if James, who paid scant attention to idle rumors, had heard murmurs, then this was certainly London's favorite subject.

"The servants," she said slowly, "may be the last people in London to hear of the killing." She was forcing herself to utter the dark words—murder, killing—as a reminder of the magnitude of Lang's actions. Of the sort of trouble she was up against. "Gossip is strictly forbidden; whispering is practically grounds for dismissal. Please, James—tell me what you've heard."

He looked startled at her use of his given name. "Of course. Though I must warn you, it'd be faster to tell you what I'd not heard. What's generally known is that Beaulieu-Buckworth was in an opium den at an interesting hour. Although his family denies that he was intoxicated, it seems much more in character for the wretch to have been drunk and behaving offensively. He was attacked—utterly without provocation, says his family—and killed.

"This is where the variations begin: some say he was the aggressor. Others say the killer was an enemy, who'd disguised himself as a Lascar and lain in wait for the opportunity. Still others say the entire den of opium smokers rushed him en masse. Some accounts have Beaulieu-Buckworth fleeing into the street, calling for help; others have him defending himself at length before finally succumbing to the sheer number of assailants. Really, there's no clear version and nothing like agreement, except on the fact that Beaulieu-Buckworth was a wild young man quite likely to die amid scandal."

"But what of his companion?" pressed Mary.

James shook his head. "In most versions he's alone; in a few, he's with a gang of young bucks, who either flee or help to defend him. There's the odd story featuring the Prince of Wales—but then again, when isn't there? I think that, ironically, that one's been discounted because there are always stories about the royal family. For such a prim family, they do get dragged into the most outlandish rumors."

"The queen's predecessors—her uncles and grandfather—were a rich source of gossip, and most of it true," Mary reminded him. "Perhaps it's just habit."

"Or wishful thinking."

"But as far as you know, nobody seriously thinks the Prince of Wales is involved?"

"No."

Mary was impressed. Although Her Majesty's influence over the Metropolitan Police was purely unofficial, it was fascinating to see how absolute that command was. "So only the royal family, two top-ranking officers at Scotland Yard, and you and I know the truth."

"Should I be impressed?" grumbled James. "The Prince of Wales should testify, not hide behind his influential parents. He's the only person who knows the truth about Beaulieu-Buckworth's death. Regrettable as the young man's life seems to have been, he still deserves justice."

Ah, yes—James the just. His absolute ideas about right and wrong were part of the wedge between them, and she flushed a little at this reminder. "So far, he's not been able to remember anything. He was quite thoroughly intoxicated, and his impressions are jumbled. The concern is whether exposure to public scrutiny and question in a court of law would serve any purpose at all."

James's mouth twisted. "And this is the future king of England: drink addled, incoherent, standing by while his so-called friends are stabbed by opium-addicted foreign criminals."

"We can't all be as perfect and morally upright as you are," she snapped.

"Surely the prince has more reason than most to try. And why are you so indulgent toward his inadequacies, anyway? Don't tell me you're defending him!"

She said nothing. If James thought she meant Prince Bertie, so much the better. For how could she explain her instinctive, passionate defense of a murderous Lascar?

He stared at her for a moment, then raised his lantern and directed the light at her face. "Yes, I do believe you are: you're trying to defend the Prince of Wales!" His expression was one of incredulity—disbelief that was quickly doused by a scowl. "I hope you're not developing tender feelings toward such a pathetic excuse of a man."

"What?" she said, startled by the very idea.

He leaned closer, as though trying to read her thoughts.

She swatted the lantern away. "Stop looming and glowering at me."

"You are, aren't you? Just a little. Not because he's dashing and rich and blue blooded, but because he's such a sniveling little pup." He made a sound of disgust. "Typical."

"Typical *what*?" She was thoroughly exasperated now.

"Typical soft-hearted, romanticizing, nurturing female. He's not worth your time or your heart, Mary. He's an inbred, overindulged, undisciplined excuse for a man. But I suppose my saying so will only make you pity him the more." He appeared angry now—an emotion that seemed utterly out of place.

Her own anger, however, felt entirely justified. "First of all," she said, pushing him back, "I'm neither romantic nor nurturing; you should know that, above all others. And second, you've completely misread my—my position and my attitude toward the Prince of Wales."

He blinked at her. "I have?"

"Of course you have! As though it's remotely appropriate or likely that I'd feel that way! Do you think I'm attracted to intellectual mediocrity, or self-indulgence, or drunkenness?" She felt like howling. "And third, why are we even having such a pointless spat?"

He grinned at her and seemed suddenly to relax. "Well, we often do. . . ."

She glared at him for a minute longer before sighing. "You are a deeply infuriating person."

"I think I've said this before, but . . . pot and kettle."

"Stop shining your lantern in my face."

"It's such a lovely face."

"That's enough nonsense," she grumbled, trying to tamp down a little rush of pleasure at his compliment, no matter how strangely gained. "So what do we know? Only that there's a secret tunnel with no apparent purpose. It doesn't seem recently or regularly used—it's absolutely full of cobwebs. And it connects to the main sewer."

"I've interviewed the flushers who maintain this portion of the sewer. They swear blind that they know nothing about it, that they thought it was merely another ventilation grille."

"What d'you mean, a ventilation grille?"

"One of the risks inherent in sewers is that dangerous gases build up. Some can suffocate a party of men; others may cause explosions, especially in the presence of flame. Ventilation grilles allow the gases to escape upward, aboveground."

Mary considered her lantern with new respect. "Do you believe them? About the grille?"

"Well, it makes a degree of sense. They can't all be lying. And if anyone had investigated and realized it was a proper tunnel, it would surely have been mapped and brought to the palace authority's attention by now."

Mary nodded. "Shall we take a look?"

Seventeen

They splashed their way to the opening, a rough circle about two and a half feet in diameter that occupied the upper half of the tunnel wall. It seemed entirely innocuous to Mary: no loose or broken bricks, no irregularities in the curved entry. It was simply a smooth oval opening, skimmed with mortar to make it uniform, and barricaded in a makeshift fashion with wooden planks.

"This is your work, of course." It was merely something to say. She already knew the answer.

"The tunnel's structurally weak here. See those rotting bricks? You could scoop them out with a teaspoon."

Mary did see. "Is it safe to be here now?"

He shrugged. "It's unlikely to cave in tonight. . . ."

"That's not very reassuring."

He grinned. "I thought you enjoyed danger."

It was wiser to ignore that. "Was it just the structural weakness that made you block it off?"

"It's clearly not a drainage pipe. Doesn't appear on

sewer maps. It's dry. And I don't like the idea of open dead ends. Enough fools try to creep into the sewers, thinking they'll find their fortunes in here—silver teaspoons and gold sovereigns, ripe for the picking. There's no sense in leaving them a hiding place."

Mary nodded. "So until you began work, the tunnel was easily accessible from the main sewer."

"Yes. And is likely to have been that way since it was built."

They stared at each other in mutual perplexity. It simply didn't make sense. And without knowledge of when the tunnel had been built, they couldn't even begin to theorize about its original use—or whether it might be in some way connected with Honoria Dalrymple's interest in it.

In that moment of silence, there came a mundane but entirely unexpected sound—something that made Mary freeze, any further questions forgotten. It was a faint but definite cough. And it came from some distance away.

James's head snapped round. Clearly she'd not imagined it. He turned back and she nodded, replying to his unspoken question. Swiftly, silently, they shuttered their lanterns. It took a moment for their eyes to adjust to the dark. Yet it wasn't completely black—somewhere, in the far recesses of the tunnel behind James, there was something other than inky darkness. It wasn't so much light as the possibility of it, a faint aura of yellowy illumination that had yet to reach them.

As Mary's eyes grew accustomed to the shadows and vague shapes, she felt James pivot to face the intruder. He, or she, was coming from the opposite direction. Farther downstream, closer to the Thames. James took a slow, silent step, then another. There was no need to hurry—the third party was making his way at a steady pace. They could hear his legs swishing through the water, the soles of his boots squeaking occasionally. As they drew closer—Mary had no idea how far down the tunnel he was (a hundred yards? more? impossible to say when she'd no perspective, no knowledge of the tunnels)—she began to hear a low vocal sound, too. It was like a cross between wheezing and muttering.

James's hand bumped against her elbow, signaling her to stop. Not that she had a choice: his back filled her line of vision, and she couldn't get round him without alerting their quarry. She could only wait for James to make his move.

The intruder splashed closer, his lantern's glow bobbing and growing stronger by the moment. His steps were measured, neither swift nor slow. They suggested that he was prepared for this adventure, knew what he was doing—neither a youngster larking about nor a casual opportunist. Mary clenched her lamp tighter, wishing it were something more substantial—something more like a weapon. From the way James gripped his lantern, it was clear he shared her thoughts.

The intruder rounded a final curve, and finally they

saw him directly: a golden dazzle of light and a shadowy form behind that brightness. Middle height, middle breadth. Face shadowed by a deep-brimmed hat. Mary thought she glimpsed an expression of grim intent—but then who wouldn't look that way, striding through a sewer on a dark February night? She squinted, trying to discern his features.

"Stop!" The voice was James's, loud and commanding, echoing off the bricks. With a swift gesture, he opened his dark lantern. The sudden burst of light blinded her, and she flinched despite herself. "State your name and business."

The man scarcely hesitated. But instead of speaking, he hurled his lantern straight into James's face. There was a crash of broken glass, a clatter of metal, a frantic splashing, all amplified by the hollow tunnel. Everything went dark.

"Are you hurt?" Mary dropped to her knees and tore off her huge, clumsy gloves. She'd seen James try to protect his face. Seen him drop his own lantern in the attempt. What were the chances of an explosion, with flame and grease in sudden, violent contact? And if a fire caught now, in this long, narrow space . . . She stopped her train of thought. Her fingers met oilcloth, coarse and slick over a broad, convulsing surface. His back. "Speak. Are you injured?"

"He's running away!"

"Are you burned?" She found his shoulders, tried to maneuver round to face him.

"No—ouch! I don't think so."

"Sorry—did I hurt you?"

"No. Chase him down, damn it!"

Mary turned toward the sound of distant and fast-receding splashing. "Not till I'm satisfied you're all right. Besides, he's got a head start."

"And whose fault is that?"

Such irritability, she decided, was a sign of good health. "Fine. Don't do anything stupid while I'm gone." She retrieved her lantern and, moving as quickly as her oversize boots would allow, set off down the tunnel. The water grew deeper as she went, pressing against the backs of her thighs, as though urging her on. She kept her lantern dark, her movements smooth. It was just possible that thinking himself safe, the intruder would stop. *And then what?* she wondered, but pushed on nevertheless.

She rounded a final curve and blinked with surprise. Here, the sewer gradually broadened like a cone, and deepened, too: she was submerged nearly to her waist, and the floor continued to drop away before her. She halted, uncertain, and now she heard a new sound from her quarry. The rapid splashing ceased. There came a scraping sound, and then a different sort of watery ripple. It was too dark to see—she knew only that he wasn't within arm's reach—and so she listened for a few moments longer. There was nothing she could make out simply through sound. She thought of James, in all probability bloodied and lacerated, with oozing filth lapping at his wounds.

She couldn't return without an explanation, could hardly swim on blindly, risking lantern and life. And so, steadying herself against the ceaseless flow of water, she opened her dark lantern with a swift, decisive snap.

Black water, swirling all about her.

Dark, rotting bricks, gleaming darkly above.

And, perhaps fifty yards ahead, a small punt nosing its way Thames-ward, steered by a figure in dripping oilskins. He glanced back to the source of the light and caught sight of Mary. She couldn't make out his expression, but it seemed to her that he stared intently. There was no triumph or glee in his opportune escape.

For half a moment, she weighed the possibility of throwing her lantern into his boat. Regrettably, the ceiling was too low and the tunnel too narrow for her to throw anything such a distance with accuracy. She had to content herself, instead, with watching him glide through the currents, learning what she could. He punted with competence but lacked the economy of motion one customarily saw in river men. Only when he disappeared from sight did she begin the long trek back to James. She hoped that he'd followed her order, to do nothing stupid, with more success than she had his.

They retraced their steps in grim silence. Despite his injuries, James insisted that Mary climb the ladder first, and the first thing she saw as she surfaced aboveground was Barker's accusing face.

He sprang down from the driver's seat, and as she turned to give James a hand, Barker pushed her aside without ceremony or apology. "Lucky to be alive, sir," he said in a gruff tone, hauling James from the manhole with such swiftness that they both stumbled slightly.

"Don't be so melodramatic, Barker," said James, sounding quite his usual exasperated self. "And how d'you know we didn't just take a pleasant stroll?"

"Echoes, sir. Heard your voice hollering, a way away."

"Well, we're fine. That is, I'm fine. And Mary chased the villain down half a mile or so of sewer, so I presume she is, too." He swung round to look at her. "Isn't that right?"

She nodded. "You're bleeding."

"Where?" He raised his hand to his face, but she knocked it aside.

"Not with those filthy gloves," she said quietly. She turned to Barker. "I don't suppose you've anything like bandages and something to cleanse a wound."

To her surprise, he answered with something less than utter hostility. "There's a small case beneath the rear-facing bench."

She was already shucking off the coat and waders, scrambling to smooth down her skirts in a semblance of modesty. Oh, who was she trying to fool? "Get in," she said to James. "No time to lose." She opened the carriage door and motioned him inside.

"I'd make the most of this opportunity if I weren't

covered in slime," he murmured, waggling his eyebrows in the fashion of a music-hall villain. Then he flinched. "Ouch. That's where I'm bleeding from, isn't it?"

She laughed. "Just get inside. We've things to discuss while I clean that disgusting gash."

His injuries were much less severe than they might have been: a jagged two-inch cut along his brow bone, and several smaller nicks. The thick flusher's gloves had served him well there, too: if the lamp had shattered against his bare hands, he'd have been both burned and badly lacerated. As it was, his injuries came only from tiny flying splinters of glass. As Barker had said, she found a small case containing bandages, clean compresses, scissors, and even a pair of tweezers. Someone—likely James—had anticipated the need for rudimentary medical care in unusual circumstances.

She picked four glittering shards from his cheeks and laid them carefully in a clean handkerchief. "This will hurt," she warned, uncorking a flask of whiskey.

"It's only fair; I did the same to you two years ago, in this very carriage."

She smiled at the memory. "In the middle of the night."

"Do you still carry the marks?"

She showed him her hand, still etched with Angelica Thorold's fingernail punctures. "A little. But don't worry: I daresay your scar will look positively dashing."

He bore her very thorough cleansing and bandaging in silence, the only sign of pain a tightening of his jaw when the alcohol burned his raw flesh. "Any reason you're saving these?" he asked, pointing to the glass fragments.

His skin was very warm beneath her fingers, his breath soft against her cheek. She concentrated on wiping the cut clean. "Don't you want to know who that man was?"

"I did ask. . . ."

"Yes, and look how well that went."

"It was the reasonable thing to do," he protested. "What would you have done—attacked first and asked questions later?"

"Hold still—you're making the wound bleed again." She finished her work and selected the largest piece of broken glass, a rough triangle, fingernail-size and somewhat tinged with red. "Look."

"And?" he asked with exaggerated patience.

She held it up to the carriage lamp. "There. At the edge."

"I don't see what—oh." The slight frown between his eyes suddenly deepened. "Is that *etching*?"

"Yes." Her eyes sparkled with excitement. "Instead of a dark lantern, he was carrying an oil lamp with etched glass. Quite an expensive item for a sewer robber, wouldn't you say?"

"Odd, certainly. It could be stolen goods, though. He might even have pinched it himself."

"For the purpose, you mean? Lamps like this are expensive, even when they're sold as stolen goods. And if you were going to the trouble of stealing one, wouldn't you choose a sensible one, like a dark lantern?"

"What are you suggesting, Mary?"

"I think our intruder is no ordinary opportunist. As you pointed out, he'd have to learn the tide tables and have special waterproof clothing. But he didn't have the right sort of lantern—I'd argue that he simply took the nearest item to hand."

"So he's middle-class, at least."

"Or more. He had a punt waiting—it was clearly an organized attempt to navigate the sewers. And his punting style may be significant: he certainly wasn't good enough to be a river man."

"That still leaves the greater part of the population of London."

Mary chafed at this skepticism. There was something—a feeling, a detail she couldn't manage to identify that formed the core of her certainty. She closed her eyes and brought to mind the image of the man, floating down the sewer into the open river. Watchful. Thwarted. Learning from this incident. And suddenly she had it. "It's his bearing—he was so focused and disciplined. Almost military in his posture."

James snorted. "A renegade army officer storming the palace?"

Mary remained in earnest. "Is there a rule against criminals being affluent? Or perhaps he's not a criminal at all; maybe his intentions were generally harmless, and he simply panicked when confronted."

"Mmm. I suppose a patrician sewer invader is more

likely to be connected with your lady-in-waiting . . . what's her name?"

"Honoria Dalrymple. The Honorable."

His lips twitched. "The Honorable Honoria?"

"Clearly her parents weren't thinking."

"Right. So you *are* imagining two high-born sewer rats, one of whom may be responsible for all this? But what for?"

She sighed. "No idea. But one of them isn't imaginary."

"In that case, we'd better focus on her."

She met his gaze, startled. "'We'?"

He offered her his most winning smile. "Say no, if you like."

The precious seconds ticked by as she struggled.

She couldn't.

Mustn't.

Oughtn't.

And yet, it made sense. He had legitimate access to the sewers. He was an intelligent, entirely trustworthy partner. And there was a sense of inevitability to this newest partnership. It always seemed to come down to James. This case, which had begun so dully, was fast becoming most complex—for her personally, at least.

His grin turned smug. "Thought so. Now, tell me all about the Honorable Honoria."

Eighteen

Wednesday, 15 February

Buckingham Palace

It was very late — or, more properly, rather early — when Mary crept back into the palace. This was just as well: she didn't want to risk the horror of seeing Octavius Jones in Amy's bed. But when Mary dared enter their shared bedroom, it was quiet but for Amy's peaceful snores. She stayed only long enough to wash off the grime, clean her boots, and change into a fresh uniform before slipping downstairs, only slightly earlier than usual. She had a great deal of work to complete if she was to steal away for an hour — hopefully with Amy covering for her.

It may have been worth missing a night's sleep just for the expression on Mrs. Shaw's face when she came into the breakfast room to see the place settings already laid, the napkins folded into triangles (the housekeeper specified a different shape for each day of the week), the coffee cups arrayed like squat soldiers, their handles pointing to four o'clock.

She contented herself by sniffing and saying, "I hope those napkins have been sufficiently starched."

Mary merely bobbed her head. Starch was not her department, and well Mrs. Shaw knew it. It was as close as she could come to acknowledging that nothing was amiss.

On her way up to Her Majesty's private sitting room, Mary caught a glimpse of Amy at work in the Blue Room, and she stopped in the doorway for half a minute to watch the girl. Amy was steady and neat fingered, going about the task in an orderly fashion—quite unlike the impatient girl who gossiped with Mary or sneaked her lover into the servants' quarters. Mary wondered what conflicting passions lay within others.

"Good morning, Mrs. Jones," she said, slipping into the room.

Amy jumped and emitted a little shriek. "Lord, how you startled me!"

"I didn't mean to."

"It was good of you to stay out so long last night," said Amy, resuming her work. "You're a dear."

"I hope everything went to plan."

Amy made a face. "Close. He didn't actually propose. Though he did give me a present." She plunged one hand into her chemise and drew out something shiny for inspection.

Mary blinked. It was a large, gilt-edged brooch—a crudely cut cameo of a generic Greek goddess with a large chin. "My stars" was her honest response.

"Pretty, ain't it? Tavvy says he chose this one because the lady looks a bit like me."

Mary couldn't help noticing that some of the "gold" border was starting to flake off, but there was nothing to be gained in slighting Jones's gift, no matter how cynically chosen. "Well, that's a step in the right direction."

"A slow one, though."

"Think he'll propose by month's end?"

Amy smiled at that—a broad, cheeky grin. "You want a wager, do you?"

Mary grinned back. "I'd put my money on you, anyway."

"That's only right and sensible, my dear. But see here, can I do aught to return the favor?"

Mary raised her eyebrows. "Well, I have got a little project of my own to see to. . . ."

"You never told me you had a sweetheart, you sly thing!"

"I've not. It's something else. But d'you think if I slipped out after dinner for an hour or so, you could . . ."

Amy nodded. "'Course. It's only right, after what you done for me last night. And I'd do it anyway, you're such a love."

A day that began with such promise, however, became complicated in late morning, when Mrs. Shaw appeared in the Yellow Room, a more than usually pinched expression on her face.

Mary stopped her dusting. "Yes, Mrs. Shaw?" She looked the housekeeper full in the face and saw, with real surprise, turmoil in those normally dull eyes.

"I have received another highly irregular request from the Prince of Wales. I am duty-bound to warn you, Quinn: this behavior is utterly inadvisable."

Mary blinked. "I beg your pardon?"

"This intrigue with the Prince of Wales. It doesn't make you special. It doesn't make you unique. And it's certainly not a way of gaining promotion. Not in my household."

Mary took a deep breath. "Mrs. Shaw, I don't understand your accusations. I'm not carrying on an intrigue with the Prince of Wales."

"Then why has he asked for you?"

"Now?"

"Yes, now."

"Is it possible that there's been a misunderstanding?"

Mrs. Shaw's eyes narrowed. "Playing the innocent doesn't become you, Quinn. I know what you're about. I suppose you think yourself very clever, skirting round the rules like this. But you mark my words—" She shook a bony finger at Mary. "One misstep . . ."

Mary suppressed a sigh. Bit her tongue to keep from reminding her, *You said this yesterday*. There was nothing she could say to persuade Mrs. Shaw that, far from this being her ambition, she wanted none of the prince's attentions. The housekeeper had already made up her mind, and she was a woman who prided herself on never changing it. Mary's remaining time at the palace was to be even more closely monitored.

And she was further than ever from finding answers.

The kitchen staff was sour when Mary asked them to make up a last-minute breakfast tray for the Prince of Wales. Naturally, Mrs. Shaw was unwilling to intervene in this instance and so Lizzie, the most senior cook-maid, had her way with a curt "We've enough to do without that lazy young gent."

Mary loitered, half impatient and half unwilling, until the tray was ready: nearly half an hour. She'd no desire to ingratiate herself with the prince and was rather afraid of what she might be forced to do if his interest in her continued as predictably as it promised to. Was it possible that he only wanted to talk some more, or were Mrs. Shaw's suspicions correct? And if so, how did one refuse royalty?

Mary's confidence sagged as she left the servants' corridor—until she caught Mrs. Shaw's vinegary look. At that, her spine straightened, her shoulders dropped, and she inclined her chin with frosty grace at the housekeeper, borrowing from the manner of touring royalty. One spoiled man-child was not going to upset her investigation. The person most likely to ruin that was Mary herself, through stubbornness and impetuous action—both traits she'd learned to temper over the past year and a half.

The prince's equerries were, supposedly, wellborn companions of the wise and sober sort, a few years older than he. They were charged with giving the prince timely doses of advice. In practice, however, these were the same attendants who'd managed to lose the prince on that now-infamous night in Limehouse—rather a dubious testament to their good judgment and desirable influence on the prince.

As she arrived at the Prince of Wales's apartments, Mary was unsurprised to see a pair of them lounging just outside the door. They leaned against the wall with a negligent air, staring rudely at Mary as she drew nearer. They neither spoke nor moved, although she nearly grazed one of them with the edge of the enormous tray. Naturally, they didn't bestir themselves to open the door for her.

Mary kept her gaze low, unwilling to draw even more attention to herself. She didn't like the expressions in their eyes. They were looking at her as they might a mildly interesting piece of horseflesh: not good for much, but perhaps worth having anyway. More than ever, she felt she was walking into a trap.

She shifted the tray, considering the pint or so of steaming coffee balanced thereon. That was certainly her best bet, if one of them made a grab at her. She didn't know what the consequences of scalding a dishonorable honorable might be. Her tension was high enough that she didn't much care. Yet they didn't move as she turned the door handle and the heavy mahogany door slowly swung open.

Like yesterday, Prince Bertie was stationed at the far end of the room, half reclined in his favorite easy chair.

Like yesterday, he wore a silk dressing gown.

Unlike yesterday, however, there was a woman in the room. A tall woman dressed in the height of fashion, her billowing skirts trailing over the arm of Prince Bertie's chair. She drooped over the prince's form, one hand resting lightly on his chest, murmuring something intimate. She was graceful, intent, predatory. She was Honoria Dalrymple. And so focused was she that she failed to notice the door swing open or the entry of a third party.

"Such an arrangement could be to our mutual benefit, don't you think, dear prince?" she murmured, her voice all honey and smoke.

"I—er. Hm. I—I'm afraid I don't know what to say, er, Mrs. D-Dalrymple."

A husky laugh. "You should say yes. I assure you, you shan't be disappointed."

"But—but Mrs. Dalrymple . . ." He was nearly panting—whether with excitement or anxiety, it was unclear. Probably both.

"But what, darling boy?"

"But you're . . . you're *old*!" The last word was wrenched from the princely throat, a half shriek of horror.

Behind Mary, the equerries burst into raucous laughter. Honoria's and Prince Bertie's heads swiveled round as they were alerted for the first time to their audience of three. Honoria blanched and toppled from her perch. He jumped up, uttering loud incoherencies and trying to help her up. She swatted away his fumbling grasp, pulled herself up with remarkable dignity (all things considered), and swept past Mary with her chin held high.

A pair of sharp slaps, flesh on flesh, echoed in the corridor, and Mary smiled. The louts had gotten a little of what they deserved, at least. Prince Bertie's entire head was the color of beetroot, his mouth slack and open as he goggled at Mary, at the tray she carried, at his still-tittering attendants in the doorway. "My God. I—I—I don't know what to say." He collapsed into the easy chair, then sprang up again as though it had burned him. Re-seated himself in a different, more upright chair. Cleared his throat. "Well. Thank God you're not my mother."

His Highness was too discomposed to do much apart from drink his coffee and wonder at Honoria Dalrymple's behavior. This was a relief to Mary—today would not be the day she had to fight off the Prince of Wales—but also a source of additional anxiety. How might Honoria retaliate against those who had witnessed her humiliation? Her influence over the equerries was dubious—louts they may have been, but they were wellborn louts. But she could certainly exact her revenge on a hapless parlor maid, especially with Mrs. Shaw's silent connivance. Mary's prospects at the palace were shrinking fast. And there was nothing to be gained in enlisting the prince's help. Even if she could make him understand her position, even if she paid his price, the young man was too weak to be of use. The only people who could help her, Anne and Felicity, were peculiarly, unusually silent.

It was with a different but equal mingling of dread and impatience that she cleared away the royal breakfast remains and hastened back to the kitchens. Prince Bertie was a late riser, and it was nearly time for the royal family's luncheon. By this time, Mrs. Shaw would be squinting at the poached fish for stray scales, reviewing the particular garnishes for each serving dish, and inspecting the platters of fruit and walnuts for perfect symmetry. With luck, Mary would be able to finish the dusting that Prince Bertie's breakfast had interrupted.

As she returned to the servants' quarters, however, there was a different mood in the air. Instead of the customary buzz of activity produced by a staff of hundreds, each quietly at work, there was a sense of waiting. Of listening. Footmen strolled past, rolling their eyes expressively. Maids performed furtive dashes of work, falling still between times.

It was unnerving, and when Mary spotted Sadie, she didn't bother with a sideways approach. "What's happening?" she whispered.

The redheaded maid, normally so cheerful, was dusting an already spotless sideboard with quick, nervous strokes. "Mrs. S. is on a right tear. There's trouble in the stillroom—some of the preserves ain't right, and she's like to go mad." It was a genuine domestic crisis: jams, jellies, and pickles were laboriously made at summer's end, sealed under wax or stored in crocks, and kept in the stillroom. If some were spoiled, that meant a flaw in the process—and a shortage as the season wore on. It was a terrible blow to any housekeeper's pride, and especially to one as meticulous as Mrs. Shaw.

"Did she sack the stillroom maid?"

Sadie bit her lip. "Aye. But it's worse. She were scolding the maid, calling her names, and our Amy, she were in the background, and Amy rolled her eyes, like, only like joking, y'know, and Mrs. S. went proper mad: foaming at the mouth, like. And she grabbed at Amy and was shaking her, and this little trinket fell out of Amy's dress, and landed on the floor, and then—" Sadie paused to draw breath.

Mary closed her eyes. She already knew how this was going to end.

"Mrs. S.—she went dead quiet. And then she smiled, evil-like. And she said now she had the answer, and that Amy was sacked for thieving. Amy were spitting mad, at first, but when Mrs. S. said that bit about thieving, she went dead quiet—like she was really scared."

"Where are they now?"

Sadie gestured with her chin. "Attic. Mrs. S. is watching Amy pack her things, and then I guess she'll get the boot."

Mary thought of Mrs. Shaw standing over Amy, enjoying herself, while Amy was losing her livelihood, lodging, and reputation. "Did Amy deny she was a thief?"

Sadie snorted. "She ain't no thief, our Amy."

"Yes, but did she say anything to Mrs. S.?"

"No . . . she didn't say no more after that."

"She was probably too frightened," said Mary quickly. "She's losing everything."

"I suppose she's got her gentleman friend."

Mary didn't think Octavius Jones represented much consolation, but said only, "Thanks," and began to walk swiftly toward the staircase.

"Where are you going?" called Sadie, bewildered.

"To see Amy and Mrs. S."

"You can't do no good that way. Mrs. S. ain't like to listen to you."

Privately, Mary agreed. But she couldn't keep herself from trying.

A terrible near silence prevailed in their attic bedroom. Mary paused in the open doorway and watched as Mrs. Shaw supervised Amy's packing, arms folded and mouth curved in a smile of grim satisfaction. Amy moved quietly, folding and stacking her possessions with hands that trembled only slightly. She paused now and then to swipe away a stray tear, but her face was set like a mask.

"Mrs. Shaw," said Mary, slightly breathless from her climb. "Amy didn't steal that brooch."

The housekeeper spun round to look at her, surprised that any minion should have the temerity to speak to her. "This is none of your affair, Quinn."

Amy's expression remained fixed.

"But I've seen the brooch. Amy showed it me this morning. It's a present from her admirer."

Mrs. Shaw's face grew fierce. "I warn you, Quinn. No more of your insolence."

"Has anybody even complained of missing a brooch?" persisted Mary. "And if not, how do you know it's stolen?"

"I am not in the habit of justifying myself to ill-bred sluts," snapped Mrs. Shaw in a tone that made Amy flinch. "But if you'd a fraction of the brains necessary to do your job well, you'd know that Amy could have stolen other items and sold them in order to buy herself such a trashy trinket."

Now she was getting somewhere. "Other things have been stolen? From the palace?"

Mrs. Shaw's cheeks flushed brick red. "That was merely an example. Now, will you return to your work, or are you asking to be dismissed along with Amy?"

"Because, again, if nothing's been stolen, I don't see why anybody should accuse Amy—"

It was Amy herself who halted the standoff. She pushed past Mrs. Shaw, who stared at her with furious surprise, and enveloped Mary in a hug. "You're a darling," she said quietly. "But this ain't helping. Keep your job, my dear. Don't argue no more."

Mary stared at her. "But . . . where will you go?"

Amy mustered an approximation of her usual cheeky grin. "I'll land on my feet, my dear—you see if I don't." And with a gentle but firm shove, she pushed Mary from the room and resumed her packing without even a glance at Mrs. Shaw.

Nineteen

The servants' dinner was a grim feast that day. It was impossible not to look at the two vacant places at table—Amy's and the stillroom maid's—and Mrs. Shaw's angry surveillance became a constant accusation aimed at the entire staff. Even the footmen, who were not subject to her discipline, seemed sobered by the morning's ugliness. Mary missed Amy already, for her giddy good humor and company, and also—selfishly—because her departure made it impossible for Mary to slip out after dinner.

Once the meal ended, instead of fulfilling the task that had haunted her for days, Mary collected a pot of brass polish, a pungent paste made up of vinegar, salt, and flour, and set off for the Blue Room. It was the largest of the reception rooms, formerly Amy's responsibility. Now it was hers until another maid could be engaged—part punishment, Mary supposed, for her having questioned Mrs. Shaw's actions.

It wasn't entirely punishment, however. This was the room from which the ornaments had been stolen. That fact, combined with Amy's uncharacteristic meekness when she'd been accused of theft, had Mary's suspicions aflame. Much as she liked Amy, all that had happened today played into her theories about Octavius Jones. All that was missing, of course, was evidence. But she could send word to the Agency. They could have Jones tailed. They could even search his home. She assumed they were still able, even if they'd not yet replied to her queries about Honoria Dalrymple, about the tunnel, about Jones.

Mary applied a thin layer of brass polish to the doorknobs and window catches, mulling over new possibilities. While Jones was her primary suspect, she couldn't yet declare the matter resolved. There was still the problem of Honoria Dalrymple, of course. Between creeping through secret tunnels and trying to seduce the Prince of Wales, the lady-in-waiting was clearly up to no good. And it was still unclear whether hers was an illegal, to-be-stopped malignancy or mere mischief making, in which case she was beneath the Agency's notice. Mary wished she and James had agreed on a more precise plan the night before. They'd left things open, each seeking to glean what they could in the course of the day. But she'd feel better knowing what James was doing, and why.

"There you are."

Mary started and turned. Surveying her from the

doorway, a stiff, quizzical smile on her lips, was the second-to-last person in the palace she wanted to see. She bobbed stiffly. "Mrs. Dalrymple." Mary was unsurprised when Honoria walked into the room and closed the door behind her. She was surprised, however, by the hints of uncertainty that hovered beneath the surface of Honoria's neutral expression. And she was downright startled when Honoria began to speak.

"This morning's turn of events was unfortunate for all present," said the lady-in-waiting in cordial, businesslike tones.

"Yes, ma'am."

"I bear no grudge against you, Quinn, for what you saw. You were simply doing your duty." Her tone was magnanimous—and perhaps rightly so. Although she was only being reasonable, wounded pride was difficult to overcome.

"Thank you, ma'am," said Mary when it became clear that some response was expected.

Honoria frowned and began to pace back and forth—signs of discomfort that surprised Mary even more. "I am not too blind to see things as they really are," began Honoria. "Although, as you heard the gentleman say, I'm rather too mature for his tastes, it's evident that you are not." At this, she wheeled about and fixed Mary with a hard look.

"Ma'am?"

"Don't trifle with me, Quinn. It's plain that Bertie fancies you. It's not every new parlor maid who's ordered to fetch him breakfast, and he in his dressing gown."

Mary felt herself begin to blush in response. "It's not like that, ma'am. Truly, I don't want that sort of attention."

Honoria's perfectly shaped eyebrows shot up. "You surprise me, dear girl. Most young women in your position would give their eyeteeth for such an opportunity."

So she was now Honoria's "dear girl"? "You may think it strange, ma'am, but I do not find the idea appealing."

Honoria sat down on the nearest chair and crossed her ankles—a relaxed posture that failed to fool Mary. "So you prefer anonymous drudgery to life as the royal favorite?"

Mary was taken aback. "There's no saying I'd be the favorite, ma'am. A young man's passing fancy would be the ruin of me."

"*Pff!* Such melodramatic words. Young women these days are all such timid things, full of shuddering prudery."

Mary permitted herself the faintest of smiles. "Are you suggesting that I try my luck, ma'am?"

Honoria sat up very straight, looked Mary in the eye, and said, "I've a proposition for you, young lady. It will make your future, if you've the stomach for it."

Mary put down her polishing rag and assumed a listening posture. Finally, things were becoming interesting.

"A woman who beds a man holds a great deal of power over him. He is often unaware of this, which makes it even more potent. She may ask him questions that nobody else dares or compel him to do things he would never otherwise consider. Do you follow me?"

"I think so, ma'am."

"This gentleman has knowledge I want, information that will make a great deal of difference to me. You may be the young woman who can dig out that knowledge."

Mary's eyes widened. "You're asking me . . ."

"To bed him," said Honoria. She seemed to enjoy the phrase, uttering it with crisp relish. "He's a young man. Almost certainly a virgin. And he desires you. It is for you to choose whether this stroke of good fortune will change your life or whether you'll continue toiling in obscurity for a pittance." She paused. "Think how easy life could be: No more work. A townhouse and a carriage. Servants of your own. Frocks and jewels and furs. These are the rewards of the best paramours."

Mary allowed her expression to glaze over with impressionable wonder. Honoria was an effective advocate for the courtesan's life, if a highly biased one. Callow, uneducated housemaids didn't reap the sorts of rewards she described; they were much more likely to end up pregnant, discarded, and in the poorhouse. However, Quinn the parlor maid wasn't meant to understand that. "All that, just for . . . ?"

A frosty smile.

"But what if he doesn't like me, after a little while?"

Honoria leaned in for the kill. "I will look after you myself. There will be a generous reward and a letter of character. All you must do is get the information I require."

Mary made a show of mulling this over—slowly enough that she saw a flicker of impatience in Honoria's eyes. "You're very kind, Mrs. Dalrymple," she said with exaggerated slowness. "But . . . I just don't know."

Honoria smiled again, and this time there was more than a hint of cruelty in her lovely face. "Let me put this to you differently: you will use all your meager charms to coax the information I require from the gentleman. The instant you cease to comply, I shall have you sacked for immorality."

Mary gaped. "But . . . I ain't never . . . I'm a good girl, Mrs. Dalrymple."

"But who would ever believe that?" Honoria's smile grew wider. "Certainly not Mrs. Shaw, once I tell her that I caught you in the Prince of Wales's bed this morning."

The two women stared at each other—one openly triumphant, the other privately so. A minute ticked past. And then another.

"I'll do it," said Mary. "On two conditions."

"As I thought," said Honoria with a smirk. "Finer mettle than first appears."

"I want this afternoon free. Will you arrange that with Mrs. Shaw?"

"I'll tell her I need you to do some sewing."

"And I can't start tonight."

Honoria's frown was instantaneous. "Why not?"

"It's my time of the moon."

"Oh, for pity's sake. Very well. When? Tomorrow?"

"Perhaps," said Mary cautiously. This ruse would certainly be short lived, but the more time she could buy herself, the better.

"Very well, then." Honoria stood up to sweep from the room, but Mary stopped her with a slight gesture. "What is it?"

"What is it I'm to find out for you?"

Honoria hovered a moment before sitting down again. "What I tell you is in complete confidence. If you repeat this to anybody, not only will I deny this entire conversation but I'll also destroy you. Do you understand?"

Mary nodded. There was something admirable about the woman's ruthlessness.

"A few days ago, a relation of mine was murdered in uncertain circumstances. The gentleman of whom we speak witnessed the murder. It is claimed by his physician that he cannot recollect the details. Of course, that is untrue. False and malicious rumors are now circulating about the manner of my relation's death. These must stop. Your task is to convince the gentleman of his duty to clear the record—or, at the very least, to learn what really happened."

Mary blinked. This was nothing short of a revelation:

Honoria Dalrymple was not only a relation of Ralph Beaulieu-Buckworth, but was so persuaded of his virtue that she was willing to prostitute herself to clear the young man's name. Having failed in that endeavor, she hadn't hesitated to blackmail a bystander into doing the work for her. Had Mary really just thought such ruthlessness admirable? Perhaps in its utter conviction. And why hadn't the Agency come through with this information days ago? It was a matter of public record. She repressed a flash of resentment and focused on Honoria's stony, elegant features. "And . . . if I can't persuade the gentleman to tell me what happened?"

Honoria bared her teeth in another predatory grimace that only just qualified as a smile. "Then you shall have to work harder."

Twenty

Wednesday evening

Tower of London

One of the ridiculous things about London was that although it was almost always faster to walk to one's destination, the streets were clogged with vast numbers of carriages, hansom cabs, wagons, omnibuses, and horses, all desperate to be somewhere, all illustrating the triumph of hope over experience. Despite the satisfaction she took in the walk from Buckingham Palace, Mary felt her confidence dip as she neared the Tower of London.

Part of this, she knew, was by design: its approach was a bleak stone wall interrupted only by arrow loops that enhanced its forbidding aspect. All the same, she felt very small indeed as she presented herself at the gate.

"Here to see whom?" The guard looked her up and down.

"A new prisoner: Lang." She was wearing her best hat and Sunday coat, and on leaving the palace had swiped an old silk umbrella that may or may not have been

Mrs. Shaw's. The overall effect was of prim respectability—a governess or a lady without much money, rather than a servant.

Even so, something about her seemed to give the guard pause. "And who might you be to the prisoner?"

"My name is Miss Lawrence, of the St. Andrew's Church Ladies' Committee. We heard of the prisoner's plight and wish to be allowed to minister to him."

"Bit irregular, this," grumbled the guard. "Usually it's a delegation of ladies."

Mary leaned forward and lowered her tone. "I hope I may rely upon you not to repeat this, sir, but this Lang was rather an unpopular prisoner within our committee. There have been so many rumors about his offense, and with some of the ladies very proud of their distant connections with the best families . . ." She smiled, a weak apology that nevertheless seemed to go a long way.

"Aye, he's a troublemaker, that Lang," agreed the guard, unlatching the gate. "And he's none too polite, neither, so you want to watch yourself, miss. He ain't above using strong language to a lady."

"Thank you," murmured Mary. Now that she was inside, she found it difficult to tolerate the guard's easy chatter. She wanted perfect silence as she picked her way through the vast, slushy courtyard; a last few moments of futile hope, aimed at the man who might be her father. Absurd. She didn't even know what she hoped for.

She turned her mind away from childish wistfulness

and concentrated on her surroundings. The Tower of London, she'd always been told, was actually many buildings within a single set of fortifications, built by different kings over hundreds of years. This made sense only now, as she stood within its bounds, craning her neck up at the different towers. She would need a map to navigate between them all. But she would remember each step of her journey to this particular tower that loomed over her, weather blackened and Gothic.

"Cradle Tower," said the guard easily as they reached its entrance and he passed her into the care of another guard. "All the best traitors have been kept here."

"History repeats itself," said the new guard in a portentous tone.

The two men chuckled, and Mary wondered how much of the gossip about Lang they actually believed. Not that it mattered. She scarcely knew herself.

The second guard was less inclined to conversation. After a cursory glance at the contents of her handbag, he led her up a narrow flight of stairs that smelled of mouse nests, circling higher and higher until they emerged on the top floor. They passed through a low, arched doorway into a dim antechamber. It smelled different here, of ancient meals, burnt tallow, and unwashed bodies.

Mary felt a lurch of fear. Somehow, she'd expected the approach to be longer, more complicated; to have time to prepare herself. Yet perhaps a dozen paces before her was a stone wall, interrupted by a door made of iron bars. She seemed unable to convince herself that the prisoner was right there.

"Visitor, Lang," said the guard in a bored tone.

Mary held her breath. The voice: would it be her father's? Yet several seconds passed, and the only reply was a soft susurration—like tree branches moved by a moderate breeze. Was Lang shuffling his feet? Chafing something against the wall?

"Lang!" barked the guard. He eyed Mary with suspicion. "He expecting you?"

She shook her head, voice temporarily lost.

The guard strode to the door and banged on the bars with his truncheon. "Get up, Chinaman. There's a lady here to see you."

Still nothing.

The jailer looked at Mary, eyebrows raised, as if to ask, what now?

She cleared her throat. "Is he always like this with visitors?"

The man snorted. "Ain't had none. 'Less you mean the chaplain, and he ignores him. He ain't violent, missy—don't let them stories frighten you. He just sleeps all day, unless he's got the shakes."

"The shakes?" Her voice echoed sharply off the stone walls.

"Drug fiend. He were found in an opium den, weren't he? And he ain't had none for four days, now. Raving, he were, the first couple of days. A regular madman."

"And now it's passed?"

"Well, he couldn't keep up that malarkey. Lord, it were tiring just to see."

"What about food or drink?"

The guard shrugged. "Prisoners, they got their notions. Most of them try a hunger strike, sooner or later."

"But if he's had nothing for four days, he'll soon be dead. He'll never make it to trial!" Mary fought to keep a sharp note of panic from her voice.

"To my thinking, it saves a world of trouble. But we got our orders. He gets whatever muck we can force-feed, three times a day, ma'am. He ain't starving."

Only in the most literal sense of the word, thought Mary. How long could a man subsist on a few spoonfuls of gruel forced down his throat? That shuffling, almost whistling sound had continued as she questioned the jailer, rising and then falling in cycles. "Will you open the door, please?"

The man shrugged again. "Suit yourself. Though he ain't like to talk to you. I ain't heard him say a word, these last two days." Still, he unlocked the iron door and stepped back, with an elaborate gesture to Mary. "Miss." He palmed the half crown she offered him with a neat gesture and, with one more obsequious bow, took himself off to the far end of the antechamber, at the mouth of the stairwell.

Mary closed her eyes for a long moment, summoning an image of her father: Lang Jin Hai. The last time she'd seen him, he'd been a handsome man in his thirties. Tall for a Chinese, with some resemblance to the prince consort—something her mother had been proud of. But that had been twelve or thirteen years ago, and she'd been a young child. Memory was an unreliable guide. At least it always seemed to be, for her.

Enough. She opened her eyes and tried to see into the cell. It was windowless and thus dark; all daylight came from a narrow window in the antechamber, and it didn't penetrate far. As Mary's eyes adjusted, she began to see shapes, perceive depth. The cell was narrow and long, furnished only with a low cot pushed against one wall. There was nothing else in the room: no chair, no table, no washstand or water jug—though judging from the fetid smell, there was a chamber pot beneath the bed that hadn't been thoroughly cleaned in recent memory.

And finally, the thing she most and least wanted to see: a small figure, crumpled on the bed, shaking beneath a thin, woolen blanket. Mary's stomach turned over. So that was the cause of the shuffling sound: a sick man shivering to death in the presence of a guard and a visitor. She wanted to charge from the cell, screaming for blankets and hot-water bottles and bowls of steaming broth. She stopped herself, with difficulty. This man had heard enough screaming and been the subject of orders too many times already.

She cleared her throat, not because it was necessary but to give him some warning. "Mr. Lang?"

Still no response, but she didn't expect one.

"My name is Mary Lawrence. I may be able to assist you." Lang remained mute, but Mary thought his shivering lessened somewhat, as though he were concentrating on her words. "I have no connection either to the police or to the family of the dead man. But I am interested in the facts of what happened that night."

There was a slight pause in the shivering, as though it were being suppressed by force of will. Very slowly, the lump under the blanket uncurled a little. And although the shaking resumed, Lang's body continued to unfurl until, very slowly, a tousled head poked, turtle-like, from one end of the blanket. The skull was capped by a shock of greasy, thinning yellowy-gray hair. The skin was almost the same color, a sallow map of a sad country, with dark, bruised craters below the eyes. And the eyes themselves—Mary repressed a shudder. They were defeat made human, a world of pain entire.

They were also her eyes.

Her lungs seized. Her heart suddenly hammered against throat. Her mouth went dry. It was out of the question. This old man, this drug-addicted, incarcerated old sailor—her father? She'd prepared herself for the possibility but now that it confronted her, found it impossible to believe.

And yet there were the eyes. They weren't hers in color; hers had always been a changeable hazel. But their shape was the same. And now they blinked at her, slowly, atop that stinking prison blanket. Blinked to clear the film that covered his eyeballs, although the weight of the eyelids seemed more than he could bear. He looked decades older than forty. He looked like death itself.

"Your name?" The voice was that of an elderly invalid — raspy, faint. He seemed to be searching her face, looking for something to latch on to.

Mary looked him square in the eyes. "Are you Lang Jin Hai, formerly of Limehouse?"

And then the unthinkable happened: he closed his eyes, turned his head away, and said, "No."

She frowned. "No to what?"

"Not of Limehouse."

He looked nothing like the father she remembered, but she couldn't be wrong about something this important. The eyes — the name — the fact that he'd asked her name . . . "If not Limehouse, where?"

No reply. Lang continued to shiver, to curl back into a ball, facing firmly away from her.

Mary waited a minute. Then two. Then three. Finally, she said, "I don't believe you. You are Lang Jin Hai, formerly of Limehouse. You were married to Maire Quinn, a seamstress."

No reply, but that near stillness again — a cessation of shaking that showed she'd struck deep.

"You had a daughter named Mary. She would be nineteen or twenty years old now."

He remained almost motionless.

Shock and disbelief passed slowly into anger. "You went to sea in 1848 or 1849. On an important mission. You left your pregnant wife and your daughter. And a box of documents in the care of a Mr. Chen, to be opened in the event you did not return." Her voice was shaking now, but still he refused to turn. To look at her. His only child. "Do you deny this, Lang Jin Hai?"

An excruciating pause. Then, so softly she scarcely heard the syllable: "Yes."

"You deny it?"

Silence.

"You unspeakable coward," said Mary, her voice low and trembling. "Have you anything more to lose by telling the truth?"

The man on the bed remained still and mute. Outside the cell, Mary heard the ravens screaming. Perhaps they were being fed.

Time passed. Her anger did not abate, but it was cold and corrosive rather than hot and fierce. She didn't want a reconciliation—not with this lying shell of a man. But she did want answers. "Very well," she said at last, after a full five minutes' silence. "You don't want to answer questions. But I can compel you to do so." She reached into her handbag, fingers closing round the slim, stoppered vial. The guard hadn't seemed to notice it when he peered into her reticule. Even if he had, a small amount of laudanum required no explanation; half the ladies in London seemed to rely upon its restorative effects. Deliberately, she let the glass clink softly against a flagstone.

The effect on Lang was instantaneous, transformative. He rolled to face her with a swiftness that surprised even Mary, his expression intent, alert—if not quite alive. "Give me that."

She whisked it out of range but let it dangle enticingly. "Answer my questions."

"I need it, you devil! I need it!" His voice crescendoed to a shriek, and Mary suddenly questioned her wisdom in forcing his hand like this.

But it was much too late to turn back. "Quiet," she said with authority. "If you scream, the guard will come back, and you certainly won't get any laudanum then."

He subsided then, but his eyes remained fixed on the bottle. "Please . . ."

Mary's mouth twisted. "Are you that Lang Jin Hai?"

"Yes, yes." But he was too eager now. He would agree to anything she asked, just for a taste of laudanum.

"Prove it. What else was in that box of documents you left before your last voyage?"

His frantic gaze wandered to her face. Returned to the bottle. Came back to her, as he tried to marshal a modicum of self-discipline. "So long ago . . ."

Mary waited, poised for flight, for combat, for any surprise she could imagine.

He swallowed hard. "A map."

"What else?"

"A letter to my daughter."

These were too generic, things anybody might guess. "Anything else?"

"A—a pendant."

Her knees buckled, despite—she told herself—her lack of surprise. "What did it look like?"

"Jade. A gourd."

She frowned. "A what?" She'd always thought it a pear or a stylized figure eight.

He made an impatient gesture. "Why does it matter? A bottle gourd. Very symbolic. A vegetable."

She'd never heard of such a thing, but she was cut off from her Chinese heritage. Why mightn't the small, seed-shaped object be a gourd? "Very well." She measured out a dropperful of laudanum and passed it to Lang's eager, shaking hands.

He downed it greedily—the first thing in days to willingly cross his lips—and immediately said, "More."

She gave him a second dropperful.

"More." This was strong stuff, the most highly concentrated tincture of opium she could procure from an apothecary, yet it seemed he could swallow the entire bottle without harm.

"I have more questions."

His eyes flicked between her and the vial, brightening slightly as the drug took effect. "Ask."

Heavy footsteps toward the cell. Mary whisked the vial back into her handbag, looked innocent as the jailer's head appeared in the doorway. He was visibly surprised to see Lang sitting up in bed, acknowledging her presence, and gaped for a moment.

"Is something the matter?" asked Mary, looking down her nose at the man.

"Beg your pardon, miss; I'd have fetched you a chair, only I never thought you'd stay this long."

"It's of no concern," said Mary, as patiently as she could manage. "I prefer to stand."

"I'm to give you ten minutes' warning, miss."

"Please—a quarter of an hour?"

He glanced about as though searching the air for permission. "Quarter of an hour, but no more. Regulations, I'm afraid."

"Thank you kindly." She waited until the footsteps had receded into silence, then looked once more at her unacknowledged, unacknowledging father. Their personal history would have to wait. "What happened in the opium den on Saturday night?"

He blinked at the change in subject. "With the toffs, you mean?"

"What else?"

He focused pleading eyes on the laudanum bottle. "I need more. You don't understand—it's like tiny drops of water to a man in the desert. Give me the bottle, and I'll tell you anything you ask."

Mary looked at him. She knew better than to believe

a drug addict, of course. He was lying. Saying whatever was necessary to feed the demon. And yet. And yet.

She held the bottle toward him, and he snatched it with eager fingers, pouring the liquid down his throat with such frantic haste that he nearly swallowed the vial, too. Coughing, spluttering, panting. He looked up at her with bloodshot eyes that were, nevertheless, alive in a way they'd not been before. Eyes that were halfway human. "Thank you."

Mary was touched, despite herself, and then angry again. How pathetic he was—and she in turn, for giving in to him. "Saturday night."

He nodded. Wiped his lips. Licked round the mouth of the vial with hope and regret. "I don't remember the start—I'd been smoking. But there wasn't enough in my hookah to keep me away properly. I heard shouting—a drunken lad's voice. Screaming and swearing. Filth. You know. The lad was falling-down drunk, but it didn't stop him from trying to kick over the hookahs—and the men lying beside them. And Sayed tried to see him off nicely."

"That's the proprietor?"

Lang nodded. "Didn't see why, at the time. First sign of trouble, Sayed's vicious at turning them out. Then I saw their clothes: toffs. And then the main one sees me, and comes staggering at me, and swipes at my hookah." Lang's breathing became louder, faster. Mary noticed that his shivering had all but subsided. He looked at her steadily. "Don't suppose you'd believe it, an old bag of skin and bones like me fighting a young man."

She met his gaze. "I suppose it depends on your level of skill. And his intoxication."

He nodded. "And the drugs. They fill you, somehow, make you theirs. You might be floating on a cloud, warm as blood, blind and deaf to all around you. This time, I was—" He stopped to consider. "I wanted him to vanish. To make him into nothing."

Mary's stomach churned. "To make him leave?"

"No. To destroy him." He looked at her again, his eyes cold but without malice. "Not what you wanted to hear? You should know better than to ask, then."

"I want the truth." And she meant it.

"You understand, I couldn't think. Felt no pain. I was in a rage, but I was numb, too."

"You couldn't reason, then." Or understand the consequences of his actions.

He seemed almost amused by the question. "In an opium dream, there is no reason."

She drew a deep breath. "So you attacked the young man. Do you remember how?"

He looked surprised. "With my hands." He held out a pair of age-spotted claws: fingers twisted, knuckles pulpy, the nails ragged and filthy. They were purple with cold, although he seemed not to mind. "The opium again. It takes strength, then gives. There were two men. A foolish one, who stood in my way—but I didn't want him. I wanted the real swine. I flew at him, knocked him down. I choked him, there on the floor." He looked down almost reminiscently, as though Beaulieu-Buckworth's supine body were there on the cell floor. "He was so weak, for such a large body."

Mary wondered. Beaulieu-Buckworth may well have been weak in every sense of the word, but a man in a drug-fueled rage could be superhumanly strong. There was a reason insane asylums kept burly warders to hand and iron rings embedded in their walls. She looked again at Lang's hands, which had fallen to his lap, palms upturned. What she saw made her gorge rise: a long, wide, dark gash that began midpalm and extended across his first two fingers. It was a dark, suppurating mess—a rank note in the fetid fragrance of this dank room—and despite her long experience of filth and stench, she recoiled. When she could speak, she said, "When did you injure yourself?"

Lang blinked, looked blank. The shivering was beginning again, and he said, in a half-pleading, half-scolding tone, "I need more."

"I haven't got any more."

"More."

"Answer my question, then: what happened to your hand?"

He was silent for a minute—sulking. Then, "He had a knife."

Mary's scalp tingled. "The second young man attacked you with a knife. How did you get it away from him?"

He collapsed into himself, a sudden deflation. "He was weak. I took the knife."

She already knew the answer but had to ask. "And then—"

"I stabbed him. I stabbed him until he stopped flopping. Until he wasn't." He sighed, resettled himself as though for sleep. "Laudanum."

She hadn't any more. What would he say when she told him? Would he fly into a rage, beat her to a pulp as he had Beaulieu-Buckworth? At this point, looking at the stinking, disheveled form of the father she'd so long worshipped, she almost didn't care.

A clomping of boots saved her. A moment later, the guard's long face appeared. "That's your quarter hour and then some, miss."

"You've been very kind," said Mary. She looked down at the matted head. "Mr. Lang, I shall call again."

For an answer, the skeleton on the bed lay down once more and pulled the coarse blanket over its head. It was neither more nor less than she expected.

"He needs a physician," she said to the turnkey as he locked the cell. "As quickly as possible."

The jailer looked dubious. "I'll ask the warden."

"Have you seen that filthy cut on his hand?" asked Mary. "Tell the warden to take a look. It needs to be seen to, if you want the prisoner to survive his trial."

"I'll tell him," said the jailer, without much conviction.

"If it's a question of money," said Mary, "our charity

will pay." Perhaps that offer was too far out of character, but the guard seemed not to notice.

"I'll tell him," he repeated in a tone that bordered now on irritation.

There was nothing else to be said. Mary had found her father at last: Lascar. Drug addict. Murderer. And as she followed the jailer down the stairs and out of the Tower, she discovered that the opium's numbing powers seemed to have affected her, too.

For the better, she thought.

Twenty-one

Mary walked back to the palace at a brisk pace, deaf and blind to the world about her but feeling otherwise her usual self—or perhaps merely frozen. It was impossible to comprehend the full import of what she'd just seen and heard. At some point, she would have to think it through. Perhaps. But for now, it was enough to know a few basic facts: Lang Jin Hai had admitted killing Ralph Beaulieu-Buckworth. Lang Jin Hai had acted in a drug-induced frenzy, without conscious intent. Lang Jin Hai had not produced the knife.

No matter who might plead for him, it was a poor defense. Lang would still pay for the murder of a young aristocrat. But a defense of temporary insanity was infinitely better than no defense at all. Mary wondered about Queen Victoria's devotion to truth and how far it might extend. Could she conceive of justice for a foreign-born opium addict? Or did her sense of fair play begin and end with respectable English subjects?

There was, too, the problem of Honoria Dalrymple. Her biases, at least, were perfectly clear. She wanted to whiten the reputation of her ne'er-do-well relation at any price—even the sacrifice of an innocent parlor maid. She would never tolerate any suggestion that Lang had not murdered Beaulieu-Buckworth in cold blood.

Finally, there was the difficulty of what would happen to Lang if, by some miracle, he failed to hang for the killing of Beaulieu-Buckworth. They no longer transported convicts to Australia. But for a man so old and frail, imprisonment on a prison hulk—a ship permanently moored along the coast, packed tight with the most desperate convicts—was still tantamount to death. Mary thought of that festering wound in his palm: four days Lang had been imprisoned at the Tower, and he'd received no treatment. Such justice was no justice at all.

She was so deeply immersed in her thoughts that the gentleman might have been following her for any amount of time. She realized this only when he finally presented himself before her and made a sarcastic bow. "My dear Miss Quinn."

"Mr. Jones." She was too startled for disdain.

"How charming to meet you in the afternoon, when you must normally be so very busy catering to Her Majesty's every whim."

The urge to slap him grew with every encounter. "What is it you want, Mr. Jones?"

"Why must you always assume I want something of

you? How very vulgar." This was typical Jonesian nonsense, but there was something forced about his performance today.

She stopped in the street. "Out with it."

"Wouldn't you like to go somewhere more comfortable?" One look at her expression, however, and he sighed. "Fine. Er . . . it's about Amy."

"I assumed that much."

"Oh. Well, then. It's like this." As he spoke, Jones kept glancing over his shoulder in a hunted fashion. "She, er, seems to have certain expectations of me. Now that she's been sacked, she thinks the logical thing to do would be for me to, er, step in, as it were."

"That's rational enough: you *are* courting."

Jones's eyes bulged, and he yelped, right there in the middle of the Strand. "No, no—that's precisely where the confusion started! Why, d'you really imagine I'd be courting a domestic servant?"

Mary tilted her head to one side. "Amy certainly believed it."

"Damn, damn, damn! Can't you see, Mary?"

"Miss Quinn."

"I beg your pardon: Miss Quinn." Jones took a few steadying breaths. "I realize that Amy may have been under the impression that my intentions were serious. But surely a lady like you—an educated woman, a journalist, a woman of the world—understands just how preposterous her expectations are. It could never be. It would be a—an inappropriate mixing of entirely mismatched parties!"

"Not merely a personal disaster but a social one as well," said Mary.

Jones seemed not to notice her tone. "Precisely! Like the Prince of Wales eloping with a barmaid—the mind boggles! You understand me!"

"Oh, I understand you perfectly, Mr. Jones."

"Then you'll help me: only a woman could persuade Amy that her expectations are absurd."

"I thought you were the persuasive one."

"The stubborn little ass won't listen!"

"But if her expectations are so absurd, why did you consummate the relationship?"

Jones hesitated. "Oh. That. Well, she was just so damn keen, y'know. It felt ungentlemanly to refuse."

"I don't believe that for a moment. I was the one who told you of the plan. That would have been the time to decline."

"You have me there." A sheepish grin crept onto his face, and he did his best to look appealing. "Come, now, Miss Quinn—I'm a healthy, vigorous man in his prime. D'you really expect me to refuse such a brazen offer? I assure you, Amy enjoyed herself just as much as I did."

"That is entirely beside the point, Mr. Jones. You consider yourself a man of the world. How could you not understand what such an invitation meant?"

He looked sulky. "I thought you understood me."

"I do; it doesn't mean I agree with you."

"So you won't help me." He made an angry, chopping gesture. "Damn it, I won't be caught this way. Look, if you can't convince Amy that it was all in good fun but I'm not the man for her, you'll regret it."

Ah. The real Octavius Jones showed himself at last. "An impotent threat, Mr. Jones. Are you really so desperate?"

"I could tell the housekeeper what you're really up to."

Mary pretended to consider. "You could, I suppose. Assuming she'd believe a word of it. And providing you could get to her before I did."

"What d'you mean?"

"All I need do is go back to the palace and explain to her why you pretended to court Amy. I'm sure she'd be fascinated to know that a scandal-seeking journalist was attempting to prize secrets out of a palace domestic." She paused. "However clumsily it was attempted." Twin spots of color appeared in Jones's cheeks, but she didn't relent. "As for the breach-of-promise suit, it would be easy to find witnesses. All the female servants saw your valentine, and I was party to your seduction of the sheltered, innocent Miss Tranter. I expect there's even the evidence of the bedsheets. . . . D'you know, Jones, I can't think of a jury who wouldn't sympathize with poor Amy."

With visible effort, he mastered his temper. It was a minute before he could speak, however, and when he did his voice was hoarse. "You're a reasonable woman, Miss Quinn. D'you think I'd make a good husband?"

"Of course not. But that's hardly the point. Amy would get substantial damages from a breach-of-promise settlement. Certainly enough to live on until she found new work."

"Then I may as well pay her off directly. Cut out the middleman, so to speak."

His attempt to sound jovial was utterly unconvincing. Mary smiled pleasantly. "Then why are you badgering me?"

"Oh, hang it all!" he cried. Again, it was a rare and unnerving example of real emotion cracking his polished facade. "I'm sick to bloody death of her! I never want to see her face again. Have some compassion, Miss Quinn, I beg of you."

Ah—now they were getting somewhere. She folded her arms. "Then make me an offer."

He glared at her, all attempts at charm abandoned. "Five guineas."

She almost laughed. "For Amy, certainly. But I don't want your money."

"What, then?"

"Information, of course: what you hoped to learn from Amy." She daren't be more direct. The thefts had been so well covered up that he'd be suspicious if she revealed knowledge of them.

"And in return, you'll call off the b—"

"In return," interrupted Mary, "I'll do my best to convince Amy that marrying you is not in her best interests and that she's better off accepting five guineas for her disappointment and suffering. I'll need a check, by the way."

"And if you fail, and she sues me for breach of promise?"

"She won't. But if she does, I won't testify on her behalf."

"That's all very well, but I need a bit more reassurance than that."

Mary shrugged. "I've never lied to you. That's more than you can say for yourself."

It was a measure of Jones's desperation that he held out for only half a minute; Amy must have been effective indeed when she ran him to earth. "Fine. It's not very juicy, anyway: there's some sort of scandal hanging about the Prince of Wales."

"Not those preposterous rumors about the death of Ralph Beaulieu-Buckworth, I hope," said Mary with feigned impatience.

"What d'you take me for?" snapped Jones. "Of course not. I've been working on Amy since early January—much too long to be distracted by that sort of half-baked gossip. No, this is something much more likely: a royal romance." He caught Mary's look of disbelief. "He mayn't seem very appealing to you, but he's still the heir to the throne. There've been a couple of sightings—the prince coming down to town at unusual times. A few letters sent. A morning ride in the park, after which the prince disappears for an hour or so."

"Who's the lady?"

Jones shook his head. "Not quite certain. It's a family of four sisters, all between sixteen and twenty-two. Name of Hacken."

"What a peculiar name."

Jones's mouth twitched. "Well, they're not *haut ton,* or whatever's left of it; otherwise it'd have a more euphonious pronunciation. Hacken *père*'s a jeweler. Done rather well for himself: big freehold pile in Mortlake, carriage and pair and all that. The older girls work in the shop. I expect that's how he met them. They're not exactly diamonds of the first water themselves"—Jones smirked at his pun—"but I suppose they're fresh and just pretty enough. And from what Amy says of the prince, he's a foolish pup. Probably he thinks he's having a grand romantic adventure, thinking and doing things nobody's ever thought or done before."

"But have you evidence that this is a romantic entanglement?"

"As opposed to what?" demanded Jones. "You think he's talking philosophy with the shopkeeper?"

Mary said nothing, except "Go on."

"Anyway, I've been trying, through Amy, to pick up any tittle-tattle about all this, but the palace is a grim little pile of stones, ain't it? No gossip, no fun, no high jinks by night."

"What made you persist, then?"

Jones shrugged. "Well, one keeps hoping against hope. And Amy was a nice enough child. Besides"—he smirked again—"why wouldn't I like a woman who ranks me higher than God? Until this, of course."

Mary smiled for rather different reasons. Even men like Jones, who prided themselves on their worldly savoir faire, could be so easily hoodwinked by girlish enthusiasm. Privately, she thought there would be little difficulty in convincing Amy of Jones's unsuitability; those five golden guineas would speak louder than words. "Why didn't you simply get a job at the palace yourself?"

He feigned horror. "My dear, the hard work! It would be the death of me."

"Yet it would be so much more reliable than other people's distilled memories."

"The newspaper pays me only so much, darling Mary—sorry—esteemed Miss Quinn. Certainly not enough to allow me to buttle. Assuming they'd have me."

Mary only half believed him. Still, there was nothing to be gained in belaboring the point. "Very well, then. Anything else you're keeping from me?"

"My dear Miss Quinn! After all you've promised to do for me?"

The answer was almost certainly yes: this was Octavius Jones, after all. But she could verify Jones's interests with

Amy herself—something he surely realized. And it was enough to rule out his interest in the heirloom thefts, Honoria Dalrymple, the death of Beaulieu-Buckworth, and the tunnels. It was the soundest bargain she'd driven since this case had begun.

Twenty-two

Wednesday evening

Buckingham Palace

Shock was an effective anesthetic, but it couldn't last indefinitely. As Mary reentered the palace grounds, she felt a strange churning in her stomach that had nothing to do with her long-ago dinner. Her chest ached, her lungs were constricted, and her mouth was suddenly parched, despite a flood of intensely salty saliva. This would never do. She flew through the service entrance, hoping she'd not run into Mrs. Shaw. Her luck held, in a way.

On her way up the servants' staircase, she nearly barreled into Honoria Dalrymple, in company with an older gentleman. Both whisked round, then Honoria relaxed. "Carry on, Quinn," she said. Mary hesitated only for a moment—her need for privacy was stronger than anything else at this moment—but as she hurried past Honoria, she heard the lady-in-waiting say, rather loudly, "I'll see you to the door, Papa." Mary kept running.

She burst into her room—the room she'd used to share

with Amy, now stripped half bare—and only just made it to the chamber pot. Retched. Choked. Finally gave up the remnants of her dinner. Dribbles of thin, sour acid. Then nothing at all, except air and muffled sobs and—yes, as they trickled down over her lips into her mouth—warm, salty tears.

She hadn't the strength to fight them now. She'd used up all her wisdom and restraint: in recognizing her father and not breaking down then and there; in bullying him into telling her his story; in not demanding personal answers of him; in leaving him there, without ally. It was time to give up the glowing, idealized father figure she had cherished all these years. The good husband. The loving father. Above all, the brave sailor who'd sailed away on a mission of justice. For two years, she'd thought of her work at the Agency as a kind of homage to her father. Following in his vanished footsteps, as best she was able. She'd dreamed of his one day finding her, after years of searching. She'd imagined it as a homecoming, a reunion.

Instead, *she* had found *him*. Her tears flowed faster as she mourned her losses. The first, of her father to the sea, when she was a young girl. The second, of the image of her father, bright and brave and untarnished. She forced herself to renounce those childish ideals and summoned an image of Lang Jin Hai as he truly was: a pathetic stick figure—shivering, unwashed, possessed wholly by the desire for more opium. A despicable figure, charged with murder and unremorseful. And, if she was very honest with herself, the deepest wound of all: a man who had been in London and failed to contact her; had, indeed, denied his identity and refused to acknowledge her.

She was soon cried out. First came the drying of tears, then the mopping and blowing, and finally the hiccups. She stood with difficulty, legs half dead from having been folded beneath her for so long. Took a long drink of stale water. Lay down on the bed to think more about her disgrace of a father.

And yet she couldn't quite join the chorus of condemnation. After all, she too had once been an accused criminal. She knew the despair that drove one to illegal acts, the instinct for survival that crowded out all others. But this was only part of the matter. For larger than empathy, larger than understanding was the fact that no matter what he'd done or who he was, this Lang Jin Hai was still her father. Of that, at least, she had no doubt.

She made it through the evening—abovestairs dinner preparation, belowstairs tea and desultory tasks—and to bed without further incident. While Mrs. Shaw looked askance at her swollen face and bloodshot eyes, the housekeeper was not usually suspicious except of excess enjoyment and leisure. Mary's symptoms were so clearly the product of misery that they went unremarked.

Sleep was a long time coming. It was unusually silent in the room; Mary had become used to Amy's chatter and snores. And try as she might to focus on the tasks at hand—Honoria Dalrymple; Prince Bertie; those ever-more-mysterious thefts—her thoughts persistently circled back to Lang Jin Hai.

Mary woke in the early hours, rather surprised to find she'd slept at all. It was a rare clear night—the rain had stopped in the early evening—and the moon shone brightly even through the tiny garret window. It was the glowing, unearthly light by which Mary, as a child, used to rob houses. Perhaps that was why her thoughts returned to Lang Jin Hai with a sudden clarity that owed nothing to adult logic, her moral training at the Academy, or her responsibilities to the Agency. Suddenly, her path became clear. Rather than frittering away time on shifty ladies-in-waiting, hopeless kings-in-waiting, and petty thefts that might never be solved, she had to address the real responsibility at the core of her life.

She had to rescue her father.

Twenty-three

Thursday, 16 February

Cradle Tower, Tower of London

It was the same sentry on duty when Mary turned up at nine o'clock in the morning. He looked surprised to see her again but admitted her readily enough. "You had a rare reception from the Chinaman yesterday" was his greeting.

Mary gave the smug smile of a certified do-gooder. "Sometimes, all these people want is a civil ear."

"Don't know why you ladies bother. He'll be swinging from the neck inside a week."

Cold terror clutched her stomach. "So soon?"

He shrugged. "Give or take. Ain't no jury going to find for a Chinee what killed a toff."

The guard was correct, of course. It was the reason she'd come. No matter how Queen Victoria felt about justice and truth, a jury of stolid Englishmen would always make a foreigner pay the heaviest price for his crime. "I don't suppose he's been seen by a physician."

The guard snorted with amusement. "Oh, aye—and by the queen herself, too."

She climbed the stairs to Cradle Tower, trying to damp down her hopes as far as possible. She'd shammed illness that morning as the simplest way of avoiding her palace tasks. It was irresponsible, of course. But nowhere near as reckless as what she was about to propose to this perfect stranger. Once more, Lang didn't bother to raise his head as the turnkey announced Mary and unlocked the cell. He was still huddled beneath that stinking blanket—he mightn't have moved since she'd last seen him—but his shaking was much diminished.

"Mr. Lang," she said quietly, reaching once more into her reticule. She sloshed the bottle gently. This time she'd provided herself with several vials, buying from three different apothecaries in order to avoid suspicion.

As if on a string, he turned to face Mary and extended an expectant hand. She waited for him to down the tincture. Allowed another minute for it to take effect. Then, without permitting herself time to reflect or regret, she began. "I asked you a number of questions yesterday. I should like to begin today by telling you about myself."

Lang blinked at her, only half focused. Those eyes were sunk deep in his head, whites yellowed, irises brown-black. And yet they were still her eyes. Today, they were bright with something other than laudanum: fever, thought Mary. It was unsurprising, given his vile surroundings, that untended gash on his right palm. She should have brought something to clean it. It was a detail she'd forgotten. One that would complicate the escape.

"I was born in Limehouse in 1841. My mother was Irish, a seamstress. My father was a Lascar." He said nothing, but his features hardened, settled into determined neutrality. "We were a poor family but a happy one—until the year 1848 or 1849, when my father sailed on a voyage that was to be his last. His ship was wrecked. He was reported missing, presumed dead. My mother was pregnant at the time, and she miscarried from grief. A year later, she died—this time from poverty.

"Somehow, I survived. I was eventually taken in by a girls' school, a charity. I said nothing of my father, concealed my race, for fear they might turn me away. But last year, I met a man who told me something of my family history. His name was Mr. Chen."

Still no response from Lang, apart from a careful blankness.

Mary steeled herself to continue, although it was a struggle to keep her voice even. "Mr. Chen showed me a cigar box containing documents my father left in his care. These included a letter in which my father explained that his voyage was more than an ordinary commercial expedition. He described it as a 'dangerous but necessary' journey, and he left documents that, I believe, would have explained his reason for going. I was never able to read the documents. They were destroyed in a house fire before I could retrieve them. Mr. Chen's body was found in the burned house." She paused again. She'd hoped that news of his old ally's death would move the man. And yet he failed even to blink. Mary swallowed. Prepared to produce her trump card.

"There was an item that didn't perish in the fire, however." She dipped a finger into her collar and drew out a thread-thin necklace. "The jade pendant you described yesterday. The gourd." The tiny stone gleamed dully in the dim light—not that Lang bothered to look at it. His gaze was fixed somewhere in the middle distance, as if he were studiously avoiding seeing his only child there before him. She waited patiently, hoping the dim light was enough to conceal the slight shaking of her hands, the way her pounding heart made her bodice tremble.

And still he said nothing.

Eventually, she spoke. It was either that or flee the Tower. "You are my father," she said in a voice shaking with unshed tears. "Do you deny that, given the evidence?"

Very slowly, his gaze sharpened and he looked her full in the eyes. "Yes."

"You deny it?"

A pause. "I am not your father."

"And what of this?" Mary snapped the necklace chain and brandished it in his face. "This pendant, which you described so accurately yesterday. It's proof."

But it was too late: he was withdrawing again, those weary eyes filming over into selective blindness.

She dropped to her knees, forcing her face into his line

of vision. "I even look like you! I have your eye shape, and your mouth, and—" To her shame, her eyes welled over. She dashed away the tears with a vicious swipe. "And I'm your only child. You're my only living relative. Does that mean nothing to you?

"Because it used to. You used to walk me round the streets of Limehouse at dusk while Mama prepared our tea. You used to tell me I had to grow up brave and strong, and always remember how much you loved me. You used to say that the truth would set me free, and always to tell it." She was crying now, quietly, dripping tears onto her dress, the ragged bed linens, Lang's gnarled hands. "You used to be my hero. And now you're lying to me in the face of all logic and reason and compassion and everything else you taught me to value."

She was fumbling in her bag for a handkerchief—why did she never have a clean handkerchief?—when he surprised her by speaking. "That man also used to say that character is destiny."

Mary stared at him. "So you do admit—"

"I admit nothing. But your father said that character is destiny, and with that much I agree." His eyes were sane, focused, despite their hectic glitter. "Look at me: a weak, vain man, corrupted and destroyed by opium."

"But—"

"If I were your father," said Lang, in tones so gentle that Mary nearly wept afresh, "and I were in this position now, I would never acknowledge you as my daughter."

He caught her look. "Never. Not to cause you pain—certainly not that. But to spare you the shame of having to own such a man as your father."

Her mind whirled, but only for a moment. "But I *want* to claim you as my father!" It was difficult not to shout the words, but, mindful of the jailer, Mary spoke with quiet vehemence. "I don't care what you've done, or who you've killed, or what you're addicted to. I know the worst there is to know about you, and I still want to be your daughter!"

He looked at her through half-shut eyes. "No. You are thinking with your heart right now. But once you think with your mind, you will understand that I'm correct."

"Damn it!" She pounded the mattress, and a puff of brown smoke, acrid and salt-smelling, flew up into the air and made them both cough. "This is about love and families. I *should* be thinking with my heart."

He looked down at her, and her heart staggered a beat. It was such a familiar expression of affectionate reproof, one she'd seen hundreds of times as a child. "Young woman, this is not merely about family bonds. It is also about survival. Your prospects. Your life as a free, educated, respectable *lady*." The emphasis he laid on the last word was unmistakable. "You have been torn free of your roots; that was heartbreaking. But it would be a greater tragedy still to allow past griefs and the sins of others to destroy your life now."

Mary closed her eyes, as though doing so would

also stop her ears. He spoke sense, of course. Her father always had. And opium fiend or no, murderer or not, he was acting in her worldly best interests. She pictured him as he had been in his prime—gentle, handsome, kind—and when she opened her eyes, it was not so excruciatingly difficult to fit together the two Lang Jin Hais. Not now that he'd addressed her so. "What if I want to?" she asked, rising abruptly and beginning to pace the tiny cell. "What if I want to destroy my social prospects, my English life, this lie I've been living?"

Lang was drooping a little, as though the intensity of his effort had actually bled him. "If. If you chose to sacrifice everything you had to embrace a foreign killer and opium addict, you would accomplish nothing. I would still be hanged. The aristocrat would still be dead."

"I would be your daughter."

"And what a bloody taint that would be."

"What if I chose to embrace it?" She dug in her reticule and found another vial of poison. Of salvation.

He drank greedily enough, but with a new, furtive expression. He was ashamed for her to see him like this, she realized, now that they were talking so very nearly without disguise. "Why stop at social and material suicide? What you propose is tantamount to self-murder."

Mary knew he intended to shock. He managed it all the same. Only the scrape of the guard's boots against stone compelled her to resume a prim, standing posture.

"Ten minutes, miss."

She nodded, unable to speak, afraid to look at the jailer lest he see the evidence of tears on her face.

When he left, not without a suspicious look at Lang, she bent low again. "You can't get rid of me that easily," she said. The interruption had been good for her composure. "I've one last question for you. I can help you to escape. I'll organize everything. I'll make it clean. When I call for you, will you come?"

Finally, she had succeeded in shocking him. He sagged back on the cot, hit the wall with a grunt. Waved off her gesture of concern. "I'm fine. You, however, are mad."

"It's been done before, by a priest in Elizabethan times. And there's a water entrance in this tower: direct access to the Thames. If we chose our time wisely, we could be several miles out of London before anybody noticed."

"I don't question your ability to escape yourself. But look at me." He sat straighter, holding out his arms, rolling up his ragged sleeves. He was a mess of bruised skin draped over bones, like gauze over twigs. "Had you forgotten my hand?" He showed her the hideous gash, black and cracked and oozing, with white streaks radiating from its crusted edges. "I'll never climb down a rope, or even a ladder."

"I'm not a fool. The most strenuous thing you'll have to do is walk down those stairs and climb into a boat."

"And then what? We'll sail to Greenwich and live as happy wanderers, picking berries and poaching the odd pheasant?" His impatience was clear, despite his weakness. "You daft, impulsive girl. I'm marked for death, one way or another. It doesn't matter if I hang at Her Majesty's pleasure or die of blood poisoning from this cut or if one of the jailers strangles me in the night. I'll be dead in a fortnight's time, and to hell with the means."

She hadn't been quite that stupid: her plan had been to go to ground in Limehouse for a time. She doubted the authorities would be able to identify Lang, one Chinese looking so much like another—to the English, at least. Then, perhaps after that, Bristol or Liverpool—another port town with a small Asiatic population. But she'd not thought so clearly about Lang's future. The complications of his fragile health, his addiction, his utter lack of interest in survival.

It cut bone deep. It was also so familiar. It was how she herself had felt, at the age of twelve, being tried for housebreaking. She'd not had a future then. Had seen no reason why her life ought not end then and there. But the women of the Agency had proven her wrong. It had been her first lesson at the Academy.

"If you escape," she told him, "that fatalism will be the most dangerous threat to your own life. We'll see a physician about that cut. You can wean yourself from opium. You're not an old man—forty-five or fifty? If you desire it, you can make yourself anew."

He simply shook his head.

"What does that mean? You don't believe me? You don't want to?"

"You're a brave, warmhearted young lady. Don't waste it on me."

So she'd inherited her stubborn streak from her father. Finally, after a long pause, she mustered enough calm to say, "I understand this is a large and dangerous proposal. You may wish to have time to consider it. I shall return tomorrow to tell you the details of my plan." After all, she'd need until then to work it out in detail and procure the necessary tools.

"I shan't change my mind, child."

Child. She blinked back a sudden rush of tears. "Then you can tell me that again tomorrow. Good day, Mr. Lang."

Twenty-four

Thursday afternoon

Buckingham Palace

When Mary presented herself for duty, Mrs. Shaw examined her with a grim eye. "You don't look much improved—still pasty and puffy. Are you sure you're well enough? I can't have you drooping about and fainting in Her Majesty's presence."

"I feel much better, thank you, ma'am."

"Then you may as well start with the Blue Room. Be thorough. I doubt the Tranter chit ever was."

The Blue Room was generally used in the evenings, before and after formal dinners. On occasion, Her Majesty entertained larger groups there in the afternoon, but those were special occasions, of which today was not one. Yet as Mary entered, she thought she heard the second set of doors click shut. She stopped. It was a vast hall, a former ballroom that had been converted only a few years earlier into a drawing room, and more likely than not she'd heard only an echo. But as she moved slowly down its length, she could have sworn she heard steps hurrying away.

She quickened her pace, glancing from side to side as she went. It was ridiculous to think that someone was lurking behind an ornamental screen or beside a fireplace, but she felt suspicious nonetheless. The door at the other side was indeed not quite closed, which probably accounted for the noise she'd heard: a slight draft would have made the door click as though just being shut.

She turned to begin her dusting—then turned back. For caution's sake, opened one of the doors very slowly. Nothing. See? She really was becoming overly suspicious about things like this. Even if it had been somebody closing the door, it was likely a footman about his work.

Right. Dusting. She selected a high shelf quite at random and began. The most annoying thing about dusting in the more public rooms was the sheer quantity of delicate ornaments one had to lift, wipe, and replace, all in the course of a few running feet of display space. Perhaps the most astonishing thing about the thefts, all of which had been from this room, was that they'd been remarked at all. She worked her way clockwise round the room, moving from high to low as she'd been taught.

When she got to the fireplace mantel, she frowned. There was something off here. Taking a step back, she looked at the array of treasures displayed: an ormolu clock, a small antique vase, an idyllic rural scene executed in Dresden china, various bits of shining crystal . . . Yes. The vase was missing its mate, throwing off the symmetry of the mantelpiece display. A quick check of the surrounding area showed that it hadn't been moved to a nearby table or ledge. Most peculiar. As she peered closer, Mary noticed a ghostly pattern in the accumulated dust of the mantel. There: a circle where the vase should have stood, now partly overlain by a tiny carved-ivory snuffbox.

Mary's scalp prickled. Had she been seconds from seeing the palace thief in action? She darted to the doors she'd just closed. Nothing, of course. And the hallway offered no clues—no hastily dropped monogrammed handkerchief, for example. Had she really expected such a convenient giveaway? Tempting as it was, she decided against pursuit. By now, the thief might be anywhere in the palace—perhaps even outside the palace—and a small vase like that could easily be carried in an overcoat or a handbag. She was only wasting time and ignoring the scene in which the theft had been carried out.

She returned to the mantel and looked again at the remaining vase. It was quite likely one of a pair, depicting as it did a classical scene: Persephone in the Underworld, clutching her fateful pomegranate. The missing vase ought to show Persephone reunited with her mother, Demeter. They would be able to confirm that in the register of household goods. If so, it also revealed one of two possibilities about the thief: either he or she did not possess a rudimentary classical education, or he or she had been too unobservant or too hasty to see that the vase was one of a pair. They were worth more as companion pieces than separated.

Honoria Dalrymple remained an unlikely culprit. Mary might not have considered her at all but for the night of her subterranean adventure. Even so, there was no incentive for a rich, wellborn lady to steal such relatively paltry items. Dalrymple must be after something else entirely. But all the servants remained suspects. All except Amy Tranter, of course. And that was the best news to come of this new theft: Amy might have lost Octavius Jones, but she could at least reclaim her job.

After a swift but comprehensive survey of the room, Mary hurried belowstairs, found Mrs. Shaw, and laid before her a concise explanation of what she'd found. Given her history with the housekeeper, she didn't expect praise or instant action, but even so, she was startled by Mrs. Shaw's response.

"Missing, you say?" said Mrs. Shaw with a thin smile. "Are you very sure, Quinn?" It wasn't a question.

"Yes, ma'am. I searched the entire room for the vase."

"And what makes you so certain it was missing in the first place?"

Mary bit back an impatient *I've already told you*. "The mantelpiece arrangement was strange, ma'am. Uneven." A parlor maid wouldn't know the word *symmetrical*.

"And so you deduced the missing vase."

"I think so, ma'am." It was too far out of character

to demonstrate knowledge of the story of Persephone's rescue from the Underworld. "There was a circle on the mantel that was less dusty. It looks like the base of a vase to me."

"And on this flimsy—I hesitate to say 'evidence'—this flimsy *tale,* you wish me to drop everything and report yet another disgraceful episode to Her Majesty?"

Mary swallowed her temper. "Isn't there a book, ma'am, that lists all the ornaments in each room? It would show whether there's a vase missing. Or anything else."

"It will—and I shall consult it in my own good time." Mrs. Shaw looked down her nose at Mary. "Not when an irresponsible, half-wild, would-be parlor maid tells me to."

Those adjectives weren't entirely inaccurate, Mary conceded, considering her role from Mrs. Shaw's perspective. All the same, she didn't understand the housekeeper's frosty hostility toward her. And as she would carry that reputation whether she earned it or not, she'd nothing to lose in pushing the woman a bit further. "With respect, ma'am, if the vase was stolen, you'd want to report it straightaway."

"But that's a large *if,* Quinn—especially as I suspect that your eagerness for action is because you have your own agenda."

This was half surprising, half entirely too predictable for words. "Ma'am?"

"The simplest and stupidest thing in the world for

you to do would be to hide a vase and claim it was stolen, thus exonerating your little friend Tranter."

"I give you my word, Mrs. Shaw. I never even thought of it. Please. Search my room, if you don't believe me."

"A very good idea, Quinn. But it wouldn't be in your room if you'd taken it." Mrs. Shaw smiled, very unpleasantly indeed. "You're rather deep, and very sly. I'll not find anything there. But watch your step, my girl: when I sack you, it'll be for very clear reasons. And you'll never work as a domestic again." And with that, the housekeeper swept from the room.

Mary shook her head in disbelief. What ought she do now? If the theft was later discovered, Mrs. Shaw would be certain to put the blame on her. Going over the housekeeper's head was the only way to protect herself from a future accusation of deficiency. But would an ordinary parlor maid have the courage to do so? And if so, whom would she tell? Such an act of mutiny would certainly make its way back to Mrs. Shaw, and how could Mary protect her place then?

The only course open to her was to notify the Agency. They would get word to the right person. They could investigate Mrs. Shaw's background at the same time, to shed some light on her hostile behavior. Yes. That was the best course of action. And yet, thought Mary as she went up to her room for paper and pen, she'd not yet heard back from Anne or Felicity on any of her earlier queries, whether to do with Honoria Dalrymple, Octavius Jones, or the purpose of the secret tunnel. Without their help, she was as alone here as any ordinary parlor maid. And at the moment, she'd no particular confidence that her training would help her at all. There were still too many things she didn't understand. There was too much for her to do. She hadn't a clue where things stood in relation to one another. And tonight, Honoria Dalrymple expected her to seduce Prince Bertie for the greater glory of the Dishonorable Ralph Beaulieu-Buckworth's reputation.

Mary thought of Lang Jin Hai, imprisoned in Cradle Tower. He, at least, was secure in his fate. The thought was only half formed, however, when a wave of shame and self-loathing turned her stomach. No: she certainly didn't envy her father. But perhaps this was part of her desire to help him escape, too—to flee this sordid confusion. Living like happy wanderers was certainly impossible. But she couldn't help a deep throb of longing for an uncomplicated existence. A happy life. If such a thing actually existed.

She rather suspected it did not.

Twenty-five

When the summons came from the Prince of Wales, she was woefully unprepared. She'd had her thoughts fixed so firmly on tonight—after dinner, after the staff were dismissed for the day—that his timing thoroughly rattled her.

It was the beginning of the post-luncheon lull, when the servants had an hour's free time. On her way up to her room, Mary paused at the housekeeper's room to check for a return message from the Agency. Nothing. She frowned. She'd not given them much time, it was true, but Anne Treleaven was generally so efficient. Perhaps in another hour. She turned down the corridor toward the staircase and, rounding a corner, met one of the smirking, thin-lipped equerries of the previous morning.

"You're a lucky girl."

She cursed silently. "Are you speaking to me, sir?"

He glanced about elaborately. "Who else?" It was

true: they were quite alone in the hallway. "His Highness wants a word with you."

"A word?"

That smirk again. "Perhaps more than one. But I doubt you'll be doing much talking."

In any other circumstances, she would have kicked him in the groin and fled. The prospect remained tempting in her situation: while defying Prince Bertie's wishes would certainly get her the sack, so would complying with them, once Mrs. Shaw could secure proof of her immoral behavior. Between these two scenarios, her continued employment was extremely precarious. For now, she elected to obey the equerry, as she stood more of a chance of influencing the prince than she did Mrs. Shaw. With a grim look, she turned on her heel and stalked toward the Prince of Wales's apartments. It would be a long walk; she was now at the farthest end of the palace from his rooms.

The equerry—they were so alike she'd never attempted to tell them one from another—tagged along behind her. "I say, are you going just like that?"

She ignored him.

"I mean, oughtn't you, er, perform your toilette, or some such?"

She looked down her nose at the lumpish attendant—not difficult, despite the fact that he towered over her. "I haven't the faintest idea what you mean."

He crimsoned, then scowled. "Hoity-toity for a

common little bit of skirt, ain't you? Just because you caught the prince's eye."

She kept walking.

"You ain't even that pretty."

Mary thought, *The next thing he says will be: "Dunno what he sees—"*

"Don't know what he sees in you, myself."

As they crossed through the portrait gallery, Mary hoped for somebody—one of the princes or princesses, a visiting dignitary, even the prince consort himself—to appear. No such luck: they came upon only an occasional domestic who, in the equerry's presence, instantly turned to face the wall. Mary's mood darkened. There would be witnesses capable of bearing a tale, but nobody capable of stopping this nightmare.

As they exited the Long Gallery, the young man drew near and said in an ugly tone, "Don't you dare behave as though I'm invisible." A few moments later, he was so close she felt his breath, hot and wine sour, on her neck. "Or I'll make you sorry."

Mary's pulse roared. She swallowed hard and checked the desire to utter a smart retort. She couldn't walk faster without breaking into a run, but three long corridors lay between her and the Prince of Wales's apartments. She'd no idea which place was safer.

The answer came a moment later, when thick fingers bit into her upper arm and she was dragged toward a doorway. "Too daft to listen," he sneered, shoving her against the wall, rattling the door handle. His face was dull red, his breathing hoarse.

Mary glanced about, trying not to show her panic. They were the only two souls in the corridor.

"No one's coming to save you, you worthless jade." His free hand rummaged her skirts, and she knocked it away with a swift blow that made him howl. She twisted away, but even as she began to run, he grabbed her by the hair and slammed her into the door so hard that her shoulder crunched and bounced off it again. "You like a scrap, eh? I'll give it to you rough."

The door was locked, but that didn't deter him. He pulled her tight against him, her back against his chest, his breath loud and moist in her ear. His arm was locked about her waist—he was surprisingly strong, despite his doughy appearance—and he fumbled her skirts again.

He wanted her to struggle.

He wanted her to cry, to beg, to be terrified.

He hadn't the first clue with whom he was dealing.

"You stupid little boy," she said in a clear, acidic voice. "What d'you think Bertie's going to say when I tell him what you're trying to do?"

Instantly, he went still.

"Do you really think the Prince of Wales will allow you to molest me and go unpunished?" Silence. She swung about to face him, trying not to flinch as the movement jarred her shoulder. "I'm about to become the new favorite. If you ruin me, he'll raise hell." She ticked off the points on her fingers. "You'll lose your post, of course. But also there'll be the cost of paying me off. Do you have that sort of ready money? And there's the scandal: you'll have to explain things to your father. D'you really want to tell him that your entire family lost favor with the future king all because you couldn't keep your mitts off a parlor maid?"

He stared at her, hatred glittering in his eyes. But though his hands were curled with rage, they remained by his sides. A sudden globule of saliva gushed from the corner of his mouth, and he swiped it away. Swallowed hard. "Devil take you," he growled. But despite the curse, his voice was hoarse. "Get out of my sight."

Mary obeyed.

Twenty-six

She arrived at Prince Bertie's apartments in a state that couldn't have been less appropriate for a tryst. Trembling from her near escape. Undeniably sweaty. Hair perfunctorily tidied. Skirt torn. And, above all, in a rage. She would never see justice between these walls—would never hear an apology or see that equerry shamed and stripped of his privilege. But more than justice, in this moment she wanted to kill him with her bare hands. None of this boded well for her encounter with the prince, for which she was so unprepared.

She dallied as long as she dared, pacing the hall and trying to calm herself. She succeeded, to a certain extent. But pain shot through her shoulder whenever she tried to move it, and the bitterness of fear and anger was strong at the back of her mouth. If he tried to kiss her, she'd probably punch him in the throat. Perhaps she ought to return to her room, wash her face, and wait a quarter hour. Yes. It was only wise, and she doubted the equerry would inform the prince of what had happened in the meantime.

As she turned to go, the door to Prince Bertie's apartments clicked open and she heard his querulous voice: "Is that you, Mary?"

Damn and blast. She dredged up the closest thing she had to a mild expression and turned. "Yes, sir."

He wore a smoking jacket—peculiar, at this time of day—and a small frown that made him look nearsighted. "Why were you going away?"

"I—I was afraid, sir."

"Of me?" He blinked. "Oh—because of who I am?"

She twisted her hands, relaxing into the role of timid ingenue. "Yes, sir."

"You mustn't think of that. Come in."

Mary allowed herself to be led into the prince's sitting room and given a glass of wine. She sipped it cautiously. "It's very nice, sir."

His smile was patronizing. "Of course; it's a good French claret." They sipped in silence for an awkward few minutes before he spoke again. "You must know, by now, how very much I admire you, Mary. I fear I haven't been subtle in showing it."

"Mrs. Shaw warned me against immorality, sir."

"Pooh! Pure jealousy, on her part. Mrs. Shaw never set a male heart speeding in her life. I suppose she said you'd be ruined."

"She did, sir."

"Well, you needn't worry about that; I'll take care of you. And you needn't call me 'sir,' either. Not when we're here, like this." He edged his chair nearer to hers, so that their knees were touching.

Mary battled a wave of nausea. She'd avoided thinking about the physical details of this encounter until now. That had been an error. "Wh-what shall I call you?"

"Call me Edward."

"Not Prince Bertie?"

He pulled a face. "My mother calls me Bertie. When she's not calling me Albert Edward Wettin."

"I see." And she did. This seduction was an attempt to balance his feelings of childish impotence. It was hamfisted and grossly thoughtless, but it might serve to help him feel like an adult.

"Drink your wine, Mary."

Her glass was very nearly full. "I don't want it to go to my head, sir."

He smiled. "Ah, but I do."

Mary battled another queasy tremor. Dipped her head and drank. What was she doing? Was there anything on earth she could say to extricate herself while preserving her cordial relations with the prince? In all her far-from-sheltered life, she'd never imagined losing her virginity this way.

"That's better," he purred as she lowered the half-empty glass.

But when he reached to take the goblet from her, she

clutched it tighter. "Mayn't I finish it, sir? It's a pity to waste such a fine wine."

His smile was half impatient, half indulgent. "Of course. You'll be more at ease then."

Did he really believe so? She took a small sip of claret, seeking her habitual discipline, mental and physical. It hadn't entirely vanished. She still had choices: she could fight and flee, jettisoning all chance of completing this case. Or she could comply with Bertie's desires and preserve her cover a bit longer. In the first scenario, she would sabotage her first case as a fully fledged member of the Agency and create doubt about her suitability as an operative. In the second, she would sacrifice her very body—the only thing that was truly hers—for the Agency's sake. Was it worth the price? She'd not heard from Anne or Felicity on any of the subjects she'd asked about, had had no contact since that mysterious Sunday summons.

Resentment flared within her, and with it panic. They'd as good as left her alone, operating without support or context. Did they deserve the sacrifice of her womanly self-respect as well? The answer came swiftly, although she'd have preferred not to acknowledge it: it was only thanks to the Agency that she had dignity at all. They had found her. Rescued her. Made her who she was. She owed them everything.

Mary drew a deep breath. She could do this. It was all a matter of discipline, and she had plenty of that. She had no expectations of her own, anyway. No beau, no plans for marriage. The only risk was to herself. The last mouthful of wine had a bitter flavor, but she summoned a shaky smile. "Well. Edward." His name was strange to utter — this felt like an enormous game of make-believe. Which it was, she reminded herself. It was all a charade.

He smiled. "You're very unusual looking. Rather beautiful. Have you Italian blood?"

"No, sir. My mother was Irish, though."

"That accounts for the dark hair and eyes, then." He touched her cheek gently, and she tried not to flinch. Her skin prickled, and she fought the urge to scrape her face clean. It was a poor effort, but again he seemed not to notice. "Would you like another glass of wine?"

"I had better not, sir."

"Edward."

"Edward."

"Well, then —" He removed the glass from her reluctant fingers. Here, however, his polished seduction scene halted. He stared at her for a moment with an expression of frank, almost tortured longing. Then, without further preliminaries, launched himself toward her.

She toppled back into the chair with a startled gasp. His lips were surprisingly cool and not entirely unpleasant. They tasted of claret and tobacco. His mustache was a surprise: she couldn't help but think of James Easton, the only other man she'd kissed, who was clean shaven. Instantly, she regretted the comparison.

Bertie drew back for a moment to look at her. "Your first kiss," he said with pleasure. "I can tell." He reapplied himself, now folding her into his arms, pressing forward. She stayed still and passive, hands by her sides, still trying to convince herself that this would be all right. It was remarkable how the same acts—a kiss, a caress—could feel so different. There was nothing technically *wrong* with Bertie: he didn't smell bad or cause her physical pain. And yet her skin crawled at his touch, her stomach roiled in protest.

She focused on peripheral details—the steady ticking of a clock in the background, the soft swell of the chair cushion behind her shoulder blades. But try as she might, the squeamish reality of what she was doing reasserted itself: Bertie's lip-smacking technique, the pressure of his knee against her thigh, the scent of his pomade suddenly made so intimate.

"You taste so sweet," he murmured. It was as though he were reading aloud from a script for the first time.

Mary said nothing, kept her gaze anywhere but on his face.

He removed her maid's cap and dropped it on the floor. "That's better." He kissed her again, apparently unconcerned by her total lack of response.

She was doing well. Even when Bertie grasped her injured shoulder, she managed not to flinch. When his hand closed over her calf, she tensed only slightly, although even through thick, unglamorous woolen stockings, her skin prickled with revulsion. He didn't seem to notice, however, and instead began to delve into her skirts, rucking them up, muttering something incoherent. His breathing was faster, heavier, and Mary wondered if she could safely count on this being a short encounter.

But when his fingers met the bare flesh of her thigh, her brittle self-control snapped. "No!" She pushed his hand away with a force that surprised both of them and sprang to her feet. "I'm very sorry, Your Highness. I—I can't."

He'd tumbled backward and landed on his bottom, and now stared up at her with shock and hurt. "What did you say?"

She scarcely believed it herself. "I thought I could do this to please you. But now I find that I can't."

"Why? What's wrong with me?"

"Nothing in the world, Your Highness." She wished he would stand up instead of gaping up at her from the carpet.

"I thought you liked me."

She drew a deep breath. "I think you're a very kind gentleman."

He pulled a face. "'Very kind.' Hell's bells." Then, suddenly angry, he scrambled to his feet. "But you came here. You drank wine with me. You let me kiss you!"

"I—I was honored by your attentions, sir." If he was blind to the complexities of refusing the heir apparent, she was not the person to explain them to him.

"Then you can continue to be honored, damn it!" He seized her by the elbows and kissed her again, a kiss that was both angry and desperate.

Mary pushed him away firmly. "I'm sorry, sir, but no." She tasted blood on her lower lip. "I apologize most humbly for having given you the wrong idea. I didn't mean to change my mind; I thought I could—go through with it, to please you. But I can't."

Bertie glared at her for a long minute. She stayed perfectly still, wondering if he would try to force her, as his equerry had done. He was a smaller, softer man than his attendant; she could hurt him badly enough to make him stop if she fought without reservation. But how could she possibly do that to the Prince of Wales? If she did, she'd be lucky to escape jail. Yet she knew herself incapable of doing anything other than refusing him.

The moments stretched long, parlor maid and prince staring at each other in furious tension. Then, quite suddenly, Bertie seemed to buckle. He staggered back, face crumpling like that of a small child, and fell into his armchair, emitting a high animal shriek. It took Mary a second to recognize it as a sob.

She stood over him, feeling distinctly foolish. What was the proper etiquette for comforting a prince one had just rejected and made cry? Could she offer him a clean apron to blow his nose with?

"Y-you—felt—sorry for me?" Bertie gasped, between sobs.

"Er—well, I wouldn't put it quite like that. I wanted to try to please you."

"Why?"

"Well . . . because you're the Prince of Wales. And you seemed keen."

"So it *was* pity!"

Mary watched with horror as he collapsed into huge, shuddering sobs and curled himself into a ball. It didn't help that he was correct. Pity hadn't been her main incentive in agreeing to prostitute herself, but it had certainly helped make the prospect of doing so a shade less loathsome. There was nothing she could say now to improve the situation. It might be wiser to leave, before he recovered and was doubly furious with her—first for changing her mind and then for witnessing his breakdown.

Yet she balked at simply running away. It was true that he'd be ashamed afterward. He would resent her all the more for having seen him bawl. But he was appallingly vulnerable just now. The back of his neck—the only skin visible to her in his balled-up position—was pink with emotion. There was nobody to ring for: he'd not thank her for bringing the queen or another servant or an equerry to the scene. And so Mary waited.

Twenty-seven

As the minutes dragged on, however, she became increasingly concerned: rather than crying itself out, Bertie's histrionic grief seemed only to intensify. Indeed, after ten minutes or so, it seemed to pass from sobbing into a sort of frenzy. Most physicians believed hysteria to be an exclusively female ailment, but it was the closest description Mary could find for the prince's condition.

She stepped closer and said, quite loudly, "Your Highness."

No break in the keening.

"Edward." No, that was no good: he'd only adopted that name for his grown-up charade. "Bertie!" Her tone was loud and forceful but caused only the slightest hitch in his pattern of wails. The merest touch caused him to roll into an even tighter ball—like a hedgehog, she thought, protecting its tender belly. It was a disrespectful analogy but a distressingly apt one as well: the hedgehog had no other defenses. The young man before her was the future king of England—and the hedgehog defense was still all he could manage.

Damn Ralph Beaulieu-Buckworth, she thought angrily. Bertie had enough work to do with ordinary growing up. Who knew how far the trauma of seeing his friend stabbed to death might have set him back? It occurred to her that she ought to curse Lang Jin Hai more, but she pushed that thought away with ruthless injustice. She approached Bertie, gripped his shoulder firmly, and delivered a resounding slap across his left cheek.

He flailed wildly, arms churning the air until he clipped her solidly under the chin.

Her neck snapped back. Ears rang. A bright flash of light blocked out vision for a moment. And then she saw him cradling his hand, still wailing, still beyond himself. "No!" he screamed, eyes dilated in panic. "I did nothing! Wasn't me!" Bertie's eyes were fixed with horror on a spot some two feet from Mary. It took her several moments to realize what might be the matter. He was in a nightmare of sorts, a recent and familiar one. She watched as he tracked an invisible figure, flinched as the figure approached, then moved past him. His attention was riveted just a few feet away and he gasped at what he saw. "Don't, Bucky—just—no—somebody"—he glanced sightlessly about his bedroom, looking for someone to intervene—"oh, God, Bucky, don't do it!" His eyes dilated further, and he flinched as at an invisible blow. "Stop it! Oh, somebody stop him!"

Mary could take no more. She found a decanter of dark amber liquid and flung its contents into Bertie's face. He half screamed as the liquid filled his mouth and soaked his face, then promptly began to splutter and hack. His shirt and smoking jacket were very wet, and the room suddenly reeked of brandy. It was a long coughing fit—his ears were purple before he'd finished—but eventually, he blinked up at Mary with watery, bloodshot, focused eyes.

"What—what the devil did you do that for?" He clutched his red, tear-streaked face and gazed up at her with reproach.

"With respect, sir, I thought it unhealthy to allow you to continue. You seemed . . . beyond yourself."

He gazed at her, struggling to comprehend. "I was crying?"

"Among other things."

Bertie's expressions were utterly transparent. He frowned, puzzled. Had a glimpse of insight. Then, his jaw slackened and he gasped in disbelief as memory rushed back. He stared at Mary with a blend of horror and excitement. "Could I have been dreaming, do you think?"

"I don't know, sir." She forced herself to be honest. "I thought you might be either dreaming or remembering."

"Yes." He nodded, slowly at first and then with increasing conviction. "Yes. I remember. I'm remembering! I think I've been dreaming about it, too—every night since it happened—but I've never been able to recall my dreams, never in my life. But this—this is different. I'm remembering, not inventing, I'm sure of it. I'd swear to it." His elation collapsed. "I expect I'll have to, once I tell Mother."

She had to know. It was none of her concern, officially, but she couldn't bear the suspense. "Do you mean—the dreadful thing that happened to you on Saturday night, sir?"

He stared at her, suddenly shamefaced. "Yes. I expect you've heard all about it."

"Not from the servants, sir—gossip's strictly forbidden. I know only what you told me the other day."

His relief was almost comical. "Of course! Right. Yes. Well, that's best. Gossip's a dangerous thing."

But he was going to tell the queen. That was what mattered. Although, of course, it no longer mattered as it once had. Mary no longer felt capable of appreciating irony. "I'm sorry about the brandy, sir."

He blinked down at his soaking-wet clothes. "No harm done, I suppose—though I'll have to explain to Mother how I got through that much brandy in such a short time."

"There are always your equerries, sir. . . ."

He half smiled. "Yes. They may finally be of use."

"Are you sure you're all right, sir? Are there medicines you're meant to take?"

He shook his head.

"Even after the . . . the tragedy? Your physician left nothing, no special instructions?"

Another denial and then, suddenly, "Oh, no—wait. He left some blue pills. And some calming drops."

Mary's mouth twisted. "A good idea just now, I think. Where is the bottle?"

"Dunno."

She waited.

"Dressing room, perhaps. But I'd rather have more wine. That calms me, too."

"Let's begin with the medicine," said Mary as she left the sitting room. "I'll fetch some dry linens, too."

Bertie's bedroom was a strange place. The bed and night table were old and good yet almost puritan in their austerity; the bed was plainly made up with a woolen blanket. These, presumably, represented the prince consort's ideas about the unpretentious simplicity of healthy young manhood. But sprinkled throughout the room were the lavish items preferred by his son—embroidered silk dressing gowns and gold-filigreed opera glasses, an ornate clock with mother-of-pearl inlay, and a rather good oil painting of a voluptuous maiden clutching a trailing scarf to preserve her modesty.

Mary smiled and wondered if the painting disappeared when Bertie's parents inspected his bedroom, as they almost certainly did. The dressing room was a small place, probably not originally intended for an adult's use, jammed with row upon row of apparel: crisp linen shirts, silk cravats, morning suits, evening suits, an entire rack of top hats, riding costumes, fishing jackets, cricket whites, fencing costumes, and even a pair of boxing gloves. Mary picked her way through these excesses to a small chest of drawers whose surface was, again, a cramped abundance of pomades, lotions, colognes, shaving implements, ivory-handled hairbrushes, and other mysterious male beauty products. There was no room here for unwanted medicines.

With a hesitant hand, she explored the drawers one by one: silk stockings and rolled-up pairs of braces; undergarments, again silk; and in the bottom drawer, nightcaps and handkerchiefs, neatly pressed. She was taking a couple of handkerchiefs with good conscience when her fingers brushed against something hard and smooth.

She froze. Had she the right to pry like this? Fetching medicines and linens was one thing, sifting through the contents of Bertie's closet quite another.

She heard his voice, reedy and querulous, from the sitting room. "Mary? What's taking you so long?"

"I'm sorry, sir," she said. "I can't see the medicine. What sort of bottle was it?" She twitched aside the next handkerchief to uncover a small porcelain vase decorated with a neoclassical painting of two women embracing: Persephone and Demeter, reunited.

"Never mind the medicine," came Bertie's voice, anxious now. "I don't need it. Just—come back here and have another glass of wine with me."

"I—I ought to find it, just in case. You may need it later."

A moment's silence. And then Bertie appeared in the doorway of the dressing room. "Just don't open—"

She turned to him, revealing the open drawer, the bright gloss of glazed porcelain.

He swallowed. Flushed. "Oh. I see you've found . . . er . . . I bought the vase for my mother's birthday. Don't tell her, will you? It's a surprise."

"Her Majesty's birthday is in May."

"Well, yes. I like to be prepared. Sometimes you just see something, don't you, and you think, *That's it! It's perfect.*"

Such desperate, transparent lies saddened her more than anything. It must have been evident in her expression: he fell silent. She stood the vase on the last few square inches of space on the chest of drawers, nudging aside a hairbrush and a jar of unguent to make room. "It's a charming vase," she said quietly.

He swallowed, said nothing.

"May I take it out to the sitting room? The light's better there."

"I'd rather you didn't."

"All right." She stood, closed the drawer, and followed him back through the bedroom to the sitting room.

He found his wineglass and knocked back its contents. "You've been kind to me. Not only today, but during our past conversations. I suppose that's what gave me the courage to—you know." He gestured. "Anyway. That's all I meant to say."

It was a clear dismissal, but she stood her ground. "I'm afraid I have something more to say, sir."

He refused to look at her.

"It's about the vase, sir. I noticed it was missing yesterday as I was cleaning the Blue Room."

"Don't be ridiculous: how could you know it's the same vase you think might be missing?"

"The things on the mantel were rearranged, sir. And the vase—it's one of a pair. It's the paintings, sir." She hoped he wouldn't ask for specifics: she couldn't see a housemaid explaining the myth of Persephone to the classically educated prince.

He remained silent and still.

"I imagine you have your reasons for having taken it, sir. . . ." Although she couldn't imagine what they might be. He was heir to all this vast wealth. And he had a generous allowance now from his parents. Was it a game of sorts? A new and indirect way to distress his mother? Mary doubted it: Bertie lacked that sort of subtle cruelty.

He spoke quite suddenly. "Yes, I have. I incurred some debts—the horses, y'know. I hope you'll have the decency to keep this quiet, Quinn." At her surprised look, his tone became defensive. "It's only a vase. There are thousands more scattered throughout the palace and in its stores. It's not especially valuable. And if you don't report it, chances are nobody will ever notice it's gone." He forced a grin. "So how about it, eh? We're friends now, aren't we?"

Mary stared at him with—yes, more pity. "Your Highness, if this were my decision alone, I would keep quiet. Truly, I would."

He folded his arms over his chest. "But . . ."

"But there's been more than one theft, hasn't there?"

His jaw hardened. "Has there?"

"Yes. And a maid's been sacked over them. She's out on the street—no job, no letter of character, no money. And now the housekeeper thinks I stole this vase to try to clear her name." She watched the unwelcome news sink into Bertie's brain. Watched him deny. Struggle. And then, very gradually, relent.

"So if I don't come forward . . ." he said, very slowly.

"Amy Tranter will never find work in service again. And I'll be out of a job as soon as Mrs. Shaw finds a good enough reason."

"Oh, God." Bertie buried his face in his hands, this time in simple despair rather than hysteria.

It was difficult not to reach out to console him, rub his head. Spoiled, entitled, and weak he might be, but he was a fundamentally good-hearted young man attempting to live up to very public expectations that were perhaps unrealistic.

After a short eternity, he raised his eyes to hers. "I'll do it. I'll tell my mother."

"Thank you, Your Highness. It's—"

He interrupted her with a gesture. "Never mind that. Just go."

"Yes, sir." As she left the room, she cast one last glance at the prince. He stood in the window, hands planted flat on the wide sill. His eyes were closed, and he appeared to be thinking or praying.

Her sympathy was worth nothing to him, but he had it all the same.

Twenty-eight

The Bertie episode had taken a great deal of time, long enough that Mrs. Shaw would demand an explanation for her absence. Mary was quite looking forward to it. Having so unexpectedly succeeded in completing her original assignment, she would now take great pleasure in being sacked. It would, in theory, be even more satisfying to resign first, but that was strictly against Agency protocol: an agent never left her post in a showy or confrontational fashion. Even Mary's sore shoulder and ringing headache felt like reasonable sacrifices now that things had unfolded so neatly.

As she approached the housekeeper's room to request some willow-bark powder—and, of course, to initiate the fateful conversation with Mrs. Shaw—she heard the housekeeper declare, "I decline to summon any member of my staff at a stranger's request. Furthermore, I fail to understand how you gained access to this part of the palace."

The voice that followed sent an electric tingle across Mary's skin. "The latter is no mystery, ma'am: I walked in through the servants' door. But can I not impress upon you how urgent my errand is? I must speak to Miss Quinn."

Laughter bubbled up in her throat, and she didn't bother to repress it. The Agency's rules about showy departures clearly didn't allow for this sort of complication. She ran the last ten paces and barreled into Mrs. Shaw's room. "I'm here, James. What's the matter?"

He swung about at the first syllable. "Mary, thank God. It's an emergency."

Mrs. Shaw rose, outraged. "This childish prank is entirely and regrettably like you, Quinn. You are—"

As James caught her arm and drew her into the corridor, Mary heard herself dismissed in the most outrageous language Mrs. Shaw knew, but she hadn't attention to spare. James wasn't the panicking type, but he was utterly rattled now. "How can I help?"

He spoke quietly. "Find the queen. Tell her she must evacuate the palace. Royal family first, but all staff, too. You're all in grave and immediate danger."

She stared at him, mouth dry. He was in deadly earnest. Mrs. Shaw had followed them into the corridor and stood behind him, continuing her furious harangue against Mary's many sins and shortcomings.

James wrapped his hands around hers, pulled her close. "Mary. Please. There's no time for me to go through official channels. You're the only one."

He didn't look mad. But surely . . . "James, I need a reason. I can't just ask the queen to do something without an explanation."

"You're not asking her; you're telling her. I've just found explosives in that underground tunnel: crates upon crates of guncotton. She needs to clear out immediately, then call the army to dispose of it."

Mary nodded. "How far need she go?"

"I don't know exactly. A mile, at least."

"I'll suggest that she go to Kensington Palace. Anything else?"

"No. Yes. You're to evacuate with them! Wait there until I send word."

She half smiled at that, but he remained deadly serious. "James, this is a stupid thing to say, but—be careful."

A brief smile. An even swifter kiss, right there in the corridor, under Mrs. Shaw's nose. "You, too." And then he was gone.

"Sacked! Do you hear me, Quinn? Pack up your things this instant."

Mary started down the hall at a run. It was teatime. Her Majesty would be in her private parlor, two stories and half a palace away. "Quinn! You're going the wrong way!"

She spared a glance for poor, overwrought, furious Mrs. Shaw. "Yes, ma'am."

Her entry into Her Majesty's presence was a shade more circumspect: she entered the private parlor at a brisk walk, eyes lowered, and immediately prostrated herself in a deep curtsy.

Even so, Queen Victoria frowned and two burly footmen instantly caught hold of her, poised to march her from the royal presence. "This is highly irregular," said the queen.

"I apologize for intruding, Your Majesty. I have done so only as a matter of national security." Mary raised her eyes—although not her head—and caught a glimpse of the queen staring at her. Honoria Dalrymple stood in a corner of the room, riveted by Mary's sudden appearance.

"Continue."

She nearly sighed with relief. "Your Majesty, the engineer engaged in repairing the tunnels beneath Buckingham Palace has discovered a grave danger. To preserve your safety, you must evacuate the palace immediately."

The queen stared at her for a full ten seconds. "We have not been informed of any danger by the palace guards. What sort of danger?"

"A high explosive known as guncotton, Your Majesty. Sheets of cotton impregnated with nitric acid. They're highly unstable." Her training in the use of explosives had been brief, but it was enough for her to know and fear the extreme danger of guncotton. Her heart squeezed painfully as she thought of James making his way back down into the tunnels. She couldn't afford to think further or imagine the worst.

"Impossible!" That choked utterance emanated from behind the queen. Honoria Dalrymple's skin was ashen, her eyes wide and staring.

"I'm afraid not, ma'am. Mr. Easton, the engineer, is entirely reliable. He says this is a task for the army."

"Leave us," said Her Majesty.

Mary felt the footman pulling on her shoulders. "Please, Your Majesty, I assure you—"

"Not you," said the queen. "We were addressing the others."

Honoria and the two footmen gaped at her. "But Your Majesty, this is clearly . . ."

Even the footmen added their silent protest, dragging Mary a step closer to the door.

"Release this person and leave us now. Time is of the essence."

With reluctant, dazed steps, the three exited the room, so utterly startled that they failed to observe the rules of precedence.

The instant the door clicked behind them, Queen Victoria spoke again. "Your name?"

"Quinn, ma'am. Mary Quinn."

"And how, Mary Quinn, are you so privileged as to know about threats to the empire before anybody else?"

She bowed her head. "I'm acquainted with the principal of Easton Engineering, ma'am. He told me because it was the swiftest way. Your Majesty, I implore you to believe me."

"This is logical enough. But you must offer some form of proof of your reliable character: any sufficiently determined and resourceful mischief maker could report such a tale. One could even heap some boxes in a disused sewer and pretend they contained explosives."

She was perfectly correct, of course—and as reasonable and logical as Mary dared hope. "Your Majesty, I am the person recently engaged to resolve the matter of a string of petty thefts. I offer my employment as a character reference."

Queen Victoria's eyebrows shot up. "Indeed." Her unspoken thought was clear: *Not what I expected at all.* But she soon rallied. "I see. And if I were to ask for the emergency password?"

Mary tried not to grin. She'd never before had the opportunity to give the phrase that identified her to the client. "I would say 'Adrift in Zanzibar,' ma'am."

Her Majesty flashed a neat, vivid little smile that was promptly replaced by her usual gravitas. "In that case, we've no time to lose, Miss Quinn. Kindly ring that bell."

Not for Queen Victoria panic and its attendant chaos. Within a quarter of an hour, the young princes and princesses and their attendants had been bundled into coaches for the short drive to Kensington Palace. The queen had then summoned the most senior domestics and explained with admirable brevity the need for them to vacate the palace immediately and without fuss. And she'd ordered the highest-ranking army officer in London to meet her at Kensington Palace. Now the Queen of England and Empress of India stood outside, wrapped in a plain woolen overcoat, overseeing the departure of her staff of hundreds. Behind her, standing at almost military attention, was the prince consort.

"Your Majesty, with respect, time is short," said Mary.

Her Majesty nodded at the carriage that awaited her, not twenty yards off. It was an anonymous black coach, an irreproachable choice for discretion. "It is our responsibility to safeguard those in our employ."

"Yet your safety is of the utmost importance, both for your family and for the country."

The queen gave her a sharp look. "And what sort of general would flee before the enemy, leaving his troops to scrabble their way to safety as best they could?"

"Please, ma'am, at least stand away from the building. Every bit of distance is essential."

Queen Victoria agreed to this minor modification, but for Mary it was a nerve-racking wait while the last of the staff trickled from the palace. They were an orderly crew, although many, ignorant of the real reason for their departure, were distracted or fussy or generally reluctant. As they passed beneath the queen's gaze, however, each seemed suddenly tidied by an invisible hand: spines straighter, shoulders squarer, any whispers or giggles instantly quelled. When at last they were all safely beyond the palace gates, walking in neat procession through the parks like so many schoolchildren being given an outing, only then did the queen permit her husband to hand her into the carriage.

From her perch on high, she looked down upon Mary. "Well? Aren't you coming, Miss Quinn?"

Mary shook her head. "It's most kind of you, Your Majesty, but I'm needed here."

The queen elevated her eyebrows ever so slightly. "Mr. Easton said this was a task for the army."

"Yes, ma'am. But until the army arrives, he'll need my help."

A long, hard look.

"Please, ma'am—your safety."

"She is right, Vicky," said Prince Albert.

"Very well. We shall pray for your success, Miss Quinn."

Mary curtsied very low. "Thank you, Your Majesty."

She waited only until the carriage was in motion. Then, with one last look at the gray, drizzling world aboveground, she hurried back into the palace.

Twenty-nine

Thursday afternoon

Buckingham Palace sewers

James stared at the crates of guncotton, wishing they were a hallucination. This was entirely his fault. Immediately after that bizarre midnight episode with the man with the etched-glass lantern, he ought to have sealed all sewer entrances and placed them under constant guard. Yet the idea of banning the flushers, of obstructing routine maintenance, had seemed excessive. He'd been reluctant to create panic where none was necessary, draw attention to a weakness that remained exposed. And this was the price for having been cavalier.

Now he was responsible for the hysterical threat to, and possible destruction of, Buckingham Palace. He knew precisely when the boxes had been moved in: at midmorning, he'd been called away from the site by a mysterious letter offering information about the midnight sewer explorer. Like a fool, he'd succumbed to the ruse. Left the manhole under a watchman's supervision. And returned three hours later, none the wiser, to find that the watchman had absconded. It had been annoying and worrisome. But even then, he'd not expected the full horror of what awaited him in that strange antechamber just off the main sewer.

It had taken time to work out what the boxes contained. One of guncotton's dangerous traits was its innocuous appearance. After all, it was merely cotton or wood fibers impregnated with nitric acid and left to dry. A crate full of guncotton looked like so much harmless fabric—unless one's suspicions were already flaring, as James's had been. He'd prized open each of the dozen boxes, dry mouthed and sweaty palmed the entire time. The slightest impact, a moment of clumsiness, and the whole tinderbox could have gone off.

The simplest way to neutralize the guncotton was to wet it again. He'd brought a pair of buckets with him and was busy filling them with rank water, hauling them up to the antechamber and carefully, nervously, pouring it into each crate. It was slow work: at this time of day, the sewers were down to a trickle, and he had to travel downstream a few hundred yards in order to fill his buckets. The first time he'd tried to douse the guncotton, he'd held his breath, certain that it would ignite instead. But it hadn't.

He was filthy. Soaked to the skin. Shaking with nervous tension. He'd no idea whether Mary had been successful. He could hear constant, irregular rumbles that echoed up and down the tunnels—the clatter of carriage wheels on the cobblestones above, translated through layers of stone and earth and brick. But he couldn't hear activity from within the palace, not even the scurrying of feet on flagstones. And yet, even as he listened, there came a new sound: light, tentative footsteps, coming from the palace's access tunnel, just above this room.

He tensed. Set down his empty buckets. He had the advantage in some ways: he'd been down here longer, knew where the crates ended, could see general outlines even in the gloom. And this other person would have just descended a ladder. But he was at a disadvantage, too: he didn't want to die down here in the sewers and was intensely aware of the risks involved simply in being where he was. He forced himself to unclench his fists, to balance his weight lightly on the balls of his feet. To be ready for anything.

The footsteps were careful, unhurried, yet steady. From the click of the shoe soles on the ladder's metal rungs, the person wasn't wearing waterproofs and waders. Not a flusher, then. He waited, wondering if he'd positioned himself as well as he'd thought: the crates were behind him, so that he might block the intruder's access to them. Perhaps he ought to have stayed behind them, for an opportunity to see the person before he showed himself. But it was too late.

In the near darkness, he saw a pair of smallish boots descending the last rungs, showing a clear three inches of ankle beneath a dark skirt, and he was instantly seized with panic and anger. He couldn't possibly recognize a pair of buttoned boots. It was ridiculous. And yet, as the owner of the boots touched down with a soft thump and turned about, it seemed inevitable that it was she.

"I told you to evacuate with the rest of the staff," he snapped.

She dusted off her hands. "So you did. And good afternoon, by the way."

"It's not, actually. Get out. Go."

And yet she came toward him, eyeing the looming stack of crates with respect. "That's an enormous quantity of guncotton."

"Enough to blow us up a hundred times over," he agreed. "Which is why you're leaving this instant."

"Only if you come with me." She held out her hand.

He stared at it, tempted. "Someone's got to guard the crates until the army can dispose of them."

"That's what I thought. I've come to help."

He squinted at the ladder and its chute, wondering if he had enough clearance simply to throw her over his shoulder and carry her up by force.

"It's no good," she said in a sweet voice. "I'd only struggle. And that would leave the crates unguarded."

Not for the first time, he was tempted to shake her. Instead, he drew a deep breath. Contained his anger. "Mary. Is there nothing I can say or do to induce you to leave?"

"No. You need help. Now tell me what to do." She

was already rolling her sleeves, turning up her skirts to knee height for freer movement.

He sighed. Gritted his teeth. Then said, "We'll make a relay: I'll fill the buckets and pass them to you; you soak the guncotton and return the buckets at the midpoint."

"Very good."

"Seems a long way from good to me."

She rolled her eyes. "All right: very sensible."

She was irresistible. He leaned down and planted the swiftest of kisses on her lips. "I do love a sensible girl." And then he turned away, bucket in hand, before she could think of a riposte.

Thirty

Once they'd settled into a rhythm, Mary found it difficult to believe in their imminent danger. It was hard work, of course—dirty, cold, slippery, splashy—but the guncotton looked so harmless. Nevertheless, they labored on. After nearly half an hour, they'd fetched enough water to soak through two-thirds of the crates. The emergency would soon be averted. And yet Mary remained troubled by the use of a substance that was so volatile.

When she next met James to exchange buckets, empty for full, she said, "Doesn't it seem strange to you, the use of guncotton?"

"How d'you mean?" He sounded distracted and squinted down the tunnel at some invisible end point.

"The whole scheme seems oddly uncalculated . . . more like a general, irrational gesture than a specific threat to the Crown."

"I'd say that planting any type of explosive beneath Buckingham Palace is irrational."

"Yes," she persisted, "but isn't the use of guncotton extra foolish? If one wanted to murder the queen, there are more direct ways. She rides out through the parks nearly every day; it wouldn't be difficult to swarm her carriage or put a gun to her head. It's happened before."

"But the palace is an important symbol. Perhaps it's a gesture aimed at the building and what it represents rather than at the monarch."

"Even so, the risk of carrying in all the guncotton . . . no sensible person would run such a high personal risk. Unless he was extremely desperate or utterly indifferent." He turned toward her, holding her gaze for a long moment. He looked deadly serious and—odd moment for her to choose to notice this—as handsome as one could look in near blackness.

"You're talking about a lunatic."

"Or someone too reckless to care about his own safety."

"In practice, it's not that different. It means we're much less able to anticipate what he'll do next."

She drew breath to reply—and was interrupted not by speech, but by a sudden dazzle of light. In truth, it was likely no more than a warm glow. But after such prolonged murkiness, it had a blinding effect. Both froze. Held their breath. Narrowed their eyes.

James's hand bumped against her arm, and he pushed her gently upstream, a silent order: *retreat*. She began to move slowly, using the noise of the newcomer's splashing to cover the sounds of her own motion. A brief retreat was all very well—it offered time to think, to plan their next move. But it had to end soon—the last thing they wanted was live flame near the guncotton. As they rounded the curve, they came to a halt by unspoken agreement.

James pulled her near, put his mouth to the curve of her ear. "Go," he said. "Fetch help."

"Come with me. Nothing to be gained by staying."

"I'm going to try to reason with him." He pushed her gently once again. "Go. It's our best chance."

"You can't reason with a madman," she hissed. "Come on. We need to get clear of the palace before he blows it up."

"There's no time."

"Precisely!"

They glared at each other. Had the situation been less serious, Mary would have burst out laughing—this was so typical of their entire history. But the more time they wasted bickering, the more certain their deaths. Even now, as she looked into James's eyes, his gaze frantic, insistent, she couldn't imagine that she'd see him again. This was simply a ploy to get her to safety. To save her life at the cost of his. She could either accept that gift or throw it back in his face, achieving nothing.

He pushed her again, firmly this time, and she relented. She wound one arm about his neck and pulled him down, planting a fierce kiss on his lips. "James.

I—" His eyes locked with hers, and suddenly her throat closed. "I—". She tried to shape the next word, bring her tongue up to her palate. She couldn't do it.

The intruder's splashing grew louder, and she spun away, unable to look at James for a moment longer. As she picked her way upstream, tears already misted her vision. She clenched her teeth and forced herself to place one foot before the other. A fine thing it would be if she ruined James's great gesture, her futile attempt to get help, by slipping and falling.

She came so very close. She was mere steps from the guncotton room when the light suddenly flared bright and she heard James say, "Good afternoon." His voice was steady and cool. "I wondered when you might return."

There was a distinct pause. She dared not move, lest sudden motion cause the intruder to panic. Then a new speaker said, "Ah—you're the fellow who was mucking about down here the other night." The voice—male, patrician, chalky with age—instantly made Mary's mind whirl. She knew those tones. Had heard this man before. But when? "Meddlesome chap."

"Hardly," said James. He managed to sound slightly amused. "The safety of these tunnels is my responsibility. If anything, *you're* mucking up *my* work."

The reply was prefaced by a metallic click. "Care to repeat that bit of insolence?" said the intruder, testy now. A short silence. "I thought not. You might cheek an old man, but not his trusty assistant."

Mary frowned, trying to make sense of the bobbing shadows and brilliant, inconsistent rays of light that obscured more than they revealed. And then her eyes caught a glimpse of the "assistant": a sleekly gleaming handgun, pointing unwaveringly at James's chest. Her heart seemed to stagger, and she stifled a useless impulse to run toward them.

"Now," said the intruder, sounding rather pleased with himself, "March. Go on. You know where I want to go."

"You must have paid the watchman a neat sum," said James, holding his ground.

The man snorted—an authoritative, impatient sound that was maddeningly familiar to Mary's ears. "Don't stall, young man; I'm not here to play about. March, or I'll shoot you here and now."

The sound of steady, sloshing footsteps came as a relief to Mary. While James was no fool, he was quite capable of asking one too many questions. She squinted toward the light but could see only James's profile and a flare of lantern light—nothing beyond that. There was no way of timing her escape, and so she remained, statue-like, a yard from the half step up to the guncotton room. She was so very near. There was less to be gained from blind risk than from caution.

The intruder's snort still echoed in her ears. Where had she heard it before? She summoned the last—the only—image she had of him, punting that little barge downsewer. Physically confident. Square shouldered. Intent.

A total stranger, and yet not quite.

She almost gasped when, at last, it came to her: Honoria Dalrymple's stepfather, the Earl of Wintermarch! He was the intruder. The man who'd bowed out of dinner with the queen at the last moment. The man who prowled through the sewers by night, looking for the secret access point. The man who'd instructed Honoria to find the access tunnel from the palace kitchens. She'd seen him the previous night on the servants' staircase, in confidential conversation with Honoria. And the snort was familiar as a masculine version of Honoria's own sound of disapproval and disbelief.

But even with this identification, she still hadn't a clue as to his motives. It made no sense: Honoria's family was part of the elite, and her position as lady-in-waiting affirmed that. Despite her family connection to the disreputable Ralph Beaulieu-Buckworth, they were still part of the inner circle. Why would her stepfather—a retired general, she knew, and by reputation a very distinguished gentleman—want to do the queen harm?

She ought never to have been this much in the dark. If Anne and Felicity had given her the background information she'd requested, it was just possible that this entire crisis might have been avoided. It was an unusual slip, a grave one—and yet it wasn't the first, even during the space of this assignment.

She still couldn't see where Wintermarch's gaze might be focused, but the two men were drawing perilously near. She had to move. In three slow, gliding steps she reached the half wall. So far, no alarm. But the most difficult part still lay before her: climbing up to the raised chamber. She risked a glance at the men—and almost immediately that voice barked, "Who's there?"

She went perfectly still. Lowered her eyelids but kept her gaze on the source of the light.

"A rat, probably," said James. His tone was passably dismissive, but Mary couldn't miss the underlying tension in his tone. "What else might it be?"

"Well, now, that's an interesting question. Keep moving."

A long pause.

A wave of the gun.

James's steps resumed, slower now, his unspoken reluctance practically audible in the silence—to Mary, at least. "Where are we going?"

No reply, the answer being only too obvious.

They were perhaps twenty-five yards away. It was either stay here and be trapped or risk being seen. Mary grasped the ledge, found the smallest of toeholds in the crumbling brick, and began to pull herself up.

"Halt! Don't move."

She ignored this command. A moment later, bruised shoulder burning in protest, she lay sprawled with less elegance than efficiency on the ledge. She was there. She had done it. She had only to climb the ladder and make her way through the tunnel. Surely the army had arrived. Surely she could convince them of the truth.

"There's nothing there, you old fool." That was James's voice.

"In that case, your confederate won't flinch if I put a bullet in your thick skull."

Mary went still.

"Precisely. A pointless bluff," said James. But his bold words were followed by the faintest of gasps.

It was enough to make Mary glance over her shoulder. James's back was to the wall, the barrel of a pistol at the center of his forehead. Wintermarch had thoughtfully raised the lantern to illuminate the metal's dull gleam, James's defiant expression.

"Hear me, sirrah?" called Wintermarch down the tunnel, making it ring with echoes. "Show yourself, or this young piece of impertinence dies." He paused, then added as an afterthought, "And then I'll keep shooting. Either the guncotton will explode or this moldering heap of bricks will collapse on you. Either way, you're both dead."

"You're talking to the echoes," said James. He sounded more angry than afraid. "Wasting time."

A soft, unpleasant chuckle. "We'll see about that." Wintermarch turned his head toward Mary, pressing the muzzle hard into James's forehead. She flinched involuntarily at the sight, and a faint smile curved the old man's lips. "Show yourself. I'll give you to five.

"One.

"Two."

He meant it. What had she said about madmen?

"Three.

"Four."

"Don't shoot." Her voice was hoarse, and for a panicked moment, she thought he'd not heard. "I'm coming."

"God damn it, Mary, run!" shouted James, apparently oblivious of the gun pressing against his skull.

But Wintermarch only chuckled. "As I thought. Although I'll confess I didn't expect a woman." He turned toward Mary. "Show yourself then, missy."

"She's done nothing wrong. Please let her go." There was a faint tremor in James's voice that moved her more than any protestation of devotion.

Mary clambered down. Despite the icy knot of fear at her core, she felt a ravening curiosity. What on earth did the Earl of Wintermarch hope to accomplish with this scheme? It defied all logic. She walked toward the two men, into the circle of light. He was carrying, she noticed, another etched-glass lantern, like some sort of lunatic's calling card "Here I am, your lordship."

Wintermarch's eyebrows, a pair of thick, tufted caterpillars, shot up. "Got it all worked out, have you, missy?"

She inclined her head very slightly—an imitation of Honoria's haughty manner. "The Earl of Wintermarch, of course. Stepfather to the Honorable Honoria Dalrymple,

Her Majesty's lady-in-waiting. And a not-so-distant relation of the Honorable Ralph Beaulieu-Buckworth."

The old man actually grinned. "At your service. You'll forgive my not asking your names; I don't much care for rabble."

Mary stepped forward so that she stood next to James, the two of them facing Wintermarch side by side. "Rabble we might be, but we uncovered your scheme. You're too late, you know—the palace was evacuated nearly an hour ago. The queen is safe."

Amusement flickered across his corrugated features. "Balderdash. That incompetent she-toad could never bestir herself so quickly."

"Have you not had word from Mrs. Dalrymple?" asked Mary, genuinely startled. "Even the servants have escaped."

He was suddenly annoyed. "Enough chitter-chatter. Move." He brandished the gun in the direction of the guncotton room.

"It's an excellent question: what do you hope to accomplish in blowing up an empty palace?" asked James, even as they began to walk. It was a curious sort of death march, accompanying an armed madman with live flame into the presence of explosives.

"I'm not here to satisfy your desire for a story," sneered Wintermarch. "Especially with such clumsy questioning."

"You don't feel even the slightest inclination to boast

of your clever scheme?" asked Mary. She felt cheated. If she was to die, she at least wanted some answers first. And more than cheated, she felt angry. She was going to die in this sewer, at the caprice of a crazed aristocrat who didn't care whether he himself lived or died. Her death wouldn't even be useful or meaningful.

For an answer, he waved the pistol. "Up."

First she, and then James, climbed into the room. The earl remained in the tunnel, smirking at them. "Would you like a hand?" asked James.

Wintermarch snorted. "I may be old, but I'm not a fool. You want to push me off balance, or at least wrest the gun from me. No, thank you, I'll do very well standing right here."

"But what are you going to do?" asked Mary. "You'll not achieve much by blowing up the palace and murdering a couple of commoners. And in present circumstances, you can't even manage that without killing yourself, too." She was scarcely able to keep her voice from shaking, from fury rather than fear. She thought of Lang, sick and alone in Cradle Tower, waiting for a visit that would never happen. He would assume she'd changed her mind, turned coward, broken her promise. Disastrous reversals seemed to run in the family.

Wintermarch scowled. "That's enough. If you were my wife, I'd beat some civility into you."

The idea was enough to make her snort. "Asking logical questions is hardly uncivil."

He frowned and turned to James. "You want to teach her some respect."

James smiled and shrugged. "She's entirely correct."

The old man growled, set down his lantern, and muttered something unflattering about the present generation. All the same, he seemed off balance for the first time since his sudden appearance—rather as though their joint impertinence had robbed him of momentum.

Mary's muscles twitched with long tension. Could she simply rush him? Would he fumble the gun, be reluctant to fire—especially at an unarmed woman? Reactionary noblesse oblige could work to her advantage here, but only if Wintermarch behaved in a logical fashion. With a rational villain, she stood a chance of anticipating his next move. Wintermarch's utter unpredictability, however, kept her frozen.

It was during this lull—gun wavering, Wintermarch gnashing his teeth, Mary and James watching, calculating, doubting—that a most unexpected thing occurred. It was perhaps the most surprising development possible. A new pair of boots dropped rather heavily from the ladder onto the guncotton-room floor. An extremely familiar but utterly improbable voice said, "Oof." And the small, plump form of Queen Victoria appeared from behind the crates.

The three of them gaped, too startled to speak or even make a sound. In this subterranean cavern, lit by a single wavering lantern, with the sound of trickling sewage in the background, the queen's familiar face seemed most likely to be a hallucination brought on by fumes and tension.

Yet even as they stared, the apparition spoke. "A rather clever false alarm, Wintermarch, but we fail to see what you hope to accomplish with this stunt."

The earl blinked and stammered, "I sh-should have thought it rather obvious."

"No," said Her Majesty decisively. "Not at all."

"Well, I've proven that you're vulnerable. That your defenses and security practices are inadequate."

"That will always be the case, Wintermarch; our security is ever at risk. But our life is in God's hands, and we endeavor our best to rule despite these constant, remote possibilities."

"It's not so remote now," he sneered. But it was a weak sort of gibe.

"It is true that an individual monarch's life may be snuffed out at any moment. But what have you really achieved?" asked the queen. "After our death, we have four male heirs to the throne; the continuation of the House of Saxe-Coburg-Gotha is assured. The prince consort would make the finest of regents and is a young man yet; his advice shall be available to the future king for decades. You may kill a single monarch, Wintermarch, but you achieve nothing in the act of regicide."

Her Majesty paused, but Wintermarch appeared unable to reply.

"Furthermore," she went on, "dare you imagine your treachery so subtle, so utterly original, that we have not been aware of your treasonous desires for some time? It is the reason your stepdaughter has been so recently elevated and honored, for we keep our enemies close. As our predecessor, Queen Elizabeth, famously said, 'I have but the body of a weak and feeble woman; but I have the heart and stomach of a king, and of a king of England, too.' Have you so forgotten your history, Wintermarch?"

The revolver flashed again, held in shaking hands but aimed directly at the queen. Instinctively, Mary and James both moved to stand between the monarch and her would-be assassin, but she waved them away.

"Fear not: the earl's time is past. He has long whispered against our authority, complaining of rule by a woman. The ruination of a kingdom and an empire. Yet his own scheme is irrational. Ineffectual. It will achieve nothing, leave no mark."

"Won't it?" shrieked Wintermarch, bracing his arm to shoot. "I'll prove you wrong, you—"

A sharp, hissing sound.

A sickening thud.

The earl's face contorted, and a moment later he toppled forward, his body crumpling as though the legs were made of rags. The lantern barely tottered, coming to rest on its base, its small flame wavering but unextinguished.

Mary and James stared at the queen, then whirled to

face Wintermarch's body. It lay slumped and prone, a long stick planted in its back like a flag. An arrow, Mary realized, her fuddled senses slow to interpret the evidence of her eyes. Behind her, the queen gave a small sigh—the only indication of emotion she'd shown throughout this swift, strange unraveling.

And now Mary heard a pair of boots splashing swiftly upstream toward them: the archer who'd killed Wintermarch. He knelt by the body, assessing his work. Glanced up at the queen and saluted. "The shot went through the heart, ma'am."

"A fine piece of marksmanship, Captain Mathers."

"Thank you, ma'am. If you'll pardon the noise, ma'am." The archer bowed deeply and whistled shrilly three times down the tunnel. In response Mary heard a whistled reply and the marching of boots. How long, she wondered, had the army been poised and waiting?

Queen Victoria sighed again. This time, Mary noticed her weariness, saw evidence of strain in the tiny beads of perspiration that dotted Her Majesty's forehead. "A bad end for a proud and foolish man."

James appeared speechless still. Eventually, Mary said, "Yes, ma'am." But her mind whirled with questions. How had the queen learned of Wintermarch's treachery? Where was Honoria Dalrymple now? And what had inspired Her Majesty to come down here herself? Despite her fine rhetoric about the royal line continuing, she'd risked her life in order to confront a madman.

Had she died, the tragedy would have changed the arc of history.

"We shall thank you both for your loyal efforts at a suitable time," said Queen Victoria. "For now, Miss Quinn . . ."

"Yes, Your Majesty?"

"We should be grateful for your assistance in climbing this rather rudimentary ladder. We are not so agile as we once were."

Thirty-one

On the road to St. John's Wood

Mary couldn't have felt more bewildered had the queen turned her upside down and shaken her vigorously. As she walked north through the relative tranquility of Mayfair, she found it difficult to stop thinking about Queen Victoria's astonishing arrival in the sewer. Her Majesty had behaved less like a doughty monarch and mother of nine, and more like a member of the Agency! Even her handling of Wintermarch—the clever conversation, stalling him until the archer was in position to shoot—was extraordinary. Not to mention the speed with which she'd organized the army and the judgment she'd shown in anticipating Wintermarch's attempt at high treason.

It had been tempting for Mary to forgo all etiquette and bombard the queen with questions. In the end, she'd not had the chance: Her Majesty was anxious to be reunited with her family and to establish a measure of normality at the now-overrun Kensington Palace. She expected the removal of the guncotton to be swift, and to return to Buckingham Palace by nightfall. And so, very little the wiser, Mary made the journey back to the Academy.

It was to the Academy she needed to return—not the Agency. She was in no state to report to Anne and Felicity. What she sought was a quiet room with a lock on the door, a place where she might think without disruption. There were distractions enough in her thoughts. She slipped in through the kitchen door, putting a finger to her lips and smiling when she met Ellie, the Academy's long-standing cook-maid. Ellie smiled indulgently. She was accustomed to the girls' comings and goings and blessed with an utter lack of curiosity.

Despite all that had happened today, it was still only late afternoon and the girls were still in their classes. Mary gained her room without meeting a soul, locked the door, and began to collect what she needed. From beneath a floorboard near the wardrobe, she extracted an envelope stuffed with pound notes—the fruit of her nearly two years' wages at the Agency; next, a letter of character written on fine onionskin paper, testifying to the good temper and patience of Miss Anne Hastings as lady's companion. She changed her dress for a dark blue woolen gown, the warmest and plainest she had, and put on her stoutest boots. And then she was ready.

Except, of course, that she was anything but. She sat down heavily at her desk, staring at its scarred surface, its uneven varnish. Generations of girls had used this desk, leaving their marks on it. She'd always loved the sense of continuity suggested by the Academy—that she was part of a new tradition, a brave enterprise on the part of impoverished young women. Was she ready to abandon this life, this identity, entirely? For that was what she'd promised Lang.

She'd meant it with her whole heart. Yet now, sitting in her bedroom in the only home she'd known in over a decade, she wondered what it meant to abandon one family for the sake of another. Anne and Felicity had proven their devotion to her. They'd educated her, housed her, trained her. They had given her life purpose. Her loyalty to Lang was born only of history, of an irrational desire to feel a blood bond with someone, even if he refused openly to acknowledge it. It was true that the Agency had failed her in small ways on this most recent case. Yet its silence was a minor failing, especially when compared with Lang's spectacular record of absence and violence. She could hardly expect perfection of Anne and Felicity when she herself was so far from faultless. And yet.

And yet.

She stood and pushed back her chair. Looked about the room one last time in farewell. There were no personal effects missing, nothing that would suggest that her disappearance had been planned. She knew this room so well, she could have sketched its every detail—the ancient washstand, the trim about the window, the shadows cast by the windowpanes by moonlight. Yet these memories would never be required, and it was best to let go of such intimate knowledge. It was as well that she had experience of starting over so many times.

A phoenix suddenly came to mind: the mythological firebird that, every five hundred years, burned its nest to nothing and rose again from the ashes. She was no phoenix, she thought with something that came near a smile, but she could do the same. Aged six or seven. Aged twelve. Aged twenty. And, she realized, once more after her father's death. His second death, she noted, with a ghost of amusement. A family of phoenixes.

She unlocked her door, drew a deep breath and walked out—straight into Anne Treleaven's hand, upraised to rap on the door.

Anne blinked. "Ah, Mary. Ellie told me you'd come back. Were you on your way upstairs?"

"Upstairs" referred to the Agency's secret headquarters in the Academy's attic, where agents always reported upon their return. Mary gaped for a very long moment. Eventually, she said in a choked voice, "Yes."

She trailed behind Anne as they climbed the stairs, steeling herself for the usual report. She hadn't a great deal to say—still hadn't much insight into Wintermarch's actions, let alone Honoria Dalrymple's involvement—but she'd tell them what she could. And then she'd leave, having at least completed her first real assignment. It was better this way, she told herself without much conviction. She touched her reticule, knowing that her future was tucked inside its lining. A strange sort of talisman, but it was enough for the moment.

As she entered the room, Mary's eyes fell on the first, most incongruous item: Anne's desk, usually a vision of order with a lone sheet of foolscap floating on its oak surface, was heaped with folders and slips of paper. Her gaze flicked to the bookcase, which looked ransacked. Finally, she turned to Anne and noticed details she ought to have seen plainly three minutes ago—and surely would have, but for her emotional distractions.

Anne Treleaven was the first person Mary had met at the Academy, the Agency manager she felt closer to. She was a thin, tidy woman with a prim, dignified air—a born governess, to look at her. Mary had seldom seen her show emotion or look less than immaculate. Today, however, her usually neat chignon was loose and the front of her hair ruffled as though she'd been running her hands through it. Behind her spectacles, her eyes were suspiciously bloodshot. She summoned a brief, tight smile. "Do sit down. I expect you're here for answers. It's taken us—me—some time to get the information you requested."

Mary stared. She'd seldom asked Anne a personal question. Even "How do you do?" sometimes seemed intrusive, depending on Anne's demeanor. Yet this scene was so startling that the words tumbled from her mouth. "Miss Treleaven, what's wrong? Are you unwell?"

Anne shook her head. "I am quite well, my dear.

But—there's something we—I—ought to tell you. Sit down."

All thoughts of Queen Victoria, explosives, James Easton, and even Lang Jin Hai drained from Mary's mind. She lowered herself mechanically into the closest chair. She wasn't going to like what she heard—of this much she was certain. "I'm listening, ma'am."

Anne did not sit. Instead, she paced the width of the room, from her desk to the bookcase and back again. And as she pivoted, Mary noticed that half an inch of Anne's slip peeped from beneath her skirt hem. This, for Anne, was the equivalent of near nakedness in others.

Mary sat in tortured suspense. And now that she had leisure for visions of doom and tragedy, a cold hand clutched her heart: something had happened to Felicity Frame. It was the only answer. Anne would never, otherwise, be alone in such a time of distress. And the obvious disorganization around her—it was no wonder Mary's requests for information had gone unanswered. "What's happened to Mrs. Frame?"

Anne's smile was weary. "You always were fond of unanswerable questions." She stopped pacing and laced her fingers together, as though about to recite a poem. "My dear, I expect you've been aware of undercurrents and tensions for some time. The day-to-day running of the Agency is a complicated affair, and Mrs. Frame and I have worked together for nearly two decades. It's quite common for colleagues, in such situations, to fall out, and you've already seen some evidence of differences of opinion between the two of us."

Mary nodded but did not speak. There was nothing to say.

"What has happened recently, however, is of graver import. There is no clever or subtle way to say this, Mary: after a fundamental disagreement about the future direction of the Agency, Mrs. Frame and I have agreed to part ways."

Mary stared. She'd expected to hear of Felicity dead or missing. Or of a case gone badly wrong. She hadn't expected this—a nasty spat, the dissolution of a business arrangement. It was both dreary and petty, adjectives she'd never associated with the Agency. So much for her childish notions of "home." "What—?" Her voice was rusty, and she cleared her throat before trying again. "What are the consequences for the Agency and its operatives?"

Anne sighed. "Both simple and complicated, I'm afraid. Mrs. Frame has, for some time, been keen to change the scope of her work. She has wanted to admit men to the Agency and to cultivate certain powerful contacts she has made in government. You've been privy to some of her suggestions—for example, that we invite your friend James Easton to join the Agency. She was also responsible for committing the Agency to the case you worked on at St. Stephen's Tower, which was so very nearly disastrous."

"Bad-mouthing me behind my back, Anne? I didn't expect that from you." The voice — rich, dramatic, slightly amused — came from the door. It was Felicity, of course — extravagantly dressed, as usual, in a garnet-colored silk gown. A scarlet woman, walking away from her home, her friends, her dependents. "Good afternoon, Mary. I see I'm just in time to balance the picture." She waved a dismissive hand at Anne. "Oh, don't ruffle up. It's best for her to hear it from both of us."

Anne swallowed something — likely her temper — and said, "True. I've just explained your desire to make changes: adding male agents and chasing your Westminster contacts."

"There's no need to make it sound grubby." Felicity turned the force of her charisma onto Mary. "Everything's changing, Mary: London. Politics. Society. The empire. Everything except the Agency. I don't think that's right, and I'm damned worried about being left behind.

"As you know, Anne and I differ on this matter. This break has been coming for some time — although I apologize if it is a complete shock to you — and I'd hoped there would be a minimum of disruption and resentment." She looked meaningfully at Anne. "But I suppose it's always difficult, breaking apart an organization."

Mary didn't like this. Of course, she hated the idea of the Agency changing. But she specifically disliked the way Anne and Felicity were sparring, sniping at each other like petty girls rather than conversing as intelligent adults. "I thought the Agency was a collective," she said. "That's how you described it to me before I even began my training."

Anne nodded. "You are correct. But over the years, Mrs. Frame and I have been its day-to-day managers. We maintain contact with clients, organize contracts, do all the background research that is so essential for the agents' success."

"In practice," cut in Felicity, "we've a choice: whether to chart a new course for the Agency or to continue straight on."

"Shouldn't you have asked all the agents for their positions? It's not right to leave us in the dark, then present this fracture as a fait accompli." She'd never spoken in such a tone to the two women; wouldn't have dreamed it possible an hour earlier.

Anne's smile was tight. "You make an excellent point, Mary. That's precisely what we ought to have done, had we been aware of the magnitude of Mrs. Frame's change of heart. I, for one, am ashamed of and disappointed in the way matters have played out."

Felicity's scowl was fleeting, almost immediately replaced by a look of regret. "My darling girl, fractures are just that: sudden and irreversible. Unavoidable, even. But you're quite correct, in that all you agents are autonomous and free to choose. And that's what I want to explain to you now.

"I shall be leaving the Agency to establish my own

intelligence organization. It will, as I'm sure Anne has mentioned to you, take a different approach to intelligence work—one that does not exclude men but treats them as allies; also one that seeks to expand its current field of expertise.

"As a fully trained agent, you are free to choose whether you wish to stay with the Agency, which will continue under Anne's direction, or to follow me. You needn't choose immediately, of course. But as our philosophical differences are quite clear, we hope this parting of ways will be swift, if not painless."

It seemed so simple, so very tidy, in Felicity's words. And yet what she was proposing was nothing less than an undoing—an undermining of the Agency's founding principles. If this reflected Felicity's real interests, the truly astounding fact was that she'd remained at the Agency for so long.

"We understand, of course, that you'll have questions," said Anne. She seemed more settled now that the news was out. Perhaps she was even buoyed by Felicity's clear, callous explanation, which said much more about its author than it did about this new, shadowy rival to the Agency.

Mary had plenty of questions—but not the sort Anne imagined. Now that the initial shock was fading, she realized she had already seen the hairline fractures in Anne and Felicity's united front. The disputes had begun during the case at St. Stephen's Tower, as Anne had said. Sending Mary onto a building site disguised as a twelve-year-old boy had been a large step sideways for the Agency, and Anne had deplored it. And when Anne had assigned Mary to the Buckingham Palace case, Felicity had grumbled at its pettiness, its insignificance, while Anne had defended it as classic Agency casework.

But despite her anger and disappointment in Anne and Felicity, their split made her path clear. She'd spent her whole life longing for family. Had found one here, at the Academy. A second, even more exciting one in the Agency. And now it was breaking up. Even had she doubted the decision to ally herself with Lang, her choices were slowly, inexorably being removed.

Thirty-two

What are you thinking?" asked Felicity.

Mary sat up straight. Organized her thoughts. "I ought to report on the assignment." She gave the briefest of summaries; it hadn't, after all, been a complex or convoluted case.

Anne and Felicity listened attentively enough. "So the thefts stopped not because of gossip or excess caution but because the prince was back at Oxford for a spell." Anne shook her head. "Sometimes the simplest explanations are the most difficult to credit."

Mary nodded. "Yes. I spent so much time thinking about palace politics and trying to work out the servants' schedules, when all the time it was just a spoiled child who wanted a bit more pocket money."

"Bit of a waste of time and resources, don't you think?" said Felicity, her voice a lazy drawl.

Mary spoke quickly, before Anne could become defensive. "Seen narrowly, perhaps. But my presence there—

combined with James Easton's—helped to avert a major disaster." As she briefly narrated the story of the Earl of Wintermarch, Honoria Dalrymple, and the crates of guncotton, she watched her soon-to-be-former managers. Felicity listened with a quizzical smile that spoke of great satisfaction. Anne, more circumspect, listened with a neutral expression, head tilted at a thoughtful angle.

When Mary finished, there was perfect silence for several seconds. Then Anne said, "We were remiss in not conveying to you the background information you requested. However, I've now gathered some details that may help to explain such a bizarre series of occurrences."

Mary shifted in her chair. There wasn't time for this. She wanted only to return to the Tower, her father, her future. Yet failing to show interest now might sabotage her sudden disappearance. No, everything had to seem entirely normal if her escape plan was to work. "An explanation of Wintermarch's actions?"

"Nothing so clear-cut as an explanation; more a possible interpretation," said Felicity.

Anne bridled at such a dismissal. "The earl, as you know, has a reputation as an extremely conservative man; his voting record in the House of Lords corroborates this. I've learned that in his own circle, and in private letters, he expresses open dissatisfaction with the idea of a female monarch. He's also strongly prejudiced against Germans and has, again, written to his intimates denigrating the royal family because of their origins. He believes them insufficiently English to reign and even questions their loyalty to the country.

"However, Wintermarch lived abroad until roughly ten years ago, when his elder brother died. He was then forced to give up his military commission to assume the title. Most of these remarks were made before he became earl and thus were, I suspect, discounted by most. It's also notable that his scurrilous remarks were never accompanied by action. It seems that only when he retired and returned to England did he have time to become bored and thus dangerous."

Mary frowned. She'd not wanted to listen, but her training was sound and she absorbed the information without conscious effort. "Are you suggesting that Queen Victoria's advisers knew of the earl's remarks but simply didn't take them seriously?"

Anne tilted her head. "Or hadn't sufficient grounds to pursue them. After all, she must be well accustomed to aristocratic tittle-tattle and backbiting."

"But his intent has changed dramatically over the past decade. His actions were those of a zealot or a lunatic rather than a disciplined military man."

Anne nodded. "That is the most troubling thing about today's events, now that the danger has been averted: there's simply no rational explanation for his actions. I can understand his attempting regicide. I could also imagine a frightening sort of prank, designed to expose Her Majesty's vulnerability. But to construct what was truly a suicide mission goes beyond any sort of logic."

"Except," said Mary, "for the logic of the mad. Just before the queen appeared, he faltered. He didn't seem to know what to do next, although he'd been very efficient up to that point."

Anne nodded. "It certainly sounds it. A portion of the plan was carried out with logic, but amid utter chaos. And frankly, history shows that those who plot against a monarch are typically unbalanced—if not unhinged, then blinded by ideological fervor. Certainly the young men who shot a pistol at Her Majesty's carriage two decades ago were declared insane." She paused. "However, we'll never know for certain. The person best positioned to know is Mrs. Dalrymple."

This wasn't nearly as dissatisfying as it ought to have been, realized Mary with a glimmer of dark amusement. She would have enjoyed a thorough and rational explanation for Wintermarch's actions, but ultimately it mattered not.

"As for Honoria Dalrymple," said Anne, "hers seems to be a simple case of blind hero worship. She adores her stepfather, would do anything to please him. She married her husband purely to do so, and that marriage was a misery. After Dalrymple died, she had time to devote to the earl once more. I doubt she's still a danger now that he's dead."

"Executed," murmured Mary.

Anne's brow wrinkled. "Yes. Well, in the circumstances one could hardly be surprised. If ever a man met his just deserts . . ."

Mary fidgeted. She disliked this new feeling of pity that now crept in when she thought of Honoria Dalrymple. To distract herself, she asked, "But the question of proximity—knowing what she did, why would the queen elevate Mrs. Dalrymple to lady-in-waiting?"

"There's an old adage," struck in Felicity, smiling slightly. "'Wise men keep their friends close but their enemies closer.' Perhaps Her Majesty found it applicable to wise women, too."

Mary wondered if she herself might ever be wise. Right now, she felt completely adrift and unable to discern even who her friends and enemies might be. She said the next thing that came to mind, quite at random. "Why does the secret tunnel even exist?"

"You are familiar with rumors concerning the private life of George IV," said Anne.

Mary nodded. Who was not? The queen's uncle had been a notorious bon vivant, in every sense of the expression. An immoderate love of food and wine, a turbulent and acrimonious marriage, numerous affairs and the illegitimate children to show for them . . . It was the stuff of private amusement and public outrage.

"I believe he caused the tunnel to be built in order to facilitate meetings with his mistress, Mrs. Fitzherbert. Although he did not live at the palace, he was on good terms with Queen Charlotte, his mother, and regularly visited her there. It is believed that Mrs. Fitzherbert was conducted into the palace via the river and up the sewer."

Mary frowned. "Was such subterfuge truly necessary?"

Anne shrugged. "In the lax society of the day, likely not; I should imagine there was an element of enjoyment in the game. But Mrs. Fitzherbert was a Roman Catholic. They were rumored to have entered into a secret marriage. There may have been a desire to evade public scrutiny—or perhaps even George's wife's attention—from time to time. Anything else, Mary?"

Mary's thoughts were an undisciplined whirl. Secret tunnels, clandestine relationships, disreputable family members . . . There was no family in the world without its secrets. "No."

"Then what of the Beaulieu-Buckworth case?" asked Anne. "Have you managed to uncover anything useful?"

"Ah, yes," said Felicity. "The Lascar."

Mary refused to squirm. They might suspect her more-than-general interest in Lang Jin Hai, but they would receive no confirmation from her. "Yes. The Prince of Wales now recalls enough of the night of Beaulieu-Buckworth's death to be able to state, with certainty, that Beaulieu-Buckworth was the aggressor." She was loath to mention the Lascar's surname. After all, it was also hers—something that both women knew.

"Very satisfying," said Anne. "Did you assist him in remembering?"

"I did nothing that compromised my identity as a parlor maid," said Mary. "It was a quite unexpected return of memory."

"Well. I'm pleased to know this case has resolved itself so favorably," said Felicity. "I must go soon—I've an appointment to keep—but you've now had a short while to think about your choice, Mary. Although we do not wish to hurry you, we should like to know of your decision as soon as possible."

Despite Felicity's words, it was quite clear that she expected an instantaneous response. Anne, also, seemed to think this an obvious matter. And to a certain extent, this was true: their philosophies were now so different—opposed, even—that choosing one manager over another had become the equivalent of declaring a creed.

Mary disliked this, too. She'd had no intention of questioning them—after all, it signified nothing to her—but pique, combined with the need to behave normally, made her ask, "What of my present connections? You're both aware that I'm once more in contact with James Easton. What would each of you have me do about that?" She regretted the question even before it was fully spoken. She didn't want to think about James. If she succeeded in helping her father escape, she would never see him again. If she failed, the same would be true.

The question startled neither manager. They glanced at each other, and after a brief pause, Anne spoke.

"My dear, the coincidences that have brought you and Mr. Easton into proximity are startlingly frequent. I would propose creating an adequate and realistic explanation—the journalistic ruse you used was good for the time being, but insufficient in the long run—before once more severing this tie. I realize this might be awkward, but it's essential to the preservation of your cover. I might even recommend some internal work for a short time, until we can properly assess the threat Mr. Easton represents to your work."

A smile hovered about Felicity's lips. She looked like a chess master about to checkmate her opponent. "And I, my dear, believe that, handled properly, Mr. Easton represents nothing like a threat—either to you or to my organization. Quite the reverse: if you follow me to this new agency, my dear, I should be most grateful for your assistance in recruiting Mr. Easton to our ranks. I believe he has the right aptitude for work such as ours. It would be a pleasure to invite him to join us."

The choices couldn't have been more divergent. Both women waited, their serene attitudes and expressions belied by the tension in the room, so thick it felt like a change in air pressure. At last, Mary said, "Thank you. I'll inform you of my decision once it's made." She paused. Then, to further the fiction of her dilemma, she asked, "Miss Treleaven, may I continue to occupy my room here at the Academy until further notice?"

Anne nodded, perhaps deflated by Mary's delay.

"You are welcome to your room, Mary, for as long as you continue to be a member of the Agency."

Ah—and if she chose Felicity, she'd be at Felicity's mercy for lodgings, as well? Suddenly, Mary couldn't leave the office fast enough.

Felicity, however, was quicker. "Take my card," she said to Mary. "You may contact me at any time by leaving a message at this address."

"Thank you," said Mary automatically. She slipped the card into her reticule without a glance.

"Oh!" Anne leaped up. "I nearly forgot."

Mary stared with fascination as Anne rummaged through the heaps of papers on her desk. She'd never before seen Anne *scrabble*. It was rather like hearing a vicar curse.

"Here." Anne passed her a square envelope. "It arrived just before I found you." She paused and added, "By special messenger."

Mary could see that much: there was no stamp on the envelope. It felt stiff between her fingers, the creamy paper thick and expensive. She could see Felicity tilting her head for a better view of the seal on the back. Mary had no desire to share this with anybody. "Thank you," she said once again, and inclined her head in an ambiguous farewell gesture. "Good day." It was a meaningless commonplace—until now. As the words left her lips, they sounded like both a mockery and a lie.

Both felt entirely appropriate.

Thirty-three

Thursday evening

Limehouse

She had an idea of what the envelope contained: the seal depicted a crown with the letter *R,* for *Regina,* across it. But she feared that the delay had already been too long. If she could evade Anne's and Felicity's probing, she could certainly let this envelope wait, too. And so she stuffed it into her reticule and made haste to Limehouse, where she had certain arrangements in mind. After some preliminary exploration, she took lodgings in a quiet house, paying a week's rent in advance and giving her name as Ellen Tan, a clerical worker soon to be joined by her invalid father.

The landlady accepted her explanation without question, her attention riveted by the three black-haired children playing by the fire. It was a decent place to go underground, thought Mary: meals included, a landlady sorely in need of income while her husband was at sea, perhaps a shade of solidarity from a woman married to a Lascar. The woman's lack of curiosity lent hope, as did her sharp-nosed interest in Mary's money. Mary might have to guard her purse while they stayed here, but such avarice would be to their advantage: even if their landlady heard of the inevitable manhunt, they stood a good chance of paying her off. While far from safe, it was as good as anything Mary had imagined.

There was little else to prepare just now. Much would depend on what Lang said to her today and on when a guard of negotiable morals would be on duty. There was no point in delaying further, and yet Mary found herself much more nervous returning to the Tower than she had been leaving the Agency and organizing a safe house by the docks. She took more time than necessary in procuring her little vials of laudanum, debating how many to buy and when might be best to start weaning Lang from the drug. Eventually, however, there was nothing else to do—and time was critical. It was getting toward dusk, after which point she'd never gain access to Lang.

A different guard manned the entrance, and he questioned her closely and inspected her reticule with care. Mary was glad she'd taken the time to distribute that sheaf of pound notes—not to mention the laudanum—in the lining of her bag and about her person. Finally, however, she found herself circling up to the top of Cradle Tower. She now understood her trepidation—and wondered at her own stupidity. It wasn't just about Lang's fate—whether he chose hope or fatalism, life or death—but about her own, too. Such an irony to think that her fate would be decided here, by a near stranger, rather than by herself. It made everything both easier and more difficult.

Up here, it was the same guard. She would have to work out their schedules if Lang was to escape. As she appeared in the doorway, the turnkey unlocked the cell door, rather as though this were part of a routine. In a sense, it was—she'd come three times in two days. He even left her a tallow candle to light the way. He then retreated to the window by the staircase, where, Mary now observed, he took advantage of the opportunity for an illicit pipe. A useful thing to know.

She entered the room, candle in hand, nervous but prepared. "Good evening. How are you feeling?"

No response from the lump beneath the blanket—only a faint crackling sound.

"Mr. Lang?"

That sparse clattering again, and then a faint whimper.

"Hello?" She peeled back the blanket with caution.

What she saw caused her to gasp, her stomach to turn over. That rattling sound was Lang Jin Hai trying to breathe, each pained gasp making the fluid rattle in his chest. His hair was soaked with sweat, clinging to his skull in streaks. His skin, even by candlelight, had a gray-green pallor. And his eyes rolled in their sockets, ghastly and unseeing.

She bolted into the larger room, her voice high and sharp with fright. "You, guard! Call a physician!"

The guard blinked, curls of tobacco swirling lazily about his head. "You all right, miss?"

"I'm fine, but the prisoner is dying. For pity's sake, call a doctor, now! You must have one somewhere in this hellhole."

The guard blinked again, as though she was speaking gibberish. "A doctor, miss?"

"This instant. Please!"

He seemed to move at a fraction of his usual sluggard's pace, but eventually he levered himself up and could be heard lumbering down the stairs. Mary considered charging after him and going for help herself—she would be so much faster—yet she couldn't bear to leave Lang to suffer alone. Her medical training was rudimentary, but even she could see that he hadn't long to live. A few hours? Perhaps a few days, if he was an exceptionally hardy and stubborn soul.

She mopped his brow with her handkerchief while the occasional tear splashed the rotting straw mattress. This was always to have been Lang's fate, she admitted now. Ever since she'd seen that jagged cut, she'd been afraid of it. Denied it. Hoped against fate. But blood poisoning was almost inevitable in an injury like his, left to fester untreated for days. And he was a frail man, his body older than his years.

Had the escape plan merely been an elaborate way to avoid thinking about her future? A deception that cushioned her unwanted knowledge that things were not entirely right at the Agency? Or perhaps merely a desperate romance built on the discovery of family? A father who'd reappeared only to vanish once more.

She knelt beside the mattress and took his parchment-thin hand. They were entirely alone now. No guard idling at ten paces, no future to fear. She drew a breath and said, very softly, "Father."

His bruised eyelids trembled, struggling against their own weight. His eyes, when they opened, were those of Frankenstein's monster—jaundice yellow, crazed with veins of red. But they were still her eyes, too. He blinked once, very slowly.

She focused on keeping her voice steady. "Father."

Another of those rattling breaths—a wrenching attempt, she realized, to clear his chest. He was too weak to cough. "Mary."

She opened a vial of laudanum and held it to his lips, cradling his head gently as he swallowed its bitter contents little by little.

After a second small bottle of the tincture, his breathing eased and a little of his agony seemed to fade.

"Father, I came for you. Are you sure you don't want to run away?"

The faintest of smiles stretched his lips—an enormous effort, she was sure. "Tomorrow."

She was crying now, utterly unable to stop the tears streaming down her cheeks. "Father, look." She fumbled for the jade pendant. "I wear it all the time. Every day possible since I found it."

He looked at the pendant, but only for a moment. Then his gaze returned to her face, drinking in her features. "You know."

"Why you went away?" She shook her head. "The pendant survived through luck—I took it first, and was going back for the papers. They were burned in a fire before I could read them."

A long silence. Then he blinked, a slow and painful movement. "Best."

Lang's mysterious departure. His so-called mission. The ruin that had befallen him: all things she would never know. Not to mention tender tales of her childhood, the story of his marriage to her mother, the privilege of knowing her father as an adult. A bubble of hysterical laughter rose in her chest as she grasped the irony of her situation. A dead father who came back to life. A man who refused to acknowledge his paternity until it was too late. A man with the answers she craved but who was too weak to speak them.

He half raised a shaking finger. "My mother's."

"The pendant?" She thought she detected a nod. "What does it mean?"

A pause. If she wasn't wrong, a slight frustration. "Too much."

Whether she was asking too much, whether it meant

too much—they were one and the same now. And that was fine, because it would have to be fine. She dabbed his forehead once more with her handkerchief. Summoning her courage, she bent and kissed him. And, oddly—but perhaps it was entirely to be expected—beneath the stale sweat, the dirt, the sweetness of laudanum and the stink of infection, he smelled familiar. He smelled like her father.

As though her kiss was the benediction he'd awaited, his eyes slowly closed and his breathing seemed to ease. A wave of panic rose within her, and she clutched at his hand. "Father!" She wasn't ready for this—not yet. She didn't know what she was waiting for, when the time would be right, but it wasn't now. Couldn't be now.

His face contorted. She must be hurting his hand. But when she released her tight grasp, he merely said, "Shhhh."

She obeyed, not without difficulty.

In the stillness that followed, she heard a new noise below: footsteps. Or, more precisely, boot steps. Her heart beat double time: a doctor, at last. She squeezed Lang's fingers gently. Disentangled herself and stood. Mopped her face, blew her nose, and hoped that the single dim candle would cover the rest of the damage.

Yet the footsteps ascended the tower staircase at a stately pace, neither sluggish nor hurried. And by the new guard's—the stand-in's—hasty response, as he knocked over his chair in his haste to rise, this was a person of some eminence. Even had the jailer kept his head, she would have known from the voice: deep, authoritative, and crisp. "I require a word with prisoner Lang."

"Y-your name, sir?" The turnkey's voice was tentative.

"Never mind that." There came the faint jingle of coins changing hands. "Now. Where is he?"

Mary frowned. She'd heard this voice before, and quite recently at that. Whether that made his refusal to identify himself more or less ominous, however, was unclear. As the footsteps came toward the cell's entrance, she stood and turned to face it. The two men filled the narrow doorway, and the deep-voiced gentleman recoiled half a step, visibly surprised to see her.

"Who are you?" His voice was sharp with angry surprise. "What are you doing here?"

Mary curtsied. "Miss Lawrence, of the St. Andrew's Church Ladies' Committee. I've been ministering to prisoner Lang in his time of need."

The man's eyes raked her, cold and analytical. "I don't see your prayer book."

"The prisoner requested a silent companionship." Mary hoped that the guard would be too overawed to contradict her on this; he must have heard the rise and fall of conversation from the cell. "And you, sir?" Her voice was sweet enough but crisp, too—the tones of a middle-class woman unaccustomed to rude treatment.

"I?" He seemed unprepared for the question, but as he glanced about, the guard's lantern illuminated his face clearly and Mary felt a surge of terror. She recognized the man now. Had first seen him at Buckingham Palace. He wasn't wearing full uniform—his blue tunic was stripped of insignia and he carried no truncheon—but it was the same man: Commissioner Russell of the Metropolitan Police. "Russell. Alfred Russell, on a private matter. If you would be so kind, ma'am, as to allow me a brief interview with the prisoner. I shan't be long."

Mary's impulse was to refuse, to make some sort of absurd, futile stand. All her instincts screamed at the notion of abandoning her father to the commissioner of police. But caution prevailed. She would be of no use to Lang unmasked and shamed. And so she inclined her head, a trifle haughtily, and stepped from the cell with her chin high.

After a moment, Russell said to the guard, "He's lucid?"

"I—don't rightly know, sir. The lady might."

Mary turned. "He is."

"And he understands English, Miss Lawrence?"

"Perfectly."

"Thank you, ma'am."

The stunned guard followed her after a moment, clearing his throat. "Afraid there's no place fit for a lady to wait, ma'am."

"This will be sufficient," she said, stopping in the antechamber. "Thank you." She willed him to remain silent, not to torment her with explanations and clumsy small talk. All her senses were trained on the cell. She heard Russell—the name he'd given was similarly stripped of rank—clear his throat. There was a long pause. Then, stepping out of the cell, he said, "Here. Guard. Send for a physician."

"Already done, sir. The lady—Miss Lawrence—asked earlier."

"Well, tell him to hurry up. This man is dying."

Such corroboration ought not to have surprised Mary. She had a more than passing acquaintance with death, having seen it all about her from a young age. Having cheated it herself. Yet when the fateful word left Russell's lips, she felt a pang. She hadn't realized just how much hope she'd held out until that moment.

With a mutter—an apology? a curse?—the guard trundled down the tower stairs, hesitating only briefly as he glanced back at Mary. The moment his footsteps faded, Mary inched closer to the cell. She needn't have bothered: Russell raised his voice to the pitch that people often use when addressing the deaf and the elderly. "Mr. Lang, I come bearing news of the case in which you've been charged: the death of the Honorable Ralph Beaulieu-Buckworth."

A pause here, but there was no response.

Russell continued. "I have recently been informed by a new source that you were not the aggressor in the altercation on Sunday morning. It is my present understanding that you were attacked, acted in self-defense, and then continued to act in a—a type of frenzy. Is this information correct?"

Mary listened, half hopeful, half fearful, entirely spellbound. Eventually, in a voice so low that it was barely a scratch, he said, "Yes."

"This changes the matter considerably, from the perspective of—an influential person. I am instructed to inform you that the charges against you have been altered. This person of influence believes that penal servitude without hard labor would be the most appropriate punishment for the killing of Mr. Beaulieu-Buckworth."

Mary drew in a short, sharp breath. This was beyond all expectations, all imaginings. And still this whole episode had the quality of a dream: the dim, flickering light; the sudden, clearly unofficial appearance of the police commissioner; the references to "an influential person," who could only be the queen. Her Majesty had been notoriously lenient in the past when attempts had been made on her life. At various times, young men who had fired pistols at Her Majesty's person had received only brief imprisonment—a direct result of Queen Victoria's compassionate nature. It stood to reason that in this case, although a life had been taken, the queen remained concerned about the life that remained.

And how little of it remained. Mary's heart felt close to bursting with a bittersweet compound of love, shame, hope, and despair as she heard Lang struggle to respond to Russell's pinch-lipped message of clemency.

He attempted to clear his chest again, with that painful rattle. In the end, he succeeded in saying nothing audible. Mary retreated just in time. In another half minute, Russell emerged, sour faced, brushing filth, both literal and figurative, from his tunic sleeves. Acknowledging Mary with the barest of nods, he stormed down the stairs.

She remained perfectly still for a moment, thoughts as paralyzed as her limbs. What on earth did this mean, really? Despite Queen Victoria's newly generous stance, it would change nothing about her father's life. He was a dying man. Optimist though she was, she knew better than to imagine he'd make a miraculous recovery. Perhaps if his wound had received prompt attention; perhaps if he'd not gone on hunger strike and been brutally force-fed; perhaps if he'd not been imprisoned; perhaps if he'd not been tormented by Beaulieu-Buckworth . . . the chain of possibilities wound on endlessly.

They had so little time left. She forced her limbs into motion, re-entering the cell with light steps. "Father. I'm back."

What remained of her father tried to turn toward her, but his head moved only a fraction of an inch. He'd used what little energy that remained listening and responding to Commissioner Russell. Still, his eyes slowly focused on her and he opened his lips. That dreadful rattling sound came again.

"Don't," she said. "Don't tire yourself talking. I'll just sit here with you."

He blinked very slowly. Tried again. "Mary."

She trembled with anticipation. "Yes, Father."

His breathing seemed to ease a little, although speech appeared excruciating. "Wanted. To find."

"Me?" she asked, breath catching.

"Shame. Opium." His eyelids drooped, becoming too heavy for him to hold open.

Mary clasped his hand tighter. "I wouldn't have cared. I would have loved you, no matter what."

The faintest of smiles softened his mouth—not a ghastly effort, as the last had been, but a yielding. A departure, Mary realized. She laced her fingers through his, straining her ears for anything that might be a word. The softest of sighs escaped his lips. And then he was still.

Mary watched, holding her breath. Waited, lest he was struggling, gathering strength, trying for something she feared to spoil or interrupt. A minute passed. Five. His cold hand began to grow colder yet, but she couldn't bring herself to let go.

Only when she heard a respectful cough behind her did she realize that the guard—the original guard—had come back. Behind him stood an irritable-looking man carrying a battered doctor's bag. Gently, she placed Lang's hand across his chest. Stood. Realized, with a shock, that not only was she not crying but she felt perfectly numb. "He's dead," she said to nobody in particular.

The doctor scowled and pushed past her, slamming

his bag about in an ill-tempered fashion. "I'll be the judge of that, miss."

Mary stood aside. Looked at the turnkey. "What's your name?"

"Baxter, miss. I mean, ma'am."

"Baxter. I'll see to the burial. Don't let anybody move him." She thrust a few coins into the man's slack hand and stepped past him. This blessed numbness was unlikely to last. But it would be enough to get her home—wherever that might be.

Outside the Tower, she found a cab without much difficulty. Climbed inside.

"Where to, miss?" asked the driver impatiently. It was a cold night, and his horse drooped miserably in the drizzle.

"St. John's Wood. No—Limehouse." As the hansom turned clumsily, she called out, alarmed, "I've changed my mind—St. John's Wood!"

The cabman cursed under his breath. "Sure now, miss? I ain't got all night."

She wasn't certain of anything anymore. But the cabman was waiting. "Yes. Acacia Road." For the last night, she hoped. And that, she realized, was the one thing of which she felt certain. What a pity that knowledge was all but useless.

Thirty-four

Friday, 17 February

Buckingham Palace

A*n audience with the queen. An audience with the queen.* The words drummed about Mary's skull in time with her footsteps as she followed a new lady-in-waiting up two flights of silk-carpeted steps. It was only when she'd woken that morning, dry eyed, that she remembered the letter in her handbag. It was a strange little epistle, exquisitely formal, signed by the queen's secretary. It commanded her to a meeting with Her Majesty at ten o'clock that morning. Mary felt no excitement, little curiosity. But she went because she could think of no reason she ought not.

Here at the palace, there was no sign of Honoria Dalrymple, no mention of her name. And the new attendant, a stout, middle-aged woman with the gown of a Paris fashion plate and the face of a fishwife, seemed to know precisely where she was going. This, combined with the strange novelty of walking down the center of a carpet runner, through the chandelier-lit, Old Masters–hung corridors of the palace, made the past six weeks of Mary's life seem a strange hallucination. Only the startled look on the underbutler's face as he'd admitted her confirmed the fact of Mary's time spent belowstairs.

She was conducted not to one of the formal drawing rooms but to Her Majesty's private parlor—a room she knew well, although she'd never before approached it without a tea tray in her hands. The lady-in-waiting stopped outside the door. "A few words of advice as to conduct, Miss Quinn. One approaches Her Majesty with eyes lowered and prostrates oneself at the edge of the Turkish carpet. One does not rise until permitted to do so. One addresses the queen as 'Your Majesty' or 'ma'am.' And on leaving, one does not turn one's back; instead, one backs out of the room."

Mary resisted the temptation to say, *One thanks one for one's advice*. A moment later, the door swung open and she was doing precisely as instructed. When she reached the edge of the specified carpet and sank low, the queen said, "Come closer, Miss Quinn."

She advanced to the chair indicated. A glance up revealed the presence of both Queen Victoria and Prince Bertie, while a thin, prim-lipped man hovered in the background: the secretary. He was not introduced.

The queen's formal manner offered no suggestion that she had ever seen Mary before this morning. "How do you do, Miss Quinn?"

"Very well, I thank Your Majesty." She hesitated. Did

one ask the queen how she did? Or ought she allude to yesterday's excitements? The fishwife hadn't covered that.

"We have asked you here today for two reasons. The first shall be explained to you by His Royal Highness the Prince of Wales." At the glance the queen gave her son, it wasn't at all clear that this was his initiative.

But, obediently enough, he drew breath. "I first wish to apologize, Miss Quinn, for the—altercation—that took place yesterday. I behaved in a less-than-gentlemanly fashion and beg your forgiveness for my actions."

Mary glanced hastily at Her Majesty, whose composed expression betrayed nothing. The prince must have confessed everything, and that knowledge made her flush with anger and humiliation. It was an unreserved apology, however—much more than she'd ever expected. Whatever good it might do. But clearly, some response was due. "Of course, sir," she mumbled.

A hideous pause. Then, at some silent signal from his mother, Prince Bertie plunged on. "The memories that were triggered yesterday—although it is too late for the late prisoner's benefit, I shall be giving my memory of events in a statement, in case the—the Beaulieu-Buckworth family should pursue a civil case." He swallowed. "That will, of course, cause much unhappiness. On—on advice, I shall undertake a tour of some sort—perhaps to the colonies—while the case is heard."

Mary heard this with mingled pity and exasperation,

as seemed ever the case with the prince. Doing the right thing, then running away from the consequences. Yet at least he'd ultimately been persuaded to behave correctly. "I wish you a safe journey, sir."

Prince Bertie blushed again and shifted in his seat. "Oh—thanks." His eyes were trained on his mother, awaiting her signal. At a glance from her, he stood hastily. "Well, I must go. It's been a pleasure to see you again, Miss Quinn, and I wish you well."

As the door closed behind him, the queen turned to Mary. "Rest assured, Miss Quinn," she said, "the Prince of Wales knows nothing of your real employment."

Mary stared at Queen Victoria's impassive features. "I—I'm very grateful for your circumspect manner, Your Majesty."

She sniffed. "Nonsense. One can't employ secret operatives, then go about exposing them to all and sundry—even to a person who is the future king. But we are straying from the subject at hand.

"The last reason we asked you here today, Miss Quinn, is to thank you for your exemplary labors throughout the confusions of yesterday. We are most grateful for your prompt, loyal, and clearheaded actions. In your absence, there might have been a genuine tragedy."

"Your Majesty is extremely kind, but the real hero of the day is Mr. Easton," said Mary promptly. "He first saw the crates of guncotton and sounded the alarm. I was only the messenger, ma'am."

The queen looked at her with reproof. "We have, of course, considered Mr. Easton's role. But this is a conversation about you, Miss Quinn."

Mary subsided.

"We remain grateful not only for the swift and effective delivery of the message but also for your return underground to neutralize the guncotton. We wish to recognize your acts of bravery and loyalty in an official fashion."

Mary's ears began to buzz—partly a result of fatigue, as she'd not slept the previous night, but mostly because the conversation, strange to begin with, had taken flight into the realm of outright fantasy.

"We have consulted with our advisers—in confidence, of course—and it appears there is no appropriate public honor to offer you. We presume that in your line of work, you would in any case prefer to avoid the sort of notice such an award would attract."

Mary bowed her head. "Yes, ma'am."

"We wish, therefore, to make you a present that will enable you to continue your work with an eye to cases that best deserve your attentions, a gift that will free you from some of the petty concerns of life as a remarkably independent female." At a signal from Her Majesty, the secretary glided forward, proffering a silver salver. On it lay a paper rectangle addressed to Miss M. Quinn.

Mary picked up the envelope as though it might scorch her fingers. Held it for a moment, wondering what preposterous three-volume novel she'd fallen into. Eventually, as the queen seemed to be waiting for her, fumbled it open. And found a check.

She nearly dropped the slip of paper—signed, so improbably, *Victoria R*—from suddenly trembling fingers. "My—Your Majesty?"

Not even the faintest of smiles. "We should, perhaps, explain the logic behind the sum. It is a block of capital that, well invested, will create for you a modest annual income."

Mary simply stared. She knew it was impolite. A breach of etiquette. And yet for the longest time, she gaped at the Queen of England, unable to summon anything like speech. When she finally spoke, eloquence escaped her. "Your Majesty, this is beyond generous. I can only thank you and say that I do not deserve your gift."

"That is for us to determine, Miss Quinn." A hint of reproof there. "Do you intend giving up your interesting and unusual work?"

"Oh, no, ma'am." She couldn't imagine sitting at home over a circle of needlepoint all day—no shape to her days, no purpose in life. She'd found a different vocation, briefly, in her father. Couldn't have imagined the void his departure after such a fleeting presence would leave.

"It is not ladylike."

Oh, dear. "No, ma'am."

"And unsuitable for a married woman."

Mary's pulse accelerated at the unspoken question. She said in firm tones, "There is no conflict there, ma'am: I shall never marry." This was to keep herself from fancy as much as anything.

A lifting of eyebrows. "Never? You are too young to make such a definitive statement, Miss Quinn. Marriage and motherhood are among the highest expressions of a woman's abilities."

What on earth could she say in reply? Did one ever disagree with the queen? Fatigue combined with curiosity made Mary reckless. "Your Majesty, you yourself are a shining example of the ability to combine domestic duties with much broader responsibilities. You must believe it possible for other females?"

Queen Victoria looked startled—it was unlikely that her pronouncements had ever been challenged like this since she ascended the throne—and then, after an agonizingly long moment, nodded. "A point well taken, Miss Quinn. But you said that you would *never* marry."

It was time for a mutual concession. "Perhaps I spoke in haste, ma'am. But I shall not marry in the near future."

The Queen nodded. "A wise decision. Marriage is a blessed state not to be entered into lightly." She paused. "Is there anything you wish to ask of me, Miss Quinn?"

This was pure formality; Queen Victoria no more expected Mary to say yes than to dance a vigorous polka. And yet Mary said, quite calmly, "Yes, please, ma'am."

Her Majesty blinked twice. "And what is that?"

"I—I believe His Highness the Prince of Wales, explained to you the matter of the missing ornaments."

Her Majesty's expression congealed. "The matter for which you were first engaged. Yes."

"One of the parlor maids working under Mrs. Shaw, a young woman named Amy Tranter, was dismissed under suspicion of having carried out the thefts."

One regal eyebrow lifted ever so slightly. "Yes?"

"It's a terrible thing to be falsely accused and dismissed without a letter of character. She has no chance of finding work in service in those circumstances. I should be extremely grateful, Your Majesty, if you could see her restored to her place."

The queen looked surprised. "Your request does you credit, Miss Quinn. It shall be done." She touched a bell. The interview was over. "We wish you well in your future endeavors, Miss Quinn. It has been a pleasure speaking with you."

"Your Majesty is, once again, too kind. I shall always be grateful for your generosity."

For the first time, the merest hint of a smile. "And we to you."

Thirty-five

Ten minutes later, Mary stood outside the gates of Buckingham Palace, feeling curiously benumbed. It was her predominant condition of late—a not unreasonable response to the violent revolutions her life had undergone in the past day and night. Secret agent. Daughter. Jailbreaker. She was none of these things now.

Instead, she was bewildered, flattered, humbled by Her Majesty's gift. Rich, too—she'd suddenly stumbled into an independence, the significance of which could not be overestimated. It relieved the necessity of choosing, and choosing swiftly, between Anne Treleaven's and Felicity Frame's visions of the Agency. It meant she need never work again, if she was frugal and practical and so inclined. It also changed her social status, in curious but tangible ways. If she didn't need to work, she could have different expectations. It meant that although not born a lady, she could be one all the same. It meant, too, that she would bring a dowry to any marriage she contracted. She might, in her own small way, become a target for middle-class fortune hunters if they knew of her windfall.

It also created new questions. Whom could she trust with her money? Where ought she invest it? Should she rent a little cottage somewhere, or would rooms suit her better? Where did she even want to live? If she lived on her own, she could employ a charwoman or a maid. Did she want to do that? Did she want the money, and its ensuing complications, at all? Had her father lived even a little longer, her decisions would have been clearer, more focused. But now, it would be simpler to give it away. She'd never had money in her life. She'd not miss its absence if she didn't become accustomed to it.

Finally, it created a terrible sense of guilty liberation. No employer, no father, nobody to whom she had to explain her windfall. No one to naysay her choices. She was freer and more powerful than she'd ever been, and lonelier as well.

Mary felt dizzy—something not difficult to comprehend, with grief, exhaustion, and hunger feeding her confusion—and sat down on a bench in the park. Ladies didn't do that, of course. Not alone, and especially not on a frigid winter morning when the world was coated in a layer of ice and grime. But she wasn't a lady yet. She did, however, regret sitting when a few moments later, a gentleman in a rumpled suit plopped down beside her in skin-crawlingly familiar fashion.

"Let me guess: you were sacked."

She took a deep breath and a firm grip on her temper. "Perhaps," she said. "It's none of your concern, though."

"You're so unfriendly," said Octavius Jones, in injured tones. "Is a little civility too much to ask?"

She ignored this. "Amy Tranter's got her job again. I don't think she'll trouble you now."

His show of surprise was genuine, and then extravagant. "And how did you manage that, missy? Let me guess: you took the blame on yourself, like an old-fashioned heroine, and begged the hard-hearted housekeeper to have Amy back."

She shrugged. "Perhaps. Don't put a stop on that check you gave me, though—I'll be giving her the money. Every girl needs a bit of capital."

"And I'm to believe you'll pass on the blunt?"

"As long as Amy doesn't come after you, isn't it money well spent?" She meant to sound defiant, but the words came out thin and weak.

He frowned, then peered at her. Poked his nose so close that he nearly touched her face. "My word . . . you look rough. Crushed."

She swatted him away. "Thank you."

"Truly, though," he persisted, not at all put off by shoving. "You look as though you've not slept for days. And when was the last time you ate?"

She closed her eyes. Perhaps when she opened them, he'd be gone.

Instead, he sighed gustily and began a rummaging sound. "You're so melodramatic, starving yourself into a pale and interesting state. Here."

She felt something bump against her hand. "All I want is for you to go away."

"Open your eyes and see first." A pause. "Go on. I'd dump it in your lap, only you'd take my head off for such a liberty."

She lifted her heavy eyelids and blinked at a paper-wrapped lump. A small patch of grease darkened one side of the paper, and suddenly she could smell it: smoke, salt, fat, wheat, yeast. Her mouth flooded so quickly, it was all she could do to keep from drooling.

Jones grinned. "You're welcome."

She eyed it, trying her best to show suspicion. "Why are you walking around with a bacon sandwich in your pocket?"

"My breakfast. But I think you need it more."

She peeked inside the paper, releasing a puff of fragrant steam into the wintry morning. The bun was golden, the bacon curling slightly at the edges. "If you ever need to poison someone," she said, unwrapping the sandwich all the way, "do it with a bacon sandwich."

He winked. "My sentiments exactly."

It was worth the risk. Mary devoured it in two minutes, heedless of the grease staining her gloves, Jones's close scrutiny, or the colossal impropriety of a lady eating in public—in a park, no less! When she'd swallowed the last bite and dusted the flour from her fingers, she felt half-way human again. "Thank you."

"My pleasure. Now, how about telling me why you left the queen's house in your Sunday best, looking half starved to death?"

"I'd rather not," she said, calm now. The urge to strangle Jones had vanished with the appearance of warm food, but she'd not lost her bearings entirely. "I've fulfilled my end of the bargain. That's that."

"What about the leads I gave you? The Hacken tarts."

She smirked. "Hackens are for hacks."

"It came to nothing?" His dismay seemed entirely genuine, but of course that was his professional amour propre speaking.

Mary thought of what the Prince of Wales's confessions had wrought. "I wouldn't say 'nothing.' But it wasn't anything like you expected." She smirked again. "No grist for your sleazy mill."

"Damn." He drooped for a moment, then cheered up. "Well, I got the best of you, then. Amy Tranter's off my back, all for the price of some useless gossip and a bacon bap."

"You seem intent on forgetting that five guineas."

"Bah." He waved a dismissive hand. "Cheap, even at that price."

"Off you go, then. There must be scandals to invent."

And yet he lingered beside her. "Care for a drink? I know a good little public house not far from here."

She shook her head. "No."

"Off home, are you? I'll see you there."

Home. She'd no idea what that might mean. "Thank you, no."

He frowned. "Sure you're all right?"

She stifled a yawn. "Of course."

"That's not very convincing."

"Oh, for heaven's sake, Jones, leave me alone."

He stood then, entirely unperturbed. "That's better. Well, then, Miss Quinn—by the by, is that your real name?"

Another question she couldn't really answer, even to herself. "It's good enough for you."

"Right then, my friendly darling. Until next time."

"There won't be one," she said automatically.

He resettled his hat. "Of course there will. I'm already looking forward to it."

She sat on the bench until a park warden, concerned by her lone presence, asked her to move on. She rose amiably enough—her feet were frozen anyway—and walked a few paces until realizing she didn't know where she was going. Despite her fatigue, she wasn't ready to return to Acacia Road. That would mean more discussions, more questions, more uncertainty. She was marooned in London, homeless once more.

There was, however, one more task to perform. One

more conversation to have before she could deem this assignment complete. And reluctant as she was to face James Easton once more, there could be no new existence—whatever form that might take—until she'd laid this present one to rest.

Thirty-six

Friday morning

46 Gordon Square

As before, the moment the cab rolled away, leaving her at Gordon Square, she panicked. It was still late morning—utterly inappropriate for a social call—and James was probably at the office. She vacillated before the glossy front door for a minute before remembering that Russell Square was quiet and nearby. She could walk there for half an hour quite decently, if she could bear the cold. She turned on her heel—just as the front door clicked open.

"Mary?"

Caught in the act, and an act of cowardice, besides. She turned with as much dignity as she could muster. "James. Hello."

A small smile hovered about his lips. "Aren't you coming in?"

"You must be on your way to work." He was wearing an overcoat and hat.

"I was coming to try to find you."

"Oh." The boldness of his confession made her shyer than ever, and she receded a step.

"Come in."

"I can't stay long. . . ."

He grinned, took three long strides over, seized her about the waist, and hauled her over the threshold. "Coward." Kicking the door shut behind him, he wrapped his arms about her and kissed her soundly. "You'll run through explosive-filled sewers and stare down the Queen of England, but you're too frightened to call on me." He kissed her again, toppling her hat to the floor.

"That's different," she said, thoroughly breathless. "Etiquette, and all that."

He laughed. "Come on, then. Upstairs."

Pure panic, shot through with excitement. "What?"

"To the drawing room, of course. We've a great deal to discuss."

"Oh. Yes. Of course."

He gave her a look. "Although we could start elsewhere. . . ."

She blushed furiously. "The drawing room is perfectly adequate, thank you."

James installed her on a sofa by the fire, rang for tea, and fanned the flames until the fire snapped and roared. Mary loved watching him. His hands were long and beautiful, and he moved with swift deftness—no wasted actions or overlarge gestures. He grinned at Mrs. Vine's surprise at the unexpected guest but said nothing to explain Mary's presence. When they were finally alone—door closed, fire blazing, tea poured—he finally sat down beside her and said, "I'm glad you came today."

Mary fidgeted with her teacup. His knee nearly touched hers. "You must be anxious to know what happened to Wintermarch and Honoria Dalrymple."

"Not particularly, no."

She stared at him, arrested. "You're not?"

"I'm mildly curious, I confess. But that's not what I've been thinking about."

"Oh."

"What were you about to say to me?" he asked. "Down in the sewers."

She felt the heat creeping up her neck, flowing over her cheeks to her ears. "N-nothing. I don't really remember." If she looked at him, she would be lost.

"Right after you kissed me. It began with 'I.'"

"I—I'm afraid I don't recall. Anyway, people say all kinds of things at moments of pressure."

"Coward," he said again.

A faint rattling sound began. It took her a moment to realize that it was her cup in its saucer, and she put it down, blushing even more deeply. "But there's something else I must tell you," she said, although it was a struggle to keep her voice steady.

"Oh? I can't wait."

Her laugh was pure shaky nerves. "You won't say that when I'm done." She was mad to plunge into this so soon. But it wasn't fair to James to do anything else. She could at least spare them both the prolonged delusion of intimacy.

James went still. "Seems to me I've heard this before." He didn't draw back, but the smile had vanished from his voice.

"I've already told you a little about my past."

"Your conviction for housebreaking, yes. And I don't care about that, Mary; I was a self-righteous prig ever to think that it mattered. You are—"

"Don't." She put a finger to his lips before he could say anything irrevocable, something he'd regret after this was done. "Please. Just listen." He always did, when she asked. It was one of his best traits. "I use the name Quinn partly because of my conviction. It was my mother's name, and I love it, and I'm glad to be able to use it. But there's another reason I don't use my father's surname, and I want to tell you what it is." She drew a deep breath. "I was born Mary Lang. I am half Chinese."

His head snapped up, eyes wide, gaze intent. He scanned her features, searched her face anew. He was putting things together—the dark hair, so nearly black; the tilt of her eyelids. She sat there and bore his scrutiny in silence, letting him look his fill. A long, long minute later, he let out the faintest of breaths. "I'd never have guessed on my own."

"No?" Her smile was slightly crooked. "My father was a Lascar."

He looked at her again, and something in his eyes changed. He stopped studying her features and simply looked at her—at Mary, his rival, collaborator, friend. "That's fascinating. I want to learn more about your childhood and upbringing. But . . . all this ominous buildup, for *this* news?"

That stung. All her careful preparation, all her anxiety . . . "You don't care to know?"

"Of course I want to know. But it doesn't change how I feel about you." He seized her arms and pulled her close, so their foreheads nearly touched. "Mary, I love you. No, no—hear me out. I am madly, ridiculously, passionately in love with you. I don't care about your past. Your race does nothing to change my feelings. I love you, you stubborn little fool. Is that clear enough for you?"

She could scarcely breathe, caught in the fierce brightness of his gaze. This was heaven. This was more than she'd ever dreamed possible. It was also hell—a merciless tragicomedy sweeping her along in its brutal torrent. "James, there's more."

"Then tell me. I dare you to put me off." He was so sure of himself, his grip on her arms firm and confident.

"I—my father—vanished in 1848 or 1849. He was reported lost at sea, presumed dead."

"Yes."

"But he came back." There was no delicate way to announce a disaster. "James, my father is the opium addict who killed Ralph Beaulieu-Buckworth."

He'd not expected that, despite his challenge to her. He sat back, his fingers slackening. Swallowed hard. Stared for a long moment. "Dear God."

She felt her composure begin to crack, like a sheet of ice on a pond. "The killing was not planned. He began in self-defense. But the fact remains that my father was a killer and an opium smoker."

"Was?" he echoed.

"He died last night." And now the tears came, hot and shameful and unwanted. "He was all but pardoned—offered imprisonment for life instead of the death penalty. But he's gone." Her shoulders crumpled. Began to shake. Tears splashed down into her lap. What did it mean that she would tell James about her father but couldn't reveal the same to Anne and Felicity? The result would be the same: Horror. Condemnation. Ostracization.

"Oh, Mary."

She felt James's arms come round her, and she shoved him away. "Weren't you listening to what I said? About my father?"

"I listened." Those arms encircled her again, pulling her tight. "And Mary, I don't care. D'you hear me? I don't care about any of that. My only concern is you."

She resisted for a moment longer, her weary mind unable to comprehend just what he meant. And then she collapsed. Lost track of time. Gave herself up to the grief within her and the arms that held her together. When she was finally sobbed out, her breath coming in jagged hiccups, her eyes salt sore, he released her.

"You never have a handkerchief, do you?" he asked, offering his own.

She half sniffled, half laughed. "No."

"I'm concerned; it's a bit of a failing."

"Like having a killer in the family?"

"Nothing at all. Your father's actions are his own; you're not answerable for them."

She twisted the damp handkerchief around her fingers. "I can't believe you were more disturbed by my housebreaking days than by my father and the fact that I'm a half-caste."

He grimaced. "Will I never live that down? The difference, in my mind, is this: there's nothing you can do about who your father was. His choices, his race—you're unable to control them, and it's unreasonable to hold them against you.

"As for the thefts . . . my first response was too rigid. I thought you'd made a choice that reflected weaknesses in your character. But when I thought more about it, I realized that as a child, you really had no choice, that it had been a question of pure survival. I'd have done the same thing in those circumstances." He laced his fingers through hers. "I suppose I got ahead of myself just now. I should have asked you first; can you forgive me for being self-righteous and judgmental?"

Mary felt the room start to whirl about her, this time not because of exhaustion, starvation, and general confusion. Rather, it was a very specific sort of disbelief and elation—and, yes, a burgeoning sense of something else that terrified her more than explosives and the Queen of England combined. "I might," she said. "But I've a few questions first."

James blinked, amused. "I should have known better than to expect instantaneous, unreserved absolution. Go on."

"You say you don't care about my heritage. Or the fact that my father died in disgrace."

"That's right."

"But earlier, you said—you suggested that—you love me."

His lips twitched. "I thought I'd been quite clear about that, actually. And the bit I didn't get round to is that one day, I want to marry you. I'm not in a position to marry now. I haven't enough money, and the terms of my father's will . . . it's complicated. But you must understand that I want you, and you only."

"Marriage makes even less sense! You were so vigilant about your brother's choice of wife, and even the Thorolds weren't good enough for you because of some distant rumours of shady business dealings. How could you possibly marry a woman on the run, living under a false name, with a father who died in Cradle Tower after killing a toff?"

"Not forgetting your racial mixture."

She glared at him. "I'm glad to see you certainly haven't."

"How could I? It's part of you."

"But you've not answered my question."

"I suppose the simplest explanation is that you've changed me, Mary. I care more for you than I do for the superficial standards I'd previously set up as being necessary to a marriage. I made those arbitrary decisions because I didn't understand the first thing about love."

"But what sort of marriage do you think we could have? Your brother would never approve. And I'd bring nothing to it—no illustrious ancestors, no business contacts." She kept silent on the subject of money.

He smiled. "I suppose I thought we'd have a madly impractical, terrifyingly modern sort of marriage. One based on love. Not to mention dangerous undertakings and hair's-breadth escapes from burning buildings, high ledges, and exploding sewers."

"And bickering."

"Always that, yes."

"Assuming I want to marry at all."

"True: I know of no good way of forcing you to do anything."

"And you're mad enough to think it could work—one day?"

He cupped her face in his hands. His smile was so

brilliant, it seemed to illuminate the room. "I think it would be heaven."

She trembled then. "You have a very strange idea of heaven."

"Kiss me and see."

In a peculiarly long and dreamlike morning, these were among the strangest few minutes. Mary had never seriously considered marrying anybody, had always assumed it impossible. And while she'd long felt James's attraction to her, these repeated, matter-of-fact declarations of love were like blinding bursts of light in a dark room.

Slowly, she stretched, her spine lengthening, chin tilting up as she reached for him. Met his treacle-dark eyes, and half smiled in anticipation. They'd never started gently or slowly, she realized. All their previous kisses had been born of impulse, momentum, long-repressed desire. And yet she felt no self-consciousness, no hesitation. This was right and true. As her lips brushed his, ever so lightly, she shivered and wondered how she'd resisted for so long.

He sighed very gently, lifted her closer, and she was lost, sinking into his delicious warmth. Dizzy once more, but without fear or reserve. When they were like this, she doubted the need for anything else—air, water, sustenance. Together, they were a world entire, and instead of being terrified, she found the thought exhilarating. And yet there was one more thing. . . .

"James."

He drew back a fraction. "There's more to discuss?"

She kissed him again. "I love you."

"You're a cruel woman, forcing me to wait so long to hear it," he murmured, burying his face in her neck.

"I started saying it in the sewers."

"That's what I'd hoped."

"I was afraid."

"I know."

She laughed and twined her arms about his neck. "Arrogance."

"Yet somehow you find that attractive." He picked out her hairpins with swift precision, and her hair tumbled down. "Come here."

She was on fire. All fatigue, all doubt incinerated by the heat of James's body, the power of his declarations. She lost herself in a haze of textures, of flesh against flesh, of silk on skin, of breath caressing lips and lashes. Only when James went still beneath her—his hands suddenly motionless against her back, her thigh—did she pause.

"I can only hope," said a stiff, half-strangled voice, "that this is a nightmare."

Mary's limbs turned leaden. Her skin suddenly prickled with shame, not desire.

James cleared his throat. Smiled reassuringly at Mary. And turned to face his brother. "Hello, George. Thought you were out."

"I just. Came. Back." George glared from James to

Mary and then back again. "Is there any point in my informing you of how unseemly this behavior is?"

"None whatsoever," said James easily.

George charged on, unheeding. "Such—carryings-on are utterly inappropriate. And this female"—he pointed a quivering finger at Mary—"is no lady."

James stood suddenly, all amusement vanished. "Miss Quinn is the woman I love," he said in quiet tones, "and you'll speak to her with respect."

George's face turned an interesting shade of purple. "You *what*?"

"You heard me. I love Miss Quinn and require you to treat her with courtesy."

George seemed to struggle mightily against an apoplectic fit. Eventually, however, he said in shaking tones, "That Alleyn chit you met in India was bad enough, but this—this—James, you go too far. I absolutely forbid you to have anything to do with this baggage."

Alleyn—was that the name of the girl in the blue dress? Mary wondered, and found within herself only the slightest pinprick of jealousy. Miss Alleyn might be rich and beautiful and have traveled to India, but she wasn't here now with James Easton.

James moved swiftly toward the drawing-room door. "George, your behavior is the most unseemly thing in this room. Go upstairs before you say something even more regrettable."

"Not while she's in the house!"

James sighed. "George, I realize this is sudden. I'll talk to you about it later. But right now, you'll be civil to Miss Quinn or you'll leave us alone."

"You've gone mad!"

"Choose." James's tone was that of an adult admonishing an obstreperous child.

"But Jamie—"

James's patience snapped. Or perhaps it was the use of his detested childhood nickname. "Go. Out." He bundled George out of the room with more haste than tact and returned a few minutes later, smiling apologetically. "He'll come round."

Mary laughed. She'd repaired her hair and was attempting to smooth her very crushed skirts. "Do you think so?"

"Well, maybe not all the way round. But he'll learn some manners around you." He took her hand and tried to lead her back to the sofa. "I'm sorry you had to see and hear all that."

"Well, I am exceedingly sheltered and delicate."

"Precisely." He kissed her again, deeply.

It was extraordinary how quickly her legs seemed to melt at moments like these. But after a minute, Mary found the strength to push back gently. "James."

"Yes?"

"You should talk to your brother."

"Later. Let him cool off a bit."

"And I ought to go back to the Academy. Make some arrangements."

He frowned. "You're still lodging at the school?"

"Not for long." She hesitated. A new scheme—a bold, foolhardy stroke of genius—had sprung up in her mind a minute before. It was either the best or the worst idea she'd ever had.

"Tell me." His eyes gleamed with anticipation.

"How busy are you at Easton Engineering?"

"I suppose you have the right to know now. Not very, I'm afraid—it's one of the reasons our marriage will have to wait. Assuming you want to marry me, of course. Anyway, one of the consequences of my going to Calcutta was that we didn't win any new domestic contracts. And George ran into a bit of difficulty with a long-term client. . . . It's going to take a while for me to rebuild things." He frowned. "Are you worried about money? I suppose I ought to lay it all out. You've a right to know what you're getting into."

Mary shook her head. "I wasn't thinking of your money."

"You should be."

"Just listen for half a minute." She laughed. "I was thinking about a joint venture. How would you like to join me in detective work?" At his look of surprise, she elaborated. "You did a little, on your own initiative, with the Thorolds. And we worked together on the clock tower case."

He looked at her strangely. "I suppose I do have a bit of experience there."

"Easton Engineering would be an effective cover. No one would wonder at clients meeting you there."

"How long have you been doing this on your own?"

"A little under two years. It all began at the Thorolds'." She hated this part: lying to James, even by omission. But if she could manage this one last time, she needn't do it again. They could start anew. Together.

He looked at her, a peculiar expression on his face. At first, she thought it was suspicion of her too-tidy history, and a little current of panic made her heart lurch strangely. "It seems so logical. . . ." he murmured.

After a moment, she realized the look was something she'd never seen before in James: indecision. "What's holding you back?"

"I trust you. I think we'd be a good team. It's a clever scheme. I think I'd enjoy it. But each time I see you in danger, I nearly go mad with terror. I don't know whether I could manage that sort of fear on a daily basis."

"It mightn't be daily," she said in a consoling tone. "Almost certainly not."

"I need more reassurance than that."

She folded her hands together neatly. Now that the scheme was hatched, she saw what she had to do. Perhaps she'd known it, at some level, all along. There was no going back to the Agency now, no following Felicity in her bold new scheme. "James, this will sound terribly like a threat, or blackmail, or something childish. It's not intended as such. But I don't intend to give up detective work. I should love it if you'd join me. But I shall continue with it, regardless."

He swallowed hard and looked at her. "You're certain."

She nodded. As certain as she'd ever be about anything, except him.

He buried his face in his hands for a minute. Then, looking up, he offered her a crooked half smile. "Well, then, Mary Quinn. Before I accept your outrageous proposal, have you any other skeletons lurking in your closet?"

"I'm a reformed housebreaker and fugitive from justice with a notorious Chinese killer for a father. Is that not sufficient?" Her tone was light, although he could surely see her pulse hammering in her throat.

"I thought maybe you were an exiled princess of the Ming dynasty."

"That would make me over two hundred years old."

He snorted. "My history's disgraceful."

She smiled softly at that. "And so is mine."

Their gazes locked. Warmed. When he spoke again, after several moments, his voice was husky. "It's apt, don't you think, that you proposed to me before I did to you?"

"We always were competitive."

He nodded. "Domineering."

"We squabble an awful lot."

"We both hate being in the wrong."

"True." She paused. "Is this your way of declining?"

He grinned suddenly, brilliantly. "Are you mad? Sounds like heaven to me."